## KANGAROO COURT

Slade looked around and stared into the muzzles of four six-guns. Behind them, Frank Tolliver and his gun hands leered. Slade glanced back at the mayor. "Who's this?"

Tolliver laughed. "I'm taking the place of the sheriff, cowboy. And we don't cotton to no killings on our streets." He glowered at Homer Akins. "Ain't that right, Mayor?"

Timidly, the mayor nodded.

"That's what I thought." The big man grunted. With the muzzle of his six-gun, he indicated Slade's Colt. "Get this hombre's six-gun and that war club, too, Dill."

Slade started to resist, but the odds were too great. He glanced around at the faces looking on. More than half appeared to be townsfolk, intimidated by Frank Tolliver and his gunnies.

Dill shucked Slade's Colt, knife, and war club. "Now, git," he said, shoving Slade toward the saloon.

Tolliver called to the angular-faced jasper with one eye missing. "Hatch! Go wake up the judge. We got us a murder trial to hold."

Other *Leisure* books by Kent Conwell:

**DAYS OF VENGEANCE**
**THE BLOODY TEXANS**
**THE LAST WAY STATION**
**CHIMNEY OF GOLD**

# SHOWDOWN AT JUNIPER PASS

# Kent Conwell

LEISURE BOOKS       NEW YORK CITY

A LEISURE BOOK®

August 2010

Published by

Dorchester Publishing Co., Inc.
200 Madison Avenue
New York, NY 10016

ISBN 10: 0-8439-6359-X
ISBN 13: 978-0-8439-6359-5
E-ISBN: 978-1-4285-0909-2

Visit us online at www.dorchesterpub.com.

# SHOWDOWN AT JUNIPER PASS

# Chapter One

Slade had no choice. The young half-breed tightened his cinch and swung into the saddle, bound for the Texas Panhandle. The snow had fallen all night, a light breeze pushing it into gentle drifts.

Leaving the thicket of piñon, he paused on the crest of a shale ridge for one final look down into the valley at the lump of snow impaled on the charred limb of a bristlecone pine, the body of his Apache brother, Nana. His vision blurred, and when he refocused his eyes on the pine, the body had vanished. Only a slender black limb stood out against the snow.

Slade jerked awake and stared into the darkness above. In one corner of his small adobe, embers blinked like wolf eyes in the *chiminea*.

Despite the chill of the winter night, sweat beaded his forehead. The same dream. Every night since his return from the high lonesome in New Mexico Territory, the same dream, but this night would be the last.

Today he would ride out of Tucson for that valley high in the Sangre de Cristos to bury his brother.

Two hours later, shortly before the sun rose over the Catalina Mountains to the east, Slade closed the freight office door behind him and filled a tin cup with six-shooter coffee. He plopped down on an empty cartridge case in front of the potbellied stove.

Cupping a steaming mug in his hands on the other side of the stove, Three-Fingers Bent rocked back in the straight back chair and grunted. "Damnation, Jake. I know you left Nana so you could get back to New Gideon to save my hide. I can't never pay you back for that, so that's why I don't mind saying you got rocks for brains heading out in this kind of weather." He cut his dark eyes to Bill Harnden, Slade's partner in the stage and freight line. "Tell him what you told me, Bill," Bent growled.

With a crooked grin, Slade glanced up at his old friend. "Yeah, Bill. Why don't you tell me?"

Harnden, his bushy brows knit, studied the lean half-breed. "Hell, I understand what you're doing. I'd do the same thing. But the fact is, we're smack-dab in the middle of one of the worst winters in years. Second, you left a heap of bad blood behind you up there in them mountains. And third, which oughta be the most important thing to you right now, is the stage line. The new route from Fort Atkinson to El Paso is running smooth, but there's only been half a dozen trips. Who's going to handle it if something goes wrong?"

"Besides," Bent put in, "them Utes is thicker'n seven cowboys on a cot up there. They'll have your scalp before you get within ten miles of that valley."

The wiry cowpoke ran his fingers through his close-cropped hair and, with the unperturbed aplomb of the Apache, studied his two friends with cool gray eyes. He knew they had his best interests in mind, but he also realized he could never explain to them the intensity of family loyalty within the Apache psyche. A knowing smile ticked up the sides of his lips. "I can't argue with what you say. I know the weather's bad, and I know there's them up yonder who would sell their own mother for my hide. But that's my brother up there." He glanced at Bent. "I left him because I had no choice."

He paused, sipped his coffee, and reached for the bag of Bull Durham. While he rolled a cigarette, he continued. "Now I got a choice. I go now because I got me a *sentir perdido*." When Bent arched an eyebrow, Slade explained. "That's Apache for a feeling of being lost. What you and me call a bad feeling. Not about me, but that Nana won't be there. I can't shake the *sentir*, but I can do something about it. As far as the stage line goes, you can run down any problems. We got good men at each of the way stations. Besides, I won't be gone more than a month."

Cantankerous as a ringy longhorn, Bent snorted. "If you're so damned bound and determined to go up there, then I'm going with you."

Bill Harnden shot a surprised look at Bent. Slade chuckled. "Forget it. Paleto's going."

Harnden frowned at Slade. "Your brother?"

"Yep." He grinned sheepishly at Bent, who picked up the moniker Three-Fingered Bent because of the loss of his thumb and forefinger in a game of chance between him and a band of White Mountain Apaches at a drunken party on the banks of the Gila River. He was a distant relative of the Bent brothers, William and George, who built the fort near the confluence of the Arkansas and Purgatory rivers in 1833, thirty-nine years earlier.

"In fact," Slade continued, "I'm meeting him up in the Catalinas midmorning. Come nighttime, we ought to reach the Hayden spread at the edge of the Dripping Springs Mountains. By heading due east, we can avoid the heavy snows."

Bent peered through the frosted windows at the brittle blue winter sky. "Well then, if I can't change your mind, I reckon you'd best get a move on while the weather holds." He flexed his left arm at the elbow two or three times. "My old bunk mate, arthritis, says we got us another cold spell coming in."

The sun was a shimmering globe overhead when Slade gave the call of a whip-poor-will. Moments later, the coo of a dove drifted down the boulder-strewn slope of the Catalinas. His Apache brother, Paleto, rode out on a craggy slope high above.

Slade held up his right hand in front of his body, pointing the index finger at Paleto, then bringing the first two fingers to his lips, the Indian sign for "brother."

With a faint smile in his eyes, Paleto returned the sign.

Slade reined up beside the wiry Apache who wore knee-high moccasins, leather leggings, and a fur-lined vest over a Yankee battle jacket. A bear-claw necklace hung from around his neck, his totem, his personal protector. A rolled bearskin was tied behind the cantle of his saddle. "You look well."

His dark face impassive, Paleto nodded. "And you, brother."

Gesturing to the north, Slade asked, "Ready?"

Paleto shook his head. "Your father wishes to visit with you."

"Santos? But I thought he was in Mexico for the winter, down with Juh's people."

Nodding to the craggy peaks towering over them,

Paleto replied, "He waits there for you." He reined around. "Come."

Slade started to protest, but Santos was his father, and the Apache son always obeyed his father. He would just have to ride harder to make up for the lost time.

# Chapter Two

A few days earlier, five hundred miles to the northeast, Frank Tolliver sat at a sunlit table out of the wind in La Plaza de los Leones, the Plaza of the Lions. He fixed his icy blue eyes on the ornately carved door of El Club del Emperador, the Emperor's Club, an exclusive watering hole for the aristocrats of Santa Fe.

A massive man, Tolliver was as cruel as he was cold-blooded. He had just ridden in. He was tired and dirty and so dry he couldn't spit.

When the door swung open and a nattily dressed man in an eastern business suit stepped out, Tolliver didn't budge. He studied the man, who with a dour expression paused on the portico and surveyed the plaza. When the man's eyes settled on Tolliver, a smug grin played over his pasty face.

He strode across the *calle* and into the plaza, stopping at the table. In a thin voice, he said, "Tolliver?"

The killer used his thumb to nudge his soiled black hat to the back of his head. "Maybe."

Wingate looked around hastily, then slipped into a chair across the table. His eyes narrowed, and his thin voice grew cold. "I'm Edgar Wingate. I'm the one who sent you five hundred dollars to meet me here. Either you're Frank Tolliver or you're not."

The testy impatience in the older man's tone surprised the outlaw. He allowed a faint grin to play over his lips. He nodded. "I'm Tolliver."

Satisfied, Wingate nodded. "Good. What would you say if I told you I would cut you in for a substantial share of a hundred-thousand-dollar deal?"

Tolliver pursed his lips and scratched the week-old beard on his iron jaw. "I'd want to know how substantial and who to kill."

"Twenty thousand."

A crooked grin twisted Tolliver's lips. "Who do I kill?"

Wingate chuckled. "I want a town, Juniper Pass. About fifty miles due east of here near the Gallinas River. Maybe thirty people live there. That's all. How you do it is up to you. I'd prefer no killing, but I want to own the entire valley. I'll send good men in to help, but I want every last soul to sign their property rights over to me." He pulled a thick wallet from inside his coat and counted out a stack of bills. He held them up. "Here's two thousand. I don't want you to do a thing until you hear from me. This should be enough to take care of your expenses until that time."

"Own the valley. Why?"

"That's my business," Wingate replied sharply. Pulling the sheath of bills back, he pushed to his feet. "If you aren't interested—"

"Hold on, hold on. I'm interested. When will I know to move ahead?"

"The last man I send will let you know."

Tolliver studied the older man several minutes before taking the proffered money. As he counted through it, he asked, "Why don't you buy it yourself?"

Wingate's eyes narrowed. "I tried. I failed. That's

why you're here. I've been told you never fail. That your methods—well—they work."

A smug grin curled the rugged gunfighter's lips. A sense of satisfaction washed over him. "You been told right." He paused and eyed the muttonchop beard on the older man's flabby jowls, figuring himself lucky for now he had a nice cozy hideout for the winter away from snooping territorial lawmen. Besides, if the deal proved profitable, he might even change his name and live out his life in New York City.

Santos looked up from the dancing flames illumining the small chamber when Paleto and Slade entered. Venison broiled on spits and a brightly painted olla containing mescal sat at Santos's side.

The old Apache, his black hair parted in the middle and held in place with a bright red headband, grunted and nodded to the far side of the small fire. Slade unbuttoned his heavy mackinaw and sat. Paleto squatted beside him.

"My father is far from his winter home."

Santos gave the remark an almost imperceptible nod. "I come when your brother tells me you journey to the north."

The wiry half-breed kept his eyes fixed on the older man. "That is true."

For several moments, Santos studied him, his eyebrows twisted into a frown, his thin lips drawn tight, ticked down at the edges. He reached for the olla of mescal and took a long drink, then handed it to Paleto. Without a word, the Apache warrior drank from the olla and handed it to Slade, who drank also.

Santos sliced broiled venison strips and, using the point of his knife, handed one to each of his sons. As he did, he said, "Nana, my son, your brother, is dead. I am an old man. Your mother, Big Calf, she grows old." He paused and a sheepish smile cracked the impassive mask that covered his swarthy face. "She would beat me with a stick if she knew I said such."

Slade and Paleto smiled, both painfully remembering the welts on their backs as a result of their mother's skill and talent with the stick.

Santos once again grew serious. His black eyes searched those of his two sons. "We are too old to lose another son. Perhaps both. And you are our son although Nez Perce blood flows through your veins." He paused and, with a faint gleam of reproach in his eye, added, "Besides, with no sons or grandsons, who will look after us when the winter of our lives begins to fill with the snow?"

Slade glanced at his brother. "I thought by now, Paleto would have given you some grandsons."

Paleto jabbed his elbow into Slade's ribs, and the two laughed.

Santos continued. "Two moons will have crossed the sky by the time you return. Nana was a true Human Being. Whether he is placed in the ground or thrown to the winds makes no difference, for he is with the Creator, who made the Tarantula, the Big Dipper, the Wind, and the Lightning-Maker and commanded them to build the earth."

Slade nodded briefly, remembering clearly the Apache version of the creation of the earth. True, Nana would be in the presence of the Creator, but without ritual burial, he would never enjoy the beauty and peace of the World Beyond.

The older man continued, his dark eyes fixed on Slade's. "While I could find the strength to continue, I do not believe your mother could if another son was taken from her. Because of her, I ask of my son that he remain here." He parted his lips to say more, but then slowly closed them, but his eyes remained on the younger man.

Well aware of the loss of pride it cost his father to ask the question, Slade winced as the tiny flames flickered across his father's eyes, revealing the old man's anguish, and the truth, the truth Santos as an Apache warrior could not admit.

Slade smiled reassuringly. "Tell my mother, I do what an Apache must." He looked deep into his father's eyes. "I do what you, my father, would do. I can do no other." He paused, then added, "I do not want to go against your wishes, but, can you not see, I am on a divided road? One is Apache honor, the other, disgrace."

Santos studied his son a few moments, then nodded. Without a word, he jabbed his knife into another strip of venison and handed it to Slade. "Eat. You must maintain your strength." He shot Paleto a disgusted look. "And try to keep this rabbit from killing himself," he added with a grin.

It was midafternoon by the time the two brothers descended the mountain and set out due east across the Arizona desert of spiny ocotillos, spreading Palo Verdes, stark ironwoods, and the candelabra-armed saguaros.

Slade's pony was a deep-chested dun with plenty of staying power. Paleto rode a smaller pony, a piebald he had freed from a white man's corral.

The sky remained clear until just before sunset, and then to the northwest, a line of dark clouds appeared over the horizon. Ahead, the tree-lined banks of the San Pedro River pushed over the horizon.

Slade gestured and shouted above the pounding of their ponies' hooves, "I know of a snug spot for the night. Good graze for the horses."

Their camp was in a wash just inside a thick bosque of cottonwoods lining the river. The arroyo was deep enough so a small fire beneath the cutbank would go unseen.

Quickly, the two men settled in, Slade readying a meal of venison and flour cakes while Paleto tended the ponies.

The wind picked up and the temperatures began to fall. "Cold tomorrow," Slade muttered, lying back on his soogan and peering at the bright moon against the dark sky. He chewed on his venison.

Paleto grunted. "Little snow. We make good time."

Suddenly a horse whinnied and startled shouts came from the river.

Instantly, Slade kicked out the fire and shucked the big Colt on his hip. Paleto came to stand at his side, both listening to the excited cries in the darkness.

As one, they vanished into the moonlit night, ghosting through the cottonwood to the willows lining the shore. They paused, looking on as two ponies struggled ashore, leaving their riders fighting the churning water in a desperate effort to keep from being swept into the swift water below.

Upon reaching shore, one of the ponies stumbled, then gained his feet and crashed through the willows. Slade reacted instantly, leaping for the bridle and ripping the lariat from a pigging string.

Quickly, he raced downstream, then waded into the water and swung the rope overhead, building a larger loop with each swing. When the first figure was within fifty feet, he released the rope.

A grin played over his lips as the loop settled over the man's shoulders. He jerked it tight. The man looked around, and Slade realized he had roped an Indian.

He didn't have time to think, for at that moment, the rushing current swept the second Indian into the rope, almost pulling Slade into the river with them.

Clenching his teeth, he dug his heels into the graveled river bottom. His wiry muscles strained as he fought against the inexorable pull of the violent current. His heels began to slip. He groaned and pulled hard. Then behind him, he felt Paleto grab the rope. Together, they held their ground as the current swept the two toward shore.

As the two bedraggled Indians crawled up on the graveled shoreline, a third raced up on a pinto. He slid to a halt when he spotted Slade.

Paleto grunted. "I Mimbre."

The Indian eyed Slade warily. He touched a finger to his leather-clad chest. *"Soy Chiquito, del Tindi."* ("I am Chiquito, of the Tindi.")

The Tindi, the name of the Lipan-Apache.

Paleto grunted and nodded to Slade. "Busca: I am Paleto, son of Santos, as is my brother here."

Chiquito nodded. "Ah, Busca. The One-Who-Seeks. I have heard of you."

Slade nodded. "Chiquito. Of the Tindi."

Chiquito grunted. He nodded to the two soaked Apaches Slade had dragged ashore. "That one is Flacco. The other, Caboe."

As one, the two Apaches nodded briefly.

Paleto turned on his heel. "Come. We have food and a fire."

A few minutes later, their ponies tethered with the others, the Tindi squatted around the small fire. Chiquito cleared his throat. "We hear of the One-Who-Seeks. You are far from Tucson."

Slade and Paleto exchanged glances, each understanding the question behind the casual remark. Slade caught a sly look in Caboe's eye, one he couldn't quite comprehend. He replied with candor, "Our brother is dead high in the mountains. We go to bury him."

Chiquito and Flacco nodded approvingly to each other, but Caboe kept his eyes on the fire. A tiny frown played over Chiquito's sun-blackened face when he saw the blank expression on his compadre's face.

"And you," asked Slade, curious as to why one of the Tindis was riding a white man's pony, "why are you so far from your winter home?"

The Lipan named Caboe grinned and nodded to the silver-inlaid saddle against which he leaned. "For what we can find."

Slade arched an eyebrow. So the three were a small raiding party. He glanced at Paleto, who stared at him impassively. While they had saved the lives of Flacco and Caboe, and while there was much honor among the Apache, both Slade and Paleto knew they must not enjoy the sleep of the innocent that night.

# Chapter Three

The night grew colder, and with the cold came the snow. Paleto and Slade had thrown their soogans in a corner of the cutback that offered a full view of the camp. Something about Caboe disturbed the young half-breed.

Two of the three Tindis slumbered with only slight movement. The third, Caboe, remained motionless, a clear sign the brave did not sleep.

The fire burned low until only tiny embers winked and flamed in the darkness. Slade lay on his side, his .44 Colt in his hand, his eyes peering through narrowed lids at the unmoving Tindi. He felt no anger or recrimination toward Caboe, for the Apache, all tribes of the Apache, the Lipan-Apache, the Coyotero, the Mescalero, the White Mountain, the Mimbre, all believed that their mission in life was to take what they could, and they felt no compunction if they had to kill those who resisted their endeavors.

While he did not believe as they in that one regard, Slade knew the concept was as much a part of their lives as the marriage ceremony displacing the groom from his tribe to that of his wife's.

Several times, Slade's eyes grew heavy. Several times,

he drew deep breaths, pulling fresh, cold oxygen into his lungs in an effort to remain awake.

He dozed off and on, but the slightest sound, whether the crackling of a dying ember, the groan of a sleeping man, or the shifting of a body jerked him awake.

Before dawn, when sleep is most deep, the wiry half-breed jerked awake. His fingers tightened about the butt of the Colt. He peered through squinted lids as Caboe slowly pushed his Saltillo blanket aside and eased into a crouch. His face was lost in the darkness, but from the tilt of his head, there was no doubt in Slade's mind the Tindi was staring in his direction.

Slowly, he eased the hammer back on the Colt, hoping the faint click when it set would not carry across the bed of coals that burst into tiny flames with the wind.

Another click from the darkness beyond the camp broke the silence.

Caboe froze. From the darkness, Chiquito spoke. "Return to your blankets. They are friends."

The flickering firelight cast frightening shadows over Caboe's rage-twisted face. He hissed, "They are not of our tribe. We kill them."

"No."

Neither Slade nor Paleto had moved, but each held his revolver under the blanket, cocked, aimed at Caboe.

For several moments, Caboe and Chiquito faced each other, locked in a test of wills. Suddenly, Caboe leaped at Slade, a bloodcurdling scream ripping from his throat.

Before Slade could fire, the racketing boom of a revolver shattered the stillness of the night, and a jet of yellow fire lit the darkness.

The impact knocked the Tindi into the fire, scattering the coals.

Slade rolled to his left and swung the Colt around on the spot from where the muzzle blast had emanated.

A guttural voice said, "Do not worry. It is I, Chiquito. I mean you no harm."

Minutes later in the light of the small fire he had rekindled, Chiquito touched his finger to his head. "Last year, my friend's pony step in a prairie dog hole. Caboe lay unconscious for a moon. When he awakened, it was like the Creator had taken the old Caboe out and put in one we could not understand. I saw something in Caboe's eyes tonight." He nodded to Flacco. "The three of us have been compadres for many years, but this last year, Caboe at times forgot that he was a true Human Being. I hoped it would not be, but tonight was one of those times." He paused and fixed his eyes on Slade and Paleto. "He would have slain you for your weapons and horses."

Flacco, who had spoken nothing, added, "You saved our lives at the river. Ask whatever you wish, and it is yours. I will ride as far as the sun to serve you."

Slade nodded.

By now, the fuzzy gray of false dawn was creeping across the treetops. Slade and Paleto watched silently as the two warriors rose to lay their friend and brother over the silver-inlaid saddle on his pony and ride out.

Without a word, Slade and Paleto covered the fire and crossed the river, heading east and figuring on reaching Hayden's spread by noon.

Only a couple of inches of snow had fallen, although the leaden clouds remained, a threatening portent of more snow to follow.

The frigid air nipped at Slade's cheeks as he matched his movements in the saddle with the running walk of his claybank dun, so called by the yellowish tint to the animal's hide.

Both brothers' eyes constantly quartered the fairly level desert around them. Ahead rose the snow-covered peaks of the Dripping Springs Mountains, their distance misleading to the eye because of their size and the clarity of the air.

Inured to the rhythmic pounding in the saddle, Slade let his thoughts drift back to the adventure-filled days of his youth. He and his brothers roamed the Dragoon Mountains, playing at being warriors, always extending their excursions a little beyond the limits given them by their father, Santos. One evening, a violent storm caught them miles from the *rancheria*.

The boys took refuge in a rocky cave where they roasted a rabbit and in the innocence and ignorance of youth, frittered the night away fabricating the great deeds they would achieve in their lifetimes.

Of course, upon their return to the *rancheria* and their father's wrath, they paid the price of their disobedience by being made to perform the menial tasks of women by gathering firewood.

Still, the three couldn't erase the furtive smiles on their lips as they made a game of the gathering.

And in the distance, hidden by a blooming paloverde tree, their father watched the three with pride.

A sudden blur before his eyes jerked the young half-breed back to the present. To his left, a black-tailed jackrabbit shot across the snow-covered landscape in thirty-foot bounds while a lean but determined gray fox stayed right on the rabbit's tail.

The jack darted down an arroyo, disappeared around

a bend, then popped out on the rim and disappeared among the wolfberry and creosote shrubs that spread for miles in every direction.

Paleto chuckled. "The fox, he will not catch the rabbit."

Slade grinned, remembering the story told around the fires on cold winter nights that when the Creator made the animals of the earth, He placed a vat of lard in the animal world into which each animal would be dipped in order to determine what measure of body fat each kind would carry. Fox, always shrewd and thievish, leaped in unbidden and jumped out rotund. The angry animals squeezed out all the fat except a little in his upper arms. Never, the tale concluded, would one see a fat fox. "Maybe not. Depends on how hungry he is."

A few hundred yards farther, they spotted the fox sniffing at first one bush and then another. Paleto's eyes danced. "See."

With a chuckle, the lean half-breed observed, "He isn't done yet."

Before Paleto could reply, the fox lunged beneath a creosote bush. A piercing squeal broke the crisp air, and the grinning fox spun around, clutching the jackrabbit by the back of the neck.

Slade arched an eyebrow. "You see. Sometimes plain old, hardheaded stubbornness gets you what you want."

The wiry Apache shrugged. "If that is so, my brother must get that which he seeks most often."

A grin curled Slade's lips. "You trying to say I'm hardheaded?"

Paleto's grin grew wider. He pointed to the east at Hayden's ranch. Smoke drifted up from both the main house and the cook shack. "I say stop wasting words. I am hungry."

Orien Hayden had come to Arizona Territory when it was still part of Mexico. He was a fair man to both Indian and white, but he never hesitated to fight any threats against his own property.

More times than he could count, he had taken in both white and Indian, offering them his protection while their wounds healed.

So respected was he that often, radical groups, intent on taking over the territory, pleaded with him to lead them, but always he refused.

He knew Slade and Paleto well, having first met them during the days of their youth as they roamed the vast wilderness of the rugged Southwest.

Standing on his porch, Hayden studied the two riders approaching. One was Apache. He snorted. Takes no damned brains to figure that out, he told himself.

The other one sat the saddle in a familiar way. Hayden narrowed his blue eyes. He had seen him before, but his eyesight not being what it once was, he couldn't discern any details until they grew closer.

A slow grin split his weather-worn face when he spotted a deerskin boot on either side of the saddle. "Slade," he muttered. If he was right, he told himself, that saddle was double-cinched with an elm-wood bow in one boot and a Winchester '66 in the other.

Slade held up his hand when they were still a quarter mile distant. Hayden returned the gesture, then, knowing the two would be hungry, stepped off the porch and stomped through the light dusting of snow to the cook shack.

* * *

When the two brothers pushed through the slab door, beefsteaks sizzled on the potbellied stove while a platter of biscuits and a bowl of steaming cream gravy sat in the middle of the sawbuck table. Next to the biscuits was a pot of coffee, three cups, and a full bottle of Old Crow whiskey.

Hayden gestured to the table. "Sit, boys. Charley's just about got the steaks ready. Take a nip of whiskey to cut through the chill and dig in."

Plopping down on the bench, Slade poured a couple of fingers of whiskey in the tin cups for him and Paleto. He nodded to the cook, Charley One-Time. "Just cook 'em long enough that they can't run off the plate." He downed the whiskey and filled the cup with coffee.

The old cook cackled. "Hell, boys. I reckon you're hungry enough to eat anything I stick in front of you. But don't worry. They'll be nice and juicy."

While the two brothers poked grub down their gullets, Orien Hayden nursed his whiskey-laced coffee and sucked on his pipe. "What brings you fellers out in this kind of weather?"

Between mouthfuls of grub, Slade told him where they were heading.

Hayden's face grew solemn. "You planning on crossing the alkali flats?"

"Yep."

The older man's voice grew solemn. "I don't reckon that'd be such a good idea."

Both Paleto and Slade looked up. Paleto cleared his throat. "Why you say that?"

The older man removed his pipe from his lips and studied them a moment. "Word is there's a heap of renegade Injuns holed up in the southern Peloncillos. Were

I you, I'd head myself north around the flats, toward Mexican Springs. Stay as damned far away from the southern Peloncillos as I could."

Slade and Paleto exchanged knowing looks.

"Thanks for the word, Orien," said the young half-breed, sopping up the last of his gravy with a biscuit.

"Besides," the old rancher added with a grin, "I'd hate to see some Ute or Kiowa wearing that bear-claw necklace of yours, Paleto."

The swarthy Apache grunted. "You won't."

# Chapter Four

Slade and Paleto reined up on the edge of the alkali flats, eyeing the vast expanse warily. Overhead, the clouds blew away. With the setting of the sun, a full moon rose, illumining the flats just as if it were daytime. Slade pulled out a bag of Bull Durham and rolled a cigarette. "You got any objection to riding a few hours longer? I figure another twenty miles to Mexican Springs on the northern side of the flats. Camp up in the Pyramids, then move out at first light."

The wiry Apache grunted.

The Pyramid Mountain range was small, but rugged, providing ample shelter against the weather and security against curious eyes.

During the early morning hours, Slade jerked awake. Beside him, Paleto's soogan was empty. The young man glanced around. His brother was crouching behind a boulder, peering in the direction of the small settlement of Mexican Springs.

Without a whisper of noise, Slade knelt by him.

Down below, half a dozen riders skirted the settlement, heading back west toward the alkali flats.

Paleto whispered, "Good you and me, we ride on last night."

Slade muttered, "Yeah."

The weather held steady the next few days as they cut northeast from Mexican Springs. Paleto's keen eyesight spotted three raiding parties well before the Indians saw them, giving the two brothers ample time to slip into hiding.

Finally they topped the Continental Divide, skirted Cooke's Peak, and pulled up at the Rio Grande where Percha Creek flowed into it.

That night, a small storm blew through, leaving a few inches of snow. Next morning, they pulled out, following the river north to the remains of San Marcial, a small village that had been wiped away by a devastating flood five years earlier.

They spent the night in the ruins of the small village, and before sunup, forded the Rio Grande, heading east, staying in the foothills of the Manzano Mountains. To the northeast sprawled a lush valley, its winter grama dotted with playas.

"I'm surprised to see as many Indians around," Slade muttered as he rocked with the rhythm of his trotting pony. "Wonder what's going on?"

Paleto shrugged. "Who can say? The Kiowa and Ute have the brains of a grasshopper."

Slade chuckled. Often as a youth, he had listened in delight as the elders disparaged the other tribes, comparing the warriors to the offspring of mongrel dogs.

The morning warmed, and the light covering of snow melted in all but the shady nooks. Slade nodded to the purple mountains rising before them. "Those are the Pedernals. We ought to reach them in a couple hours."

An hour later, the distant popping of gunfire arrested their attention. Slade reined up.

Paleto glanced at him, his eyes asking the same question on Slade's mind. The wiry young half-breed shook his head and gestured to the foothills of the Pedernals. "Best we move in a little closer just in case."

Touching the heels of his knee-high moccasins to his piebald, Paleto fell in behind his brother as they rode warily in the direction of the gunshots.

Before they had covered a mile, Slade spotted movement ahead. He reined up behind an upthrust of granite. Ground-reining his dun, he shucked his Winchester and leaped lightly to the ground and quickly scaled the jagged slab with Paleto at his side, carrying his Winchester Yellow Boy.

When they reached the top, they sprawled on their bellies among the jagged shards of gray granite and peered at the battle below.

A dozen Indians in winter buckskins had two white men pinned into a small canyon. Slade recognized the tribe instantly from the hairstyle of the warriors. The right side of the hair was cut off at the ear, but the left grew long and was braided and bound with otter fur. Kiowa.

Some distance behind, the Kiowa had tied their ponies, covered with garish circles and handprints of yellow and red on the chests and ribs of the animals.

Paleto grunted. "Brothers of the Wolf Clan."

While his gray eyes quickly pinpointed each of the warriors' locations, Slade asked, "Do they still follow Black Eagle?"

"Yes."

With a grimace, Slade shook his head. Black Eagle had turned renegade. The cruel chief detested the white man for slaughtering his family, his wife, two sons, and daughter. Slade couldn't blame him. He himself knew the unquenchable fire of revenge. Such a blaze had raged in him years before when in the small town of Pinos Altos, Union soldiers murdered and decapitated Mangas Coloradas, who had been the young half-breed's mentor.

Despite Cochise's entreaties, Slade left the Mimbre Apache and joined the Confederate army in hopes of killing as many Union soldiers as he could.

Later again, the passion blazed with a fire that only death could extinguish as he pursued those who had murdered his mother, kidnapped his sister, and left him for dead.

Now, as he peered down at the fighting, his feelings were mixed. Still, Black Eagle was a cold-blooded killer, sparing no one, Indian or white, who possessed that which he desired.

Without taking his eyes off the battle, Slade spoke. "How many?"

"I count eleven."

"Twelve. The one behind the piñon."

Paleto scanned the rugged field of boulders below, finally spotting the twelfth warrior crouched behind a scrubby piñon between two boulders. "I see."

Slade turned his attention to the white men. There was no sign of panic, which told the young man that the two holed up down in the small canyon had experience fighting Indians. Still, so much lead had been thrown that their supply of cartridges had to be running short.

Without taking his eyes from the scene, Slade muttered, "Where do we begin?"

Paleto touched his fingers to his necklace of bear claws and grinned at his brother. "Like the turkey?"

Slade chuckled, his laugher mixed with nostalgia as he remembered him and his brothers ambushing wild turkeys. They always took the ones on the outside of the flock so as not to startle the others. Nana, their dead brother whom they were returning to bury, was the most proficient of the three boys. Slowly, Slade nodded. "Like the turkeys." He pointed the muzzle of his Winchester at a Kiowa crouching behind a boulder a hundred yards distant. "I'll take this one and work back to us. You start with the one below us. We'll meet at that one behind the piñon."

Paleto's grin grew wider. "Just like the games when we were boys."

Slade's reply was the boom of his Winchester. Moments later, the Kiowa warrior jumped to his feet and staggered backward.

Paleto touched off the Yellow Boy. Two hundred grains of lead exploded from the muzzle at eleven hundred feet per second. The slug slammed into the back of a warrior's head, blowing away his face.

Without hesitation, the two brothers fired at the remaining Kiowas.

One warrior spun and began firing at the puffs of smoke coming from the top of the granite upthrust. He managed two shots before one of Paleto's slugs caught him in the chest, sending him sprawling on that granite and shale slab at his feet.

Excited shouts erupted from the warriors. They attempted to return fire, but the gunfire from above was too devastating. For a few moments, the besieged warriors tried to make a fight of it, but their resolve wavered as slugs from above and from the canyon whined past. Suddenly they broke and ran for their ponies, darting between boulders and behind scrubby piñon.

# Chapter Five

Slade and Paleto lowered their rifles, but the two jaspers holed up in the box canyon continued firing until the last Kiowa disappeared down the valley.

One of the cowpokes peered up at Slade. When he spotted the wiry half-breed, he held up his saddle rifle.

The two cowpokes grinned when Slade approached. "Mighty glad to see you, partner," said the older one, extending his hand. "You sure saved our bacon." He glanced past Slade and frowned. "I coulda sworn there was two of you up there."

"There was. My brother's waiting. We figured after what you old boys have been through, you might be kinda itchy fingered."

The second cowpoke narrowed his eyes. "What do you mean by that?"

Slade chuckled. "My brother is Apache, Mimbre Apache." He gave a sharp whistle, and Paleto appeared from behind a jumble of boulders. "This is Paleto. My name is Jake."

A smile played over the second cowpoke's lips, but his eyes remained cool. "I see what you mean, friend." He waved Paleto in. "Coffee's probably all boiled down, but you're welcome to what we have. My name's Jess Cooper. This here ugly galoot is Arch Simmons."

"Coffee sounds good," Slade replied, studying the two jaspers as they rummaged around the fire. From the cool manner in which they had fought the Kiowa and the six-guns hanging low on their thighs, Slade knew instantly they were gunfighters. He glanced at Paleto, who squatted beside him at the fire.

The impassive Apache nodded almost imperceptibly. He, too, had recognized the two gunnies for what they were.

The younger of the two, Jess Cooper, sipped his coffee. "Me and Arch come up from a place called Roswell. Some gambler bought the place and named it after his old man, is what we heard."

Arch grunted and loosed a stream of tobacco in the fire.

Jess shook his head. "Damn it, Arch. You know that stuff stinks when it burns."

The older man winked at Slade. "Don't smell it, then." He paused, a quizzical frown on his weathered face. "No offense intended, Slade, but you don't look Apache."

Slade grinned. "Nez Perce. My father was white. Comancheros left me for dead. Paleto's father found me and took me in."

Arch nodded.

The younger gun hand upended the skillet, dumping the burned bacon on the dying fire. "If you're hungry, I can whip up some more. Them Injuns hit us just after I put the skillet on the fire."

"Kiowa," Slade said. "Brother of the Wolf Clan. They can be pretty mean."

A shrill war cry galvanized them into action. Slade leaped to his feet, his .44 Colt appearing in his hand like magic, but before he could fire, Jess Cooper's six-gun barked twice, slamming two slugs into the wounded Kiowa's chest, knocking him backward.

Cooper grunted. "There's another good Injun."

Arch was scanning the hills around them, his own six-gun in hand. "I don't know about you, but I'm ready to light a shuck out of here." He glanced at Slade. "We're heading up to Fort Union. I'd feel a heap better with four of us together."

"Yeah," Jess put in. "Hear some jasper up there is looking for hombres handy with a six-gun. Interested?"

Slade holstered his Colt. "No, thanks. We're heading back toward Santa Fe." It was a lie, but neither Slade nor Paleto cared for the confinement or possible ramifications two more riding partners might create.

Cooper shrugged, his eyes still cool. He holstered his six-gun and shook hands with Slade again. "We're in your debt, Jake." He nodded to the Apache. "Yours, too, Paleto. If we can ever give you a hand, just say so."

As they parted, Arch gave a last wave of his hand. Slade returned the gesture.

Paleto muttered, "The young one is fast."

Slade arched an eyebrow. "He beat me. I wouldn't be anxious to go up against him." He paused, then added, "Handy with a six-gun, huh? Makes you wonder what those two got lined up at Fort Union."

The leather-tough Apache grunted.

Slade and Paleto rode hard the next two days, their eyes constantly scanning the desert for Utes or Kiowa and the skies for threatening weather.

Finally, they spotted the Sangre de Cristos to the north. Slade grinned. "We're getting closer, my brother."

That night, they made camp in a small cave in the foothills of the Sangre de Cristos near the headwaters of the Gallinas River. As the fire burned low, Slade ambled outside, drawing the fresh crisp air into his lungs.

He glanced at the cave, noting the smoke from the fire, upon emerging from the mouth, swirled to the ground instead of immediately rising into the treetops. He grimaced. Bad weather. A sure sign despite the starry heavens above.

During the night, a storm blew in, dumping several inches of snow on the ground and drifting several feet high in arroyos and gulches.

The storm lasted all day. The following morning dawned clear and bright.

After a light breakfast of coffee and venison, Paleto and Slade, not anxious to waste any time snowbound in a cave, stomped outside and looked around. To the north beyond a distant ridge, several columns of smoke drifted lazily into the crisp blue sky.

Paleto looked up at Slade. "What town, do you think?"

The wiry young half-breed shrugged. "No idea. Let's find out."

Slade buttoned his heavy mackinaw and Paleto donned his heavy bearskin coat before they rode out. While the ridge was less than a mile distant, they didn't reach it until noon.

Reining up on the crest of a shale ridge, they peered down at the small village below.

A dozen or so buildings of clapboard, rock, log, and canvas lined either side of a wide street. At one end of the row of buildings was a small church. Puffs of frosty air jetted from the nostrils of four pairs of draft horses straining to pull a snowplow through the middle of town and out the south road.

For several minutes beneath the pine and piñon, they studied the village. Without warning, the pop of

gunfire drifted up the slope. Moments later, two cowpokes, arms flailing and feet kicking, rolled out of a
saloon and into the street. Half a dozen drunken waddies staggered out to watch the fight.

Paleto grunted. "That no place for Apache."

Slade chuckled. "Ain't no place for anyone." Without
taking his eyes off the scene below, Slade said, "Still,
we need supplies. I'll drop down and pick up some.
Meet you back up here as soon as I finish."

Paleto grunted. "Take care."

Over his shoulder, Slade replied, "Don't worry about
that."

An hour later, Slade rode into town. Though only early
afternoon, tinny music and riotous laughter poured
from all three of the saloons.

Slade kept his eyes fixed on the mercantile store next
to the Golden Queen Saloon at the end of the street. He
read the sign on the store, JUNIPER PASS MERCANTILE
AND MARKET, JUNIPER PASS, NEW MEXICO TERRITORY.

On the opposite side of the street inside the Nugget Saloon, a gap-toothed gunman watched through a dingy
window as Slade rode into town. The gunnie frowned
at the war club on the buckskin-clad man's waist and
the bow and quiver of arrows rocking gently against the
long-coupled dun's ribs as the rider grew closer. His
frown deepened. Somewhere, he had heard of a waddie
dressed in buckskins and wearing knee-length moccasins.

Suddenly his eyes popped open when he remembered. He spun on his boot heel and scurried across
the sawdust floor to a poker game in the rear of the
dimly lit room. "Jack! Jack! He's here. He's here."

Kansas Jack looked up, his bushy brows knit irritably. "Not now, Dill."

Dill Carson sputtered, "But—"

Across the table from Jack, Frank Tolliver narrowed his eyes and, seeing his opponent was distracted, grinned to himself. He tossed a dollar in the pot, then added five more. "Call and bump you five."

Dill persisted, "But, Jack, he's—"

Jack's eyes blazed. "Damn it to hell, Dill, shut your damned mouth until this hand's over."

Tolliver broke in. "You gonna play, Jack, or talk?"

Increasingly frustrated, Jack slammed a half eagle down on the table. "Call you, damn it." In the next moment, he spread his hand on the table. "Three kings." With a smug grin, he glared up at the grizzled face of his partner. "Let's see you beat that."

The larger man shook his head and frowned, not because he had lost the hand, because he hadn't, but because he liked to play mind games with Kansas Jack, who couldn't pick out a goat in a herd of sheep.

When Jack spotted the frown on Tolliver's face, his thick lips curled in a gloating smirk. He started to reach for the pot.

"Hold on," Tolliver exclaimed. "Maybe you ought to take a look at this." He laid out a six-ten mixed straight.

Jack's lantern jaw dropped, and then his eyes blazed as he glared up at Tolliver.

The big man laughed and dragged the pot. "Appreciate the handout, partner. Sure do."

Chagrined not only at losing the pot but being laughed at, Jack dropped his hand to the butt of his revolver. His fingers curled around the walnut grips. He hesitated. He was no match for Frank Tolliver. For long seconds, his black eyes burned holes into the grizzled

jaw of his partner, who was sorting through his win-
nings. No sense in getting killed over twenty bucks.

His shoulders slumped, and with a sigh, he leaned
back in his chair as Tolliver rolled a cigarette. Without looking at Jack, Tolliver muttered, "You're getting
smarter, Jack. I could have put a slug in your gut before
you cleared leather." He placed the cigarette between
his lips and touched a lucifer to it. Then his cold blue
eyes nailed the smaller man. "Don't ever try it. Don't
even think about it."

For several seconds, he stared at Kansas Jack. He was
growing tired of waiting for that damned Wingate to
send him enough gunnies to take over the town and
buy out the community. Still, he had been paid well. He
couldn't complain. A breezy grin broke over his face
and he reached for the cards. "Now, let's play poker."

Jack suddenly remembered Dill. He looked up impatiently.

"Well, what it is now?"

He gestured sharply to the pot in front of Tolliver. "I
coulda won that hand if you hadn't started all that
yapping."

Dill Carson gulped. He hooked his thumb over his
shoulder. "Out yonder, in the street."

Tolliver tossed out his ante. "Ante up."

Jack pitched his ante into the pot as he directed his
question at Dill. "What about the street?"

"A few months back, over in the Texas Panhandle."

"So?" Jack turned his attention back to the cards
being dealt him.

"So. Remember that jasper in buckskins with that
old man?"

Kansas Jack froze. His throat went dry. "Buckskins?"

"Yeah. Wore a Injun war club."

.. 

gunman's entire body tensed. Dill had his
complete attention now. "What about him?"

Dill jabbed a bony finger at the street. "He's out there
now. He just rode in from the south all by hisself."

Kansas Jack leaped to his feet, knocking the captain's
chair to the floor and hurrying to the window. "Where?"
He quickly scanned the street, spotting Slade just as the
young half-breed tied up in front of the mercantile.

His beady eyes narrowed. Slade and the old man
had been the ones that broke up a profitable rustling
operation over on the Canadian River in the Texas Panhandle a couple of months earlier.

Now it was payback time.

Tying up at the rail, Slade paused to glance up and
down the snow-covered street. Seeing nothing out of
the ordinary, he pushed through the double glass doors.
Ignoring the attention the old-timers around the potbellied stove paid to his dress, he stopped at the counter. At
the end of the counter stood two Indians patiently.

A rail-thin man wearing an apron greeted him.
"Howdy, stranger. Welcome to Juniper Pass. I'm Abner Reed. I own this place." He glanced at the drifts
out the window. "Reckon you had a time getting here,
huh? Why, that snow's bound to be five or six feet in
places."

With a faint grin, Slade replied, "Reckon it is."

"So, what can I do for you?"

Slade hooked his thumb to the Indians. "They was
here before me."

Abner Reed shrugged. "Navahos. They can wait.
Now, what can I get you?"

The wiry half-breed's eyes grew cold. "I said, they
was here before me."

Surprised, Reed hesitated, then nodded and quickly serviced the Navahos.

After they left, Reed hurried back to Slade.

Slade glanced around the room, looking over the four old men staring unabashed at him. He turned back to the clerk. "I need some coffee, beans, bacon, and flour. And—"

Two gunshots rang out beyond the wall. Abner Reed shrugged. "Don't pay no mind. Just some old boys next door in the saloon letting off steam." He shook his head and continued, a wry twist in his voice. "Been here a week or so. Mighty rowdy. I guess that's why the sheriff rode out to Santa Fe. Now, what else did you need, friend?"

"A couple cans of peaches and tomatoes if you got them."

"Right away." The store owner scurried around the store, pulling goods from shelves, dipping flour into a bag, and slicing off a slab of bacon. Deftly, he wrapped the purchases, then slapping his hands together to brush off the flour and dust, said. "Anything else? Cartridges?"

Slade shook his head. "Nope."

"Let's see." The store owner's lips moved silently as he totaled the bill. "That'll be four dollars and sixty cents."

Outside, the young half-breed packed a couple of bundles of supplies in his saddlebags and tied the remaining bag to the saddle with pigging strings. Just as he started to mount, a cold voice growled, "Turn around, Slade. I want you to see who's going to kill you."

# Chapter Six

Slade froze, one hand with the reins on the saddle horn, the other on the cantle.

"Drop them reins and turn around real slowlike."

"Whatever you say, friend." Slade turned, then stiffened when he stared into the sneering smirk on Kansas Jack's face. He nodded slowly. "Well, well, well. Kansas Jack. I was wondering where you'd crawled off to."

The smirk froze on Jack's face. "I'm going to kill you, Slade, and then I'll leave you out here for the buzzards."

By now, several of the townspeople as well as hired guns had gathered.

His brain racing, Slade ticked off his options. His mackinaw was buttoned. He'd be on the stairway to hell three times over before he could shuck his Colt. He had to push Jack, not too far, not over the edge, but far enough so the dull-witted gunnie would make a mistake. "Kill a defenseless man? That would be murder, Jack, and you got too many witnesses looking on." He paused, then decided to push a little harder. "Of course, I don't blame you because you know I'm a better man with a gun than you'll ever be."

Kansas Jack glowered. His finger tightened on the trigger. "Why, you—"

On the porch in front of the Nugget Saloon, Frank Tolliver laughed and called out, "Give the half-breed a chance, Jack. Or ain't you got the guts?"

The cowpokes around the big man laughed.

"Yeah," shouted the one called Hatch, who wore a black patch over one eye.

Ears burning, Jack stiffened. His whole body trembled as if caught in a seizure. He snarled through clenched teeth. Angrily, he slammed his six-gun in his holster and took a step back.

Slade's gray eyes turned to ice as he gingerly unbuttoned his mackinaw with one hand, never taking his eyes off Kansas Jack. Reaching behind his back with his left hand, he pulled the tail of the heavy wool coat back behind his Colt. Then, with one finger, he flipped the leather loop from the hammer of his .44.

Kansas Jack's eyes narrowed.

"Hold on, Jack. Hold on just a minute." Slade eased sideways several steps into the middle of the street. "The dun is a good animal. I don't want to see him shot. I need him."

For a moment, Jack frowned, not comprehending Slade's comments, but the sarcastic laughter from the Nugget Saloon was all he needed.

He slapped leather.

He had no sooner wrapped his fingers about the worn handle on his six-gun than a blow like a blacksmith's hammer slammed him in the chest followed instantly by a second blow.

Kansas Jack stared at the young half-breed in disbelief before a curtain of darkness swept before his eyes. He never felt the impact of the snow against his face.

Slade remained motionless for several moments, then

scanned the onlooking faces. He cleared his throat. "Is the sheriff around?"

Abner Reed looked up and down the street nervously. "Like I said, he's done rode off to Santa Fe."

Several onlookers started across the street, curious as to the conversation, among them Frank Tolliver and three of his gun hands. Tolliver was cursing to himself. Kansas Jack was dumber than a snake, but he had been good with a gun. That's why Wingate had sent him. Now he was dead. Wingate wouldn't like that. Still, the cold-blooded killer told himself, we can take over this town without Kansas Jack, and that's all Wingate cares about.

Eyeing the clerk on the porch outside his store, Slade said, "What about a mayor?"

The clerk indicated a small man in black trousers with a matching vest over a boiled shirt. "That'd be Homer Akins. He owns the gun shop."

Holstering his Colt, Slade nodded. "You saw what happened, Mayor. What do you need from me to clean all this up?"

Akins licked his lips and ran his thin fingers through what few strands of hair he had left. "Well." He looked around nervously, his eyes flickering briefly over Tolliver. "I ain't real sure."

"Look, I've got business up north that I need to get on. I'll be back this way in a couple weeks. If you want, I can write down what happened and how you can get in touch with me."

Mayor Akins scratched his head and frowned at the store owner. "What do you think, Abner?"

The slender store owner chewed on his bottom lip. "Well, I don't know. I suppose—"

A voice behind them boomed, "You might not know, grocery man, but I do. You're under arrest, cowboy."

Slade looked around and stared into the muzzles of four six-guns. Behind them, Frank Tolliver and his gun hands leered. Slade glanced back at the mayor. "Who's this?"

Akins gulped. "I—I mean—"

Tolliver laughed. "I'm taking the place of the sheriff, cowboy. And we don't cotton to no killings on our streets." He glowered at Homer Akins. "Ain't that right, Mayor?"

The mayor didn't reply.

Tolliver shouted, "I said, ain't that right?"

Timidly, the mayor nodded.

"That's what I thought," the big man grunted. With the muzzle of his six-gun, he indicated Slade's Colt. "Get this hombre's six-gun and that war club, too, Dill."

Slade started to resist, but the odds were too great. He glanced around at the faces looking on. More than half appeared to be townsfolk, intimidated by Frank Tolliver and his gunnies.

Dill shucked Slade's Colt, knife, and war club, overlooking the deadly slingshot the young half-breed carried in his shirt pocket. "Now, git," he said, shoving Slade toward the saloon.

Slade stumbled, cutting his eyes to the distant ridge on which Paleto sat. He couldn't see his brother, but Paleto's eyes were those of the eagle. A modicum of relief washed over Slade, knowing his brother was watching.

Clouds blew in over the mountain peaks surrounding the small village. Heavy wet flakes of snow began to fall.

Tolliver called to the angular-faced jasper with one

eye missing, "Hatch! Go wake up the judge. We got us a murder trial to hold."

The one-eyed gunman scurried down the street.

"Murder!" The word burst from Slade's lips. He spun, but suddenly he felt like his head exploded.

Matilda O'Connor had been widowed four times, the last being Ailin O'Connor, who came from County Clare in the west of Ireland and north of the Shannon River. O'Connor struck a small vein of gold, enough to build the single hotel with a café in Juniper Pass that would provide for him and his wife through their old age. After his mine caved in on him, Tilly held on to the hotel.

Matilda had just finished changing the linens in the second-floor front room of the hotel when she heard the commotion. She peered out the window. Her curiosity turned to alarm when she saw the young man being shoved across the street, then slammed on the back of his head. She muttered a curse. "Enough is enough," she exclaimed, spinning on her heel and storming down the stairs.

Grabbing her fur-lined coat and broad-brimmed hat from behind the counter, she spoke over her shoulder to the desk clerk as she yanked open the door. "I'll be back directly, Harold. Look after things."

Like others in town, she had tolerated Tolliver and his gang, especially after Sheriff Townsend had disappeared. The citizens were no match for Tolliver's firepower, so all the townsfolk could do was wait for him and his gunnies to leave.

Slade jerked awake to raucous laughter when Dill Carson threw a mug of warm beer in his face.

"That did it, Dill," shouted Fats Buchler, so called

because of his pear-shaped belly. "That woke that half-breed up."

Blinking his eyes, Slade tried to gather his thoughts.

He was slumped in a captain's chair in front of a poker table. The room was filled with citizens of Juniper Pass whose number was matched by a cross section of western outlawry.

Tolliver poured himself a drink and tossed it down. He glared at Fats. "Where's Hatch and that judge?"

The laughter fled the fat man's face. He shook his head. "I don't know, Frank. I'll go see."

At that moment, Jimmy Horner, a dissipated drunk in shirtsleeves and an open collar, staggered in followed by Hatch. Horner headed straight to the bar, but Tolliver pulled him away. "Not yet, Judge. We got to keep this legal. Bar's closed during trials and hangings, ain't that right?"

Swaying on his feet, Horner drew himself up and nodded somberly. "By all means, Mr. Tolliver. By all means."

Matilda O'Connor pushed through the crowd of onlookers to confront Tolliver, her Irish temper ready to explode. "Just a damned minute there, mister. There ain't nothing legal about this trial. For one thing, that jasper there's got no lawyer, and as for a judge—" She jabbed a finger at him and snorted. "Why, Jimmy Horner there was kicked off the bench five years ago for being drunk and has been a sot ever since."

Tolliver studied the feisty bantam of a woman. She was a humorous sight. Her heavy leather coat swallowed her, and her bushy gray hair stuck out under her slouch hat. "Lady, we're going to have us a trial here, and this sot is the judge. Yonder, in front of the bar, is the jury." He narrowed his eyes. "Now, if you don't like it, get out. Otherwise, you might not have a hotel to go back to."

Homer Akins hurried to her side. "Tilly, damn it to hell. Shut up. These men mean business. There ain't no sense losing all you got for a drifter."

She jerked around and glared at Akins. "You're a coward, Homer Akins." Her gaze swept the crowd. "That goes for you too, Abner Reed and Burl Henry and Matthew Leighton." She rattled off several more names before pausing. "If we let them hang this drifter, who's next?"

"Nobody," Burl Henry replied hastily. "Hush now, Tilly. Nobody's going to get hurt. Nobody important."

"Yeah," said Matthew Leighton, who owned the Leighton Freight Lines.

Tolliver growled, "You best listen to him, Tilly girl. At least somebody in this town has got good sense." He turned to the judge. "Let's have a trial." He looked back around with a hint of murder in his icy blue eyes. "Anyone who don't like what's going on had best light a shuck out of here."

No one moved.

Within five minutes, the trial was over. The jury found Slade guilty.

"Now, the sentence, Judge," said Tolliver.

Judge Jimmy Horner read the sentence in the eyes of the grizzled outlaw. "Hang by the neck until dead," he announced.

A shout of glee went up from Tolliver's men. Dill and Fats grabbed a lariat and hurried outside. The others rushed forward, grabbing Slade and shoving him to the door.

Fats and Dill came stumbling back in. "It's a blizzard. We can't see nothing out there."

The bloodthirsty crowd paused, staring at each other in confusion. Hatch shook his head. "So, now what?"

Fats grinned. "I got an idea." He pointed to the rafters overhead. "Let's hang him in here."

# Chapter Seven

Tilly O'Connor spun and shot an accusing look at Abner Reed and the others.

Before she could utter a word, Frank Tolliver's booming voice silenced the excited roar of the crowd. "There ain't going to be no hanging in the saloon."

Instantly, the room became silent as midnight in a graveyard. Tolliver continued, his blue eyes crinkled with amusement as they stopped on Tilly. "Even though we ain't got no sheriff, we need to stay legal. Hanging a jasper in the saloon ain't legal."

"Maybe not," a voice piped up from the rear of the crowd. "But it'll damned well get the job done right proper."

A smattering of chuckles rolled across the crowd.

Tolliver nodded. "Won't argue that, but we got us a hanging tree, and that's what we'll use. Besides, a body swinging from the rafters would interfere with my drinking." He turned to Fats and Hatch. "Toss this jasper in the hoosegow. Soon as the storm's over, we'll give him a hemp necktie."

Gleeful shouts of approval greeted his announcement.

"Come on, you," growled Fats, seizing Slade's arm and jerking him from his chair.

* * *

Ten minutes earlier at the end of the snow-swept street, Paleto had crouched at the corner of the Longhorn Saloon and squinted against the blowing snow. He laid his fingers on his necklace of bear claws to draw from the strength and bravery of the grizzly. The laughter and shouts from the Nugget Saloon in the middle of the block pinpointed his brother's location.

He racked his brain in an effort to figure out how to communicate with Slade. Then he had an idea.

Slipping back into the forest, he found two branches about three feet long, one with a fork at one end. Apache youth and white youth had much in common, one being the use of signals communicating information understood only by those aware of the meaning of the signal.

More times than the wiry Apache could remember, he had placed two branches in an inverted V in the ground to indicate to the others he had passed this way. And both Nana and Busca had done the same.

Pausing at the corner of the saloon, he studied the street. Still empty. Quickly, he hurried along the rear of the buildings until he was directly across from the Nugget.

Like a ghost, he slipped to the edge of the boardwalk and under the veil of blowing snow, placed the branches in the snow so that anyone leaving the saloon would see them.

Hastily, he returned to his post in the forest at the end of the street, where he pulled the bearskin coat tighter about him. All he could do now was wait, and watch.

Not long afterward, the saloon doors swung open and two jaspers holding guns on Slade stepped out into the storm.

Slade's heart jumped into his throat when he spotted the inverted V. He glanced up and down the street. For a fleeting moment, he glimpsed a dark head beyond the Longhorn Saloon.

"Get inside," Hatch snarled, shoving Slade into the single cell and slamming the door. He glanced over his shoulder at Fats. "Get a fire going while I stuff a blanket in the window."

"Fire? What for?" He nodded to Slade. "Hell, he's going to be dead in the morning anyway."

Hatch grimaced. "Not for him, for us." He shook his head.

"Us?"

"Yeah, us. Tolliver told us to stay with him, and me, I'm doing whatever Tolliver says."

Fats nodded eagerly. "Yeah."

Slade scanned the jail. Solid stone. A single window on the south side. The wooden bunk in the cell had no blanket. Beneath the bunk sat a wood-stake bucket, which, from the stench emanating from it, served as an indoor outhouse.

Twenty minutes later, the door swung open. A blast of wind and gust of snow accompanied Tilly O'Connor, who was carrying a covered basket.

Hatch frowned at her. "What are you doing here, lady? This here's the jail."

Fats's nostrils instantly picked up the succulent aroma of fried venison and homemade biscuits.

Tilly smiled shyly and replied, "Mr. Tolliver said I could bring you and the prisoner some supper from the café." She set the basket on the desk and removed the cloth. She brought out a platter of venison, a bowl of steaming gravy, and a plate heaped with soda biscuits.

Both gunnies looked on anxiously.

Finally, she set out plates and silverware, and they dug in, ignoring the silverware.

In a timid voice belied by the steely glint in her eyes, she asked, "Do you mind if I fix the stranger a plate?"

Fats shook his head, his mouth too full to speak.

Hatch mumbled around a whole biscuit he had popped into his mouth, "Don't give him no knife or fork. Let him use his fingers," he said as he reached for another slab of venison with his own dirty fingers.

"Thank you, ma'am," Slade said as he took the plate of grub. "And thanks for the words you put in for me back there. For a while there, I didn't figure I had any friends at all around here."

She smiled gently and patted his hand through the bars. "I don't know how, but we want to help you."

Slade arched an eyebrow.

The woman grimaced. "I know it didn't seem that way back at the saloon, but it's just that we've never had to face someone like Frank Tolliver and his men."

Under his breath, Slade asked, "What's someone like that doing here?"

Tilly glanced over her shoulder and leaned closer.

Fats looked up from feeding his face. "Hey, what are you two jabbering about over there? Give him his grub and back away, lady."

The young half-breed nodded imperceptibly. "My brother is outside. He's in the forest by the Longhorn. Find him. Maybe the two of you can figure out something."

"All right."

"He's Apache."

Her eyes grew wide. "Apa—"

Slade held his finger to his lips. "I'll explain later. His name is Paleto."

She nodded jerkily. "But how do I find him?"

"Don't worry." Slade grinned knowingly. "He saw you come in here."

Though the storm had slackened, the streets remained empty. Most businesses except the saloons had closed early.

Bundled in oversize coat and floppy hat, Tilly O'Connor hurried across the street to the Longhorn Saloon. She paused at the batwing doors to peer inside, just in case anyone was watching.

Moments later, she slipped around the corner and out of the wind. She peered into the shadows of the pine and piñon. Nothing moved. She moved deeper into the forest. She called out, "Paleto."

No answer.

A sudden precognition came over her. She had the feeling someone was nearby, unseen, but nearby.

"I want to help your brother. He told me to find you. I own the hotel. Come to my back door." She paused, looking around at the empty forest about her and feeling somewhat foolish for speaking as she had.

What if Paleto isn't here? What if he's in another part of town? A dozen questions filled her head, none for which she had an answer.

At the hotel, not bothering to light a lantern, she went directly to the back door and peered outside. She frowned in disappointment. No one. Slowly, she closed the door and turned back to the front.

The door creaked open and a blast of cold air rushed in.

She spun and gasped as she stared at the bulky figure before her, his dark features indiscernible in the shadows of the back room.

A guttural voice said, "I am Paleto."

Though not a shy woman, Tilly stammered for words at the moment.

In a soft voice, Paleto continued. "You saw Busca?"

Finally, she found her voice. "Busca?"

"My brother. That is his Apache name. The white man calls him Slade, Jake Slade."

By now Tilly had gathered her thoughts. "They plan to hang him in the morning."

The shadows hid the expression on his face from her. "I know the kind who watch after him. Can you get them whiskey?"

She studied him a moment, uncertain just what he was asking. Then she understood. A smile played over her lips. "Yes. His horse is still at the rail outside Abner's store. I'll put him in my barn, then take two bottles to them. I'll tell them I found the whiskey in the saddlebags and ask them what to do with it." She paused, waiting for his response.

After several moments, he chuckled. "You make good Apache. I wait outside the jail. When those two sleep, I will free my brother."

A grim smile played over her lips.

As soon as Tilly O'Connor closed the back door behind Paleto, she hurried to the front of the hotel. She had no time to waste picking up Slade's dun.

She jerked to a halt on the porch and stared in disbelief. Slade's horse had vanished.

\* \* \*

Moments earlier, Paleto had crouched at the corner of the hotel, studying the rear of the buildings between him and the jail. Next door, the tonsorial parlor had an outhouse. He hesitated only a moment, taking a chance on slipping between the two instead of spending extra time circling behind the latter.

Just as he glided up to the outhouse, the door opened, and a cowpoke stepped out, coming face-to-face with the surprised Apache.

At that second, the back door of the barbershop opened, and a second cowpoke stepped out.

The first one grabbed for his six-gun and shouted, "Injun! Injun!"

Paleto ducked his head and charged, slamming his shoulder into the cowpoke and knocking him back into the outhouse before vanishing into the forest amid whining slugs.

Tilly spun when she heard the shouting. She muttered an unladylike curse and bolted toward the jail, uncertain just what she could do now, but realizing whatever it was, time was of the essence.

# Chapter Eight

The firing continued. Cowpokes poured from all three saloons, filling the street, then bolting north as Paleto led them away from the jail.

Two doors before Tilly reached the jail, Fats and Hatch stepped out on the boardwalk to see what was causing the ruckus. The small woman ducked into a narrow space between the gun shop and Pate's tax office.

For a moment, the two gunnies stared in the direction of the gunfire. Hatch shrugged and started back inside, but then the firing intensified and excited shouting echoed from the forest. Fats and Hatch raced down the street.

After they passed Tilly, she hurried around the back of the gun shop and came in from the rear at the jail. She slipped inside and sighed with relief. Empty except for the young half-breed.

Slade swung to his feet when she burst in. He looked for Paleto, but when he didn't see his brother, he called to her, "Where's Paleto?"

Tilly rummaged frantically through the desk for the keys. "I don't know. Somebody spotted him." Finally, she found them, and with shaking fingers fumbled to open the cell.

Taking the keys from her, Slade opened the cell and

stepped out. Quickly he retrieved his weapons. "Now what?"

"Now follow me back to the hotel."

"Just a minute." He locked the cell and returned the keys to the desk drawer, then quietly closed it. He grinned wickedly at Tilly. "All right. Now let's get."

She paused at the door, peering up and down the street. Glancing over her shoulder with a broad grin on her flushed and excited face, she nodded. "Empty. Let's go. The back way."

Three minutes later, they closed the back door of the hotel behind them. Shadows lay thick over the room.

She hesitated, then in a tentative voice said, "I've got a place to hide you. When my last husband, Ailin, built this place, he put in some hidden passages because of Injun trouble back then."

Slade grunted. "Let's go."

"No, listen. Only one person besides me knows about them. He helped Ailin build the place. Jimmy Horner, the judge."

"The judge?"

"Jimmy was sweet on me before Ailin and me married. He still is. I don't think he'll tell anyone about the passages, but he could. It's a risk, and it's your risk to take."

The wiry half-breed patted the butt of his Colt. "What happens to you if they find me here?"

The diminutive woman snorted. "Nothing if them jaspers knows what's good for them." She peered into the darkness that was his face. "What about it?"

"Like I said, let's go."

Tilly grabbed his arm. "Over here. A pantry. You're going to have to feel your way." At the rear of the pantry, she pressed a hidden catch. The rear wall swung open, shelves and all. "Never had a chance to use these passages, but I reckon they'll come in handy right now.

"Give me your hand." She led the way up a flight of stairs and into a small room. She lit a small lamp.

Slade started to protest, but she explained. "This room is closed in. No light can get out." She paused, then added, "I figure Tolliver and his boys is going to be looking mighty hard for you. I'll get you some grub later, but don't worry. No one knows about this room except me and Jimmy. Come morning, I'll see how things stand. Your pony's missing, so I'll try to find you one. Best you get out of Juniper Pass as soon as you can."

Slade chuckled. "I can't argue with you there, ma'am. And, ma'am?"

Tilly paused as she started down the steep stairs and looked over her shoulder.

"See what you can learn about my brother."

A pang of sympathy tugged at her heart. She nodded. "I will."

By the time Tilly O'Connor reached the front desk, most of the shouting and shooting had died away. Through the front window, she saw excited cowpokes still running up and down the street. The search had moved farther north of town beyond the livery.

Silhouetted against the yellow glow from the batwing doors of the Nugget Saloon stood the hulking body of Frank Tolliver.

As Tilly looked on, Hatch Ahearn rushed up to Tolliver.

Tolliver frowned at his man. "What in the hell are you doing out here? You're supposed to be at the jail watching that Slade jasper."

Breathless, Hatch gulped, dreading telling the big man what had happened. "That—that's just it, Frank. He—he ain't there to watch. He's gone."

Tolliver glared at the smaller man. "He's what?"

Taking a tentative step back, Hatch nodded. "Me and Fats ran down to see if we could catch that Injun, and when we got back, he was gone."

Tolliver's rock-hard face turned purple with rage. "Why, you worthless—" He drew his arm back to hit the slender gun hand, then hesitated.

Taking another step back, Hatch babbled, "We don't know how, Frank. Honest. The keys was where we left them in the desk drawer. They hadn't been moved, and the cell was still locked. It's just like that jasper just shinnied out between them bars. I—we don't know how he got out."

For several seconds, Frank Tolliver held his massive fist drawn back. Slowly, he lowered it, and Hatch relaxed. Tolliver growled. "Hell, bustin' you up won't get that jasper back."

Hatch grinned in relief. "That's right, Frank, that's right."

Without warning, Frank Tolliver drew back and slammed his knotted fist into Hatch Ahearn's face, smashing his nose and sending blood squirting in every direction.

Hatch hit the ground and slid to the edge of the boardwalk.

Tolliver studied him a moment. "It might not help gettin' Slade back, but it sure as hell makes me feel better, you no-account little bastard."

He turned back into the saloon. "Dill! Dill! Get over here."

* * *

Five minutes later, half a dozen vigilante posses began combing Juniper Pass for Jake Slade. They stomped through every business, every home, opened every room, closet, and pantry.

Tilly O'Connor looked up behind the front desk when Tolliver and a handful of gunnies, including one-time judge Jimmy Horner, stomped in. The big man glared at the small woman. "We're here to search the place. Any objections?"

Her eyes filled with defiance, Tilly glanced past Tolliver at Jimmy Horner. "I have guests. You'll disturb them."

Leaning forward in a threatening manner, Tolliver snarled, "So?"

With a resigned smirk, she cut her eyes up the snarling gun hand. "Go ahead. I can't stop you."

Tolliver nodded to the men. "Search everywhere. Three of you take the second floor."

"Don't forget the barn out back," she said, her gaze fixed on Horner.

Still in his shirtsleeves and reeking of whiskey, he tried to look her in the eye. For a few seconds, he held her gaze, reading her mind, then dropped his gaze to the floor and followed the others.

One of Tolliver's gang, Dill Carson, caught the exchange of glances between the two. He frowned, wondering what was taking place between them.

After the handful of gunnies began their search, Tilly pulled out the Colt .44 she kept under the counter and checked the cartridges. Gently, she turned the cylinder until a slug was under the hammer, then slid the six-gun under a sheaf of papers.

Her muscles tensed as she heard the sound of

boots on the floor above. Several times, she drew a deep breath and released it slowly in an effort to relax.

She looked around the empty lobby, wishing her employee, Harold, was here to take her mind off the present.

At any moment, she expected to hear gunfire, but when she heard the thump of footsteps returning to the lobby, she relaxed.

Tolliver stopped in front of the desk and growled, "If that jasper shows up, you best not help him. Understand?"

Her eyes shifted to Jimmy Horner.

Despite the cold, sweat rolled down his flabby jowls. He smiled weakly at her. She returned the smile.

Resisting the temptation to sneak up the hidden passage and tell Slade what had happened, Tilly quickly closed the hotel down for the night and retired to her small room behind the front desk.

Outside, Dill Carson shivered in his heavy coat and frowned as he watched the small woman, holding a single candle to light her way, disappear into her room. He studied the empty lobby for several moments, remembering the odd look that had passed between Tilly and Jimmy Horner.

For a moment, he couldn't decide whether to reveal his concerns to Tolliver or not. The big man was already primed to explode, and Dill had no intention of being the spark to set him off. Still, if there was something going on and if Tolliver learned Dill hadn't told him, there would be hell to pay.

The slight gunnie shivered. That was one chance he wouldn't take. Look what had happened to Hatch!

* * *

Frank Tolliver glared up at the slender gun hand through bloodshot eyes, his rock-hard face contorted in anger. "What in the hell are you talking about?"

Dill gulped. "I ain't sure, Frank. I saw the two look at each other real funnylike when we was over there." He paused and shrugged. "Maybe there ain't nothing to it, but I got a feeling Horner knows more than he's saying."

For several moments, Tolliver studied the quaking man before him. Over his shoulder, he growled, "Get the judge."

Ten minutes later, Hatch, his one good eye blackened, and Fats ushered a bleary-eyed, staggering Jimmy Horner into the saloon. They stopped at the table. Horner swayed on his feet and finally plopped down in the chair. "What—what's going on?" He slurred his words.

Tolliver stared at the flabby man in disgust. "You tell me. What's going on between you and that widow at the hotel?"

The question threw cold water on Horner's drunken brain. He tried to collect his thoughts. "What do you mean, sir, going on?" He leaned forward, reaching for a bottle of whiskey.

Instead of snatching the bottle, Tolliver remained motionless. Let the sot get even more liquored up. "Is there anything you ain't told me about you and Widow O'Connor?"

Taking a deep slug from the bottle, Horner lowered it, stared at it curiously as if it were an object he had never before seen, then slowly shook his head. With the pomp and dignity of delivering a summation in court, he replied, "Much to my regret, no, sir. Many years ago,

I once clung to the futile hope that someday an agreement of eternal nuptials might take place between us, but alas, I was doomed to disenchantment."

Dill stared down at Tolliver. "What did he say?"

A faint grin turned up one side of Tolliver's thick lips. Keeping his eyes on Jimmy Horner, Tolliver replied, "He said nothing's going on." He looked up slowly at the slender gunnie. "And you, you're nothing but a damned fool for letting your imagination get away with you."

That night, Dill awakened in the back room of the Nugget Saloon. He knew something out of the ordinary was going on between those two. One way or another, he was going to learn just what in the hell it was. Then Tolliver would realize Dill wasn't a fool—that he knew what he was talking about.

# Chapter Nine

Next morning before sunrise, Dill Carson, fortified with a bottle of whiskey, found a comfortable nook in the blacksmith's next to the O'Connor Hotel and Café.

Maybe he was wrong. Maybe not. He'd pondered it all night, and the more he turned it over in his head, the more convinced he was that Jimmy Horner had not told them everything. With a smug grin, Dill Carson swore he'd show Tolliver who was a fool.

Peering out her front window as false dawn grayed the sky, Tilly saw several of Tolliver's men still prowling the town, still searching.

Later, after the morning rush in the hotel café was over, Tilly slipped up the back stairs with some grub for Slade.

While he ate, she told him of the search. "They must not have found your brother. I ain't heard nothing about it if they did."

"What about my horse?"

She shook her head. "Haven't had time to ask about it. Don't worry. They'll be a pony for you tonight."

Slade nodded, chewing slowly. "How long has this Tolliver jasper been around?"

With a shrug, the small woman ran her fingers

through her graying hair. "A couple weeks. Just after he got here, the sheriff, Joe Townsend, disappeared. Word was he went to Santa Fe, but I've got my own suspicions."

Arching an eyebrow, Slade sipped his coffee.

She continued. "I figure Tolliver had him killed because the sheriff was the only one standing between Tolliver and the fresh gold strike up at Cimarron Gorge."

"Fresh gold strike?"

"Yes. Boles's Mines. There's been gold up there before. In fact, the mine up there is the best customer Juniper Pass has. I don't know if we could make it on just stage travel and what few visitors we have from Las Vegas and Santa Fe. Lord knows, this ain't farming country. Anyway, the mine was petering out, but a few months back, the owner experimented with some new processes that brought out a heap more gold."

Slade frowned, puzzled. "What makes you figure Tolliver is connected with the gold?"

"Well, a few weeks back, a city dude by the name of Edgar H. Wingate come in. A banker of some sort. He was trying to buy up mining claims, but he had no luck." She paused. "So he just caught the stage out of here. A couple weeks later is when Tolliver showed up."

"You think there's a connection?"

A sheepish grin wrinkled her cheeks. "I'm just guessing, but those of us that have talked about it figure that's the only reason he's hanging around here. Something to do with the gold. And ever' couple days, two or three more gun hands ride in." She paused. "It's like he's getting ready for a war or something."

Later that morning, bundled against the cold, Tilly waded through the snow to her barn to tend her own horses. She spotted Hatch and two men on their hands and knees, peering beneath the buildings.

When Hatch saw her, he called out, "Hold on, lady. Where are you going?" The three waded through the snow toward her.

She glared at him. "To feed my horses, if that's any of your business."

Hatch eyed the barn with his one good eye. "You best let me look in there first. That Injun and half-breed is still on the loose."

Tilly bit her tongue, silencing the profanity-laced response she wanted to give. Instead, she shrugged. "Go ahead."

Drawing his six-gun, Hatch swung open the door and disappeared inside. Long moments later, he returned, holstering his hogleg. "All right. It's safe in there. You can go on in."

With a toss of her head, she stormed past him and closed the large door behind her. Before she could turn, a soft voice carried through the shadows. "Do not be afraid."

She spun and squinted into the darkness. "Paleto?"

"Sí."

The surprised woman glanced over her shoulder. "But that man—he was just in here."

From the darkness came a chuckle. "Like all white men, he is blind. I could have killed him, but I have my brother to free."

Hurrying forward, she asked, "Are you all right? Slade is worried about you."

Stepping from the darkness, the wiry Apache nodded. "These white men are blind. I am well. Tell Busca I have his dun horse. I take from livery. You know the cave behind your barn?"

Tilly frowned a moment. "By the small creek?"

"Yes."

"Is that where you have the horse?"

Paleto grunted. "Yes. Tonight after the sun goes down, there will be a fire in the saloon. Everyone will go there. That will be the time for Busca to come."

A dozen questions filled her head, but the small woman remained silent. "I'll tell him." Her eyes drifted down to the bear-claw necklace about his neck.

Unknown to her, Dill Carson watched diligently as she made her way back to the hotel. After she closed the back door behind her, he hurried over and found a spot where he could peer unseen into the back room.

No sooner had he found a snug hidey-hole than he saw Tilly enter the pantry. She was out of sight for several minutes. When she reappeared, she carried a coffeepot in one hand and an empty plate with utensils and tin cup in the other.

Where had she gone? He scratched his head, anxious to look behind that closed door.

For most, confined to a small space with nothing to occupy time could be a suffocating experience, but the fatalism of the Apache eschewed such anxieties, instead infusing the warrior to face calmly that which could not be altered.

Slade gazed unseeing at the ceiling above, his mind drifting through a fuzzy panorama of memories. A guttering candle flickered on the floor beside him.

Throughout the day, his keen hearing allowed him to pick up on the routine of the hotel, the coming and going of guests, the puttering of feet as daily cleaning jobs were conducted, and even the opening and closing of the rear door as trash was hauled out back to be burned.

Midafternoon, he heard the rear door open and close. A frown knit his broad forehead. No footsteps below had preceded the opening and closing of the door.

Someone had entered, but then, the footsteps ceased.

He remained motionless on his bed, his ears tuned to the slightest sound.

Glancing around to make certain no one was in sight, Dill Carson slipped into the back room of the hotel. He opened the pantry door and stared at the canned goods on the shelves. He frowned, remembering the coffee-pot and dishes. After a few more moments of trying to make sense of what he had witnessed, he shrugged, figuring the old woman had simply left the pot and dishes in the pantry.

He glanced around, looking for a place to hide. He considered the pantry, but decided against it. There was too much likelihood of someone coming to retrieve a food item. Instead, he slipped into a closet with a sheet of Onasburg canvas draped over the opening.

Thirty minutes later, Tilly O'Connor returned with a tray holding coffee, venison, and biscuits. She opened the pantry door and set the tray down on top of a flour barrel.

The gun hand watched in disbelief as she pressed a catch and swung the wall open. Before she could move, he threw the canvas back and shouted, "Stop right there!"

Instantly, the diminutive woman slammed the wall shut and spun to face him.

* * *

Upstairs, Slade heard the shout followed by the slamming of the wall. In one bound, he leaped from the bed to the top of the stairs, his fingers gripping the butt of his double-edged knife like molded steel.

From below, he heard Tilly scream shrilly, "What are you doing here? Get out, get out, get out."

A sarcastic laugh rolled up the dark stairs. "Not on your life, lady. I'm going to see what's in there. If it's what I think, we're going to have us a hemp party tonight."

Slade had nowhere to go but down. Quickly, he closed the door to the room, dropping the stairs into complete darkness. Agilely, he descended the stairs, pressing up against the wall beside the door.

For only a fleeting second, whoever was out there would be off guard when they stepped from the pantry onto the stairs. That's when Slade would strike.

He pressed hard against the wall, his razor-edged knife in his right hand and that hand pressed tightly against his chest, ready to whip out like a catapult.

His face grim, he listened as Tilly exclaimed, "There's nothing in there. Nothing, I tell you. I—"

The pop of a slap cut her off, and a voice growled, "Open that damned wall, lady, or I swear I'll cut off one of your ears."

Anger roared in Slade's ears, and the Apache lust for blood surged through his veins.

Tilly sobbed and fumbled with the latch. "There's nothing in here. Just another room."

"Hurry up, damn you," the voice shouted.

Finally, the wall swung open. A rectangle of light appeared on the stairway wall across from Slade. Slade pressed his rawhide-tough body against the wall. His muscles tensed.

Dill shoved Tilly, sending her stumbling through the opening. She fell to the stairs.

"Get up, old lady. You hear me? Get up."

As the small woman pushed herself to her feet, she spotted Slade.

He shook his head and nodded upstairs.

A knowing smile touched her lips. She headed up the stairs. "Up here," she mumbled. "Up here at the top of the stairs."

With a cruel laugh, Dill Carson took that first step into the passage. Now he would show Frank Tolliver who was a fool. He glimpsed a flash of silver, and then a club hit him in the chest, followed by a searing pain.

Rough hands grabbed his coat and jerked him on into the passage. The knife flew from his hand and clattered on the steps below. He opened his lips to scream, but a hand covered them, and a carefully honed blade slashed his throat.

Still holding his hand over Dill's mouth, Slade wiped the blood on the knife on Dill's coat and looked up at the trembling woman. "Are you all right?"

She nodded jerkily.

"When I leave tonight, I'll take this one with me." He glanced through the open door at the fading light outside. "From the looks of it, it won't be long." He felt Dill's body go limp, and he removed his hand from the outlaw's lips.

# Chapter Ten

Brilliant flames leaped high into the dark sky, illumining the main street of Juniper Pass. Excited shouting echoed through the town, and every citizen converged on the Nugget Saloon as flames engulfed the storage room.

Tilly O'Connor turned from the window, the flames lighting her face. She looked up into the shadows that filled the young half-breed's face. "You sure you know where the cave is?"

"Don't fret now. You've told me a dozen times." He squatted and picked up the body of Dill Carson. The corpse, wrapped in a sheet, was still limber enough for Slade to toss him over his shoulder although the cold was helping stiffen the body.

Tilly opened the back door and peered outside. "All right. Everyone's across the street," she whispered. "And good luck."

He paused at the door. "I'll be back. I've got a few unsettled debts here in Juniper Pass. You take care."

She nodded and turned back to the lobby, hurrying to join the crowd of gawkers staring at the fire.

Skirting the barn, Slade cut through the forest to the small creek. When he reached it, he paused and squinted into the darkness.

From within the dark mouth of a cave across the stream, a voice whispered harshly, "Busca! Busca!"

Moving quickly, he forded the small stream. Paleto led two horses out. When he saw the body over Slade's shoulder he frowned. "I'll explain later," Slade said, draping Dill's lifeless body over his dun's croup. He started to swing into the saddle but froze as another Indian rode from the shadows of the forest.

Paleto explained, "Do not be alarmed, my brother. This is Right Hand. He was one of the Arapahos who survived the Sand Creek Massacre and fought the white man with the Northern Cheyenne. The Kiowa have been raiding through the mountains. He knows them and the country well. He will take us to the valley where our brother lies."

Slade swung into the saddle. Remembering the previous encounter with Kiowa back to the south, he shook his head. "I can do without them."

"I know."

With a click of his tongue, Slade sent his dun up to Right Hand. "Let's ride, but we need to find someplace to dump this body so no one can find him."

The diminutive Arapaho grunted, then led off through the forest.

Twenty minutes later, he reined up at the edge of a narrow gorge. "River at bottom. Goes into mountain."

In the rear of the Golden Queen Saloon, Tolliver slammed a gnarled fist on the poker table. "What do you mean, you can't find Dill?"

Hatch shrugged. "Just what I said, Frank. Dill's bedroll and all was burnt up by the fire, but he wasn't there. There wasn't nobody in the back room when the fire started. Nobody's seen him."

Clenching his teeth, Tolliver splashed Old Crow whiskey in his glass and downed it. "It ain't like him to run off."

Fats grunted. "No, it ain't. Besides, his horse is still in the barn."

Tentatively, Hatch muttered, "You don't figure he got drunk and passed out somewhere and froze to death? The wind could have drifted the snow over him."

"Not likely," Tolliver muttered. Then he remembered Dill's feeling that maybe Tilly O'Connor and Jimmy Horner knew more about the half-breed's disappearance than they let on.

The judge had denied it. And Tolliver had believed him. However, he told himself, maybe it wouldn't hurt to question the judge again, and Tilly O'Connor while he was at it. Leaning back in his chair, the cold-eyed killer growled, "Keep looking." He turned to Fats. "You bring me that old lady at the hotel and the judge. I got a few more questions for them."

Jimmy Horner was visibly shaken when he stumbled into the Golden Queen. His eyes hastily scanned the room, nervously settling on the grizzled leader of the outlaws.

At that moment, Tilly O'Connor burst through the doors, propelled by two of Tolliver's gunnies holding her arms. She screamed at the top of her lungs.

"You no-account sons of bitches, take your hands off me! That ain't no way to treat a lady."

Hatch gave her a final shove toward Tolliver and sneered. "Get over there and shut up."

Eyes blazing fire, the diminutive woman jerked herself upright and straightened her blouse and skirt. Her hands trembled in anger. She glared at Frank Tolliver.

"Just who do you think you are, treating people like this?"

Leaning his elbows on the table, Tolliver leaned forward, an amused gleam in his eyes. "I'll treat you like I want to, old lady, so you best get used to it."

"How dare you! Why—"

Jimmy Horner attempted to calm her. "Hush up now, Tilly. Screaming won't do no good. Besides, I'm sure Mr. Tolliver has a good reason for asking us to come see him." He glanced hopefully at the leering killer. "Isn't that right, Mr. Tolliver?"

Tolliver ignored the question. The entire saloon had grown silent, the only sound the popping of wood in the potbellied stoves on either side of the room. "One of my boys, Dill Carson, is missing."

"Good," Tilly snapped. "I wish all of you owl-hoots was out of here."

"Tilly!" Horner exclaimed. "For heaven's sake."

A sneer twisted Tolliver's lips. "Heaven ain't helping nobody around here. Before Dill turned up missing, he told me something mighty curious. He said that when we was over to the hotel looking for that half-breed, you two acted like you knew more than what you told us."

Tilly O'Connor glared at him defiantly. Horner could not bring his eyes to meet Tolliver's, a move not lost on the grizzled killer.

With a smug grin, Tolliver looked up at Horner. "Now, I want the truth, Judge. Was there something you didn't tell us that night?"

Tilly clamped her lips tightly and shot Jimmy Horner a warning look. Horner gulped, and despite the chill blowing in through the batwing doors, sweat beaded on his forehead. "N-no, Tolliver. Nothing. That's the truth."

Pushing up from his chair, Tolliver sauntered around the table, slipping his black leather gloves from his belt. Horner's eyes grew wide. He gulped.

Tolliver laughed. "Don't worry, Judge. I ain't going to hit you." Suddenly his hand lashed out, slapping the startled judge with the fingers of the gloves. "I might slap you a bit, but I won't hit you."

Horner staggered back, his flaccid cheek turning red from the blow.

Tilly screamed and leaped at Tolliver, her fingers clawed. Had her nails not been broken for manual labor, she would have drawn blood. Instead, the big man shoved her away and slapped the judge once again, sending the older man spinning to the floor.

"What do you have to say now, Judge? Ready to tell the truth?"

Horner lay on his side, sobbing.

Tolliver nodded to his boys and two of them lifted Horner to his feet. Tolliver drew his hand back again, and Horner tried to back away. "No, don't hit me again. Please. I'll tell you, I'll tell you."

"Jimmy!" Tilly screamed, and tried to reach the sobbing man, but strong hands held her.

"I figured you would, Judge. Now, what was it you wanted to tell me?"

Head bowed, his entire frame trembling, he mumbled, "There's a secret passage in the hotel."

"Damn you, Jimmy Horner," Tilly exclaimed. "Damn you."

He looked at her with washed-out eyes. "I'm sorry, Tilly. Honest to God, but I—I . . ." His voice trailed away.

Tolliver grabbed a handful of the sobbing man's hair and jerked his head up. "Where is this secret passage?"

In a weak voice, Horner mumbled, "In the pantry. A catch under a shelf."

"Is that where the half-breed is?"

Horner shook his head. "I don't know, Mr. Tolliver. Honest. All I know is that's where the passage is."

Tolliver cut his eyes to Hatch and Fats and nodded to the hotel.

The two gunnies disappeared out the door.

Legs spread, Tolliver slapped his gloves into the palm of his hand. "What else haven't you told us, Judge?"

The broken man shook his head emphatically, tears rolling down his cheeks. "Nothing. That's the truth. That's all I know."

Tilly planted her fists on her hips. Fury leaped from her eyes. "You're a coward, Frank Tolliver. I knew it when you first came into town. You're a lying—"

"Shut her up," he barked.

One of the gunnies slapped his hand over her mouth only to scream and jerk it away when she bit him. Two more grabbed the struggling woman and held her while the third stuffed a ball of cloth in her mouth and gagged her, then tied her hands behind her back.

Moments later, Hatch and Fats burst in, breathless. Fats gasped. "It's there, Frank. Like he said. The half-breed ain't there, but there's blood all over the place."

"Blood, huh?" Tolliver eyed the judge coldly. He deliberately pulled on his leather gloves. "Hold him."

Tilly's ears exploded with her muffled scream when Tolliver slammed a massive fist into Jimmy Horner's face, splitting his nose and covering everyone around with a spray of blood.

"Whose blood was it, Judge? Huh?"

The battered man shook his head. Through swelling lips, he muttered, "Don't know. I—"

Tolliver hit him again and again, calmly questioning the battered man between blows.

Finally, the judge passed out.

The two rannies holding his arms dropped him to the floor.

Tolliver cut his piercing eyes on Tilly. While he glared at her, he spoke to his men. "Tie the no-good bastard to the hanging tree. At least, he's good enough for target practice."

Tilly fainted.

Cold water jerked her awake. She lay on the floor, staring up into the leering face of Frank Tolliver. He growled, "Whose blood was it?"

Ignoring his question, she rolled over and tried to rise to her feet, but she was still addled from her fainting spell. Tolliver nodded to a couple of his boys, who helped her into a chair. He gestured to the gag. When it was removed, he asked again, "Whose blood was that?"

The small woman eyed him defiantly. She wasn't ready to die, but she wasn't about to give this worthless bastard the satisfaction of knowing she was frightened. Her gaze grew hard. She set her jaw. "Whose blood? I'll tell you. It was your boy's, Dill Carson. That's whose! And I'm glad."

Tolliver stiffened. His eyes grew cold as he stared malevolently at the woman seated in the chair before him.

Fats spoke up. "You want us to tie her to the tree too, huh, Frank?"

Tilly's bright eyes dared the big man. He chuckled, realizing that was exactly what she wanted. Well, she ain't going to get it, he decided. "Nope. I don't shoot women. Burn her hotel. Break a couple of her fingers, but don't kill her. I want her to stay alive."

# Chapter Eleven

Just before dark inside the Golden Queen Saloon, Hatch squinted his good eye and peered over the batwing doors at five riders heading into town, hats tugged down on their heads and coat collars turned up about their necks. The one-eyed owl-hoot glanced over his shoulder. "Five riders coming, Frank. They look like our boys."

Tolliver looked up from his poker hand. "Go see."

With a terse nod, Hatch pushed through the doors.

The wind was from the north, sharp and cutting. Hatch huddled down in his heavy greatcoat.

He returned a couple of minutes later leading five raw-boned rannies with cold eyes and iron jaws. "This here is Joe Lazlo," he said, hooking his thumb over his shoulder at the jasper behind whose greasy, black hair hung down to his shoulders.

Lazlo stared down at Frank Tolliver. "Wingate sent me." He hooked a thumb over his shoulder. "This here is Bull Gutierrez."

Tolliver studied the gunnies through narrowed eyes. "I reckon you must be good with that hogleg, then."

Behind Lazlo and Gutierrez, a couple of gunnies chuckled. "Ain't found nobody better," one rock-jawed killer replied.

Pursing his lips, Tolliver studied them a moment longer. "Wingate send any word?"

"Nope." Lazlo unbuttoned his heavy coat and shook the snow off his Montana-crowned hat. "He just told us to get here and wait."

Muttering a curse under his breath, Tolliver shrugged. "Reckon you boys could use a bottle of whiskey and a full meal to put yourself around. Help yourself over to the bar, and Hatch will find a place to throw your soogans."

Lazlo hesitated. "See you had a couple fires around here," he said, nodding in the direction of the charred remains of the O'Connor Hotel and the Nugget Saloon.

Tolliver laughed. "You could say one was a payback for the other." He paused and leaned back in his chair, his cold blue eyes fixed on the gunman before him. He folded his arms over his chest. "I always like to make sure everything is even. That a jasper gets paid for what he does."

"That what happened to that jasper tied to the tree?"

A cruel gleam glittered in Tolliver's eyes. "Let's just say that hombre went one step too far with me. I had to show him the error of his ways."

The rawboned gunman held Tolliver's gaze as if sending him the same message. "Sounds fair enough to me."

Later, Frank Tolliver looked up from his poker hand as Hatch pushed through the batwings of the Golden Queen Saloon. "Got 'em bedded down at Abner Reed's, Frank," he grunted, picking at a piece of pork stuck between two of his rotted teeth.

"What about Reed? He pitch a fit?"

Hatch grinned, revealing his rotted teeth. "Naw."

He patted the butt of his six-gun. "He had nothing to say about nothing. He knows better than to fuss."

"What about his old lady?"

The thin gunfighter shrugged. "Gone. Reed said she took the kids and rode over to visit family in Las Vegas."

Rolling his massive shoulders, Tolliver ticked off the number of gun hands Wingate had sent in the last couple weeks. Thirteen so far. Counting his own boys, he had sixteen, seventeen including himself.

The first two days out of Juniper Pass, the fortunes of weather smiled on Slade. Right Hand led them well, averaging almost fifteen miles a day despite the rugged country.

Just after noon on the third day, Right Hand suddenly threw up an arm, halting them. While Slade and Paleto looked on, the small Arapaho drew back his bow and sent a yard-long arrow whistling through the air.

Moments later, the small Indian yipped once, then urged his small sorrel through the snow to a fallen doe. While gutting the animal, he paused once to jab the bloody blade of his knife to the north. "Deep snow tonight." He nodded to the forest. "There is cave."

After dressing the deer, he threw the haunches over his horse's rump, handed Paleto the forequarters, Slade the backbone, and swinging into his saddle, hurried on through the forest. After thirty minutes or so, he jabbed a thin finger into a motte of tall pines below a sheer bluff of shale. "We make camp there. Water in cave."

Slade was surprised that the large cave had not seen more use, but the layers of dust and the coals of ancient fires told him much time had passed since anyone had inhabited the cave.

They built the fire around the second bend, completely preventing any glow from the flames to be seen from outside. Slade fashioned a torch and explored deeper into the labyrinth of caverns. At one juncture, the torch flames leaped toward a dark tunnel that Slade had to squat to enter. The wiry half-breed followed the flame until it suddenly shot upward. He peered up into the chimney, seeing nothing but darkness.

Only the moaning of the wind made it past the second bend. The fire warmed their small nook in the cave, and the sizzling venison and flour cakes filled their bellies. Once or twice, the young half-breed wandered to the mouth of the cave, but he could see nothing, only feel the wet touch of the heavy flakes on his upturned face.

As Slade lay on his soogan staring at the mesmerizing flames of the fire, his thoughts returned to his dead brother, Nana. He couldn't shake the *sentir perdido*, the bad feeling that he would never find his brother's remains.

"My brother has deep thoughts."

Paleto's words jerked Slade from his somber reflections. He forced a laugh. "Just about what is ahead."

"Then what will you do?"

With a shrug, he replied, "Back to Tucson."

A sly grin played over Paleto's lips. "Do you ever think about marriage? There is a young Coyotero maiden who has eyes for Busca."

From the corner of his eyes, Slade saw Right Hand look over with a grin.

"Not for me. Not yet. I've got a business to build."

Paleto grinned at Right Hand. "Poor Busca. He does not know the pleasure of a smooth body against his on a cold night. All he has to share his blankets is a stagecoach." He exaggerated a shiver. "Such a thought causes the blood to run cold."

Ignoring his brother's taunting, the grinning young man nodded to Right Hand. "What about you? Do you have a woman?"

The faint smile on his face froze momentarily, then turned down sadly. "My family is beyond the sun and the moon." He paused. His brows knit, and his smile grew sadder. "Soon I will join them."

Slade and Paleto exchanged puzzled looks.

Right Hand laughed softly. "Do not worry. I will take you where you wish first."

Next morning, waist-deep drifts of snow filled the mouth of the cave, but the storm had passed, leaving a frigid blue sky above.

From the mouth of the cave, Slade eyed the heavy snowfall in frustration. "We can't move in this. Too deep for the horses."

At his side, Paleto grunted. He glanced at Right Hand. "How long on foot?"

The dark face of the diminutive Arapaho gave no indication of his thoughts as he studied the forest beyond the cave. He held up one hand, fingers spread. "Five sleeps. Two by pony. Five on foot."

"We could leave the ponies here," Slade said. "Pick them up on the way back." He paused, then added, "I don't want to waste any time holed up here."

Right Hand and Paleto looked at each other, their expressions revealing their doubts of ever reaching the valley on foot.

Without warning, the sharp crack of a rifle broke the frozen silence. Right Hand grunted and spun to the ground. "What the hell?" muttered Slade, shucking his

Colt and dropping to one knee against the wall of the cave. He glanced at the fallen Arapaho, but Right Hand had scrambled back into the cave.

Two more shots followed, the slugs ricocheting off the granite walls with the hum of angry bees.

Paleto glimpsed a dark figure darting from one pine to another. He grimaced. "Kiowa."

Slade shook his head. "What in the hell are they doing out in the middle of the winter? They ought to be curled up snug in their tipis with one of those smooth-skinned young maidens you two were talking about last night."

With a soft laugh, Paleto muttered, "You watch. I see to Right Hand."

Slade peered into the forest. Beyond the motte of pines in front of the cave sprawled a vast valley, covered with almost three feet of snow. Among the trees, less snow lay on the ground. From time to time, he caught a fleeting glimpse of a fluttering piece of buckskin, the muzzle of a rifle, the movement of an arm.

He guessed the party to be at least six, but no more than eight warriors.

From behind him, Paleto whispered, "The Arapaho is well. Only the shoulder. Peyote will dull the pain."

Slade nodded to the Kiowa. "I'm not particularly anxious to sit here for the next week."

Wryly, his brother replied, "Going out to face them is not wise."

A shout hailed them from outside.

His fingers clutching his necklace, Paleto arched an eyebrow.

Slade shouted back, "What?"

A guttural voice replied, "We are many. Give us your horses, and you can go."

Slade winked at his brother.

All Paleto could do was shake his head. "Even a fish has more brains than a Kiowa. What will you tell them?"

Cocking the hammer on his Colt, Slade took aim at the heel of a rifle butt sticking out from behind the scaly bole of a pine. "Let's let them decide what our answer is," he muttered, touching off a shot.

A saddle rifle flew out from behind the pine followed by startled yelping and a Kiowa warrior jumping out. A second shot followed, and the warrior spun to the ground.

"Now that leaves seven," Slade muttered.

"Now you duck," Paleto said, throwing himself to the granite floor of the cave as a barrage of gunfire echoed through the motte of pines and slugs ripped into the walls of the cave, ricocheting wildly.

As soon as the volley of gunfire lifted, Slade and Paleto scrambled back around the first bend. Right Hand came up behind them. "I can still fight."

Slade studied the small Indian. He would do to ride the river with. "You two stay here."

An alarmed frown knit Paleto's dark face. "Where you go?"

"Last night, I found a chimney back in the cave. It was too dark to tell at the time, but the updraft was strong. There might be a chance to climb out of this trap and come in from behind the Kiowa."

With a terse nod, Paleto turned his attention back to the mouth of the cave. "We wait here."

Pausing at the fire to sling his Winchester over his shoulder, Slade dropped a handful of cartridges in his pocket and, torch in hand, headed back into the cave.

# Chapter Twelve

The flames on the torch leaped toward the ceiling as Slade approached the chimney. He peered upward, grinning when he spotted daylight some hundred feet above his head.

Laying the torch aside, he stood upright, his head and shoulders in the chimney. He studied the jagged walls above him, noting the opening was not as much of a chimney as a gap between two faults in the granite slabs of the mountain. Except for one or two spots he might have to squirm through, he saw nothing to prevent his scaling the fault.

Sporadic gunfire echoed through the tunnel and from above.

Ten minutes later, the wiry young half-breed rolled out of the fault onto the snow-covered slope of the mountain. He eased around on his belly and oriented himself to the mouth of the cave.

The firing from below was irregular.

Slade crept forward, trying to pinpoint each of the Kiowa. After a few minutes, he grinned to himself. He had figured right, there were seven remaining. They had positioned themselves in a semicircle around the mouth of the cave. At their back, he saw a serrated ridge of granite overlooking them.

He backed away and circled around, coming into the ridge from the east, working his way through wind-blown piñons pushing through the crevices in the granite slabs.

Suddenly he jerked to a halt when he heard feet crunching on snow beyond a jagged granite upthrust. He eased into a fissure in the rock wall not a moment too soon, for a Kiowa warrior rounded the slab, heading in his direction.

Slade slipped his double-edged knife into his hand and felt the reassuring comfort of its familiar handle. He dropped into a crouch and held his breath.

A brief second later, the warrior strode past the fissure.

Slade struck like a sidewinder, leaping forward and wrapping his arm about the warrior's throat and slamming the blade into the unsuspecting brave's spine, instantly severing the spinal column.

Like a sack of feed corn, the warrior dropped to the ground without a sound.

Glancing over his shoulder hastily, Slade unslung the Winchester and clambered to the crest of the ridge, snaking his way between the jagged shards of granite piercing the air like needles.

Down below, he spotted the other six Kiowas.

Cocking his .44, he laid it on the granite beside him and threw his Winchester to his shoulder. Between his rifle and six-gun, he had twenty-one shots. "If that ain't enough," he muttered, "you shouldn't even be up here, Jake."

The first Kiowa's arms whipped out to his side as the impact of the .44 rimfire slammed him forward. In the next few seconds, all hell broke loose below as Slade methodically drew down on Kiowa warriors scrambling and darting among the pines in order to escape the new enemy.

Paleto and Right Hand joined it from the mouth of the cave. Within seconds, the slaughter was over. Through the pine and piñon along the foothill ridges, Slade glimpsed two Kiowas racing north.

Below, four lay on the ground, their blood turning the pristine snow the color of rust.

While the Arapaho watched from the crest of the ridge for any other unwanted visitors, Slade and Paleto scavenged weapons and ammunition from the dead Kiowa, then dragged their bodies to the base of a ledge, where they rolled heavy rocks over the corpses.

Slade set the last rock in place. He glanced northward, his eyes narrowed with anger.

"What troubles you, my brother?"

Slade jerked around, his jaw set in disgust. "I was just thinking how we spent an hour burying these Kiowa while our brother has been left to the animals for almost three months."

Paleto nodded slowly. "Life is not fair. That is why the rattlesnake lives."

With a soft chuckle, Slade replied, "I wouldn't mind dumping a bagful of rattlers on those Utes. Let them see what fair is like."

A shrill whistle cut through the frigid air. Slade and Paleto looked around. Right Hand was gesturing to the south. Quickly, the two scaled the ridge.

A handful of riders were plodding through the snow in their direction. Paleto squinted into the distance. "Indians."

Slade blew through his lips in disgust. "Now what?"

Right Hand grunted, "Navaho. They friends."

"Wonder what they're doing out here. I'd reckon those jaspers would be back in their warm pueblos."

The three continued to watch as the small party grew closer.

"Six of them," Slade announced. "Looks like a couple of them are children."

Right Hand exclaimed, "*Aiyee*. I know them. They are from Juniper Pass. The one in front, he is Altsoba. He is with his brother, Haloke, and their wives, Doli and Kai." He paused, then added, "I do not see Bil-agaana, the other brother."

Slade remained silent, but in the back of his head, he knew that the only reason peace-loving Navahos would brave the fierce storms of the last few days was if they had no choice, if something so terrifying had happened to drive them out.

The oncoming party rode straight up to the base of the ridge. Altsoba reined up and shrugged off the layers of brightly colored blankets in which he had bundled himself. He held up his hand. "Right Hand, my Arapaho friend. It is good to see you."

The Arapaho returned the greeting. "And what are you doing here? Why are you not in your warm home out of the snow?"

The old Navaho shook his head slowly. "Better to fight the snow than die."

Right Hand glanced around at Slade and Paleto. "Ask him what happened," Slade said.

Altsoba replied, "I know you from the white man's store." He paused until he saw recognition in Slade's eyes before continuing. "There is much death behind us. The white men come for us, but we escape before he comes."

The Arapaho looked over the small group. "Where is Bilagaana? I do not see him."

"He is dead. The white man named Tolliver kill him as he kill many in Juniper Pass."

Slade stepped forward. "White, too?"

"Yes."

The young half-breed glanced at Paleto, then turned back to the Navaho. "Come. Share our fire. Tell us more."

After the evening meal, the women retired to their soogans while the men sat around the fire, listening silently as Altsoba related the events back in Juniper Pass.

"When did it all start?" Slade asked.

"After a great fire at saloon. The white man, Tolliver, he send his men to bring back many of the town's people. He questioned them. Some he shoot."

Slade's blood ran cold. "What about the woman who owns the hotel, O'Connor? Tilly O'Connor?"

Altsoba turned to Haloke and whispered. The younger brother shrugged and spoke rapidly to his wife. She replied in the lilting cadence of the Southern Athabaskan language. Haloke spoke up. "Kai, she say Miss Tilly, they beat her. The hotel burned, but she live."

"What about the old drunk who they called a judge?"

Altsoba's ancient face filled with deep wrinkles. "That one, Tolliver, he shoot. Tie him to hanging tree and use him for target."

Slade clenched and unclenched his fists as anger surged through him. Treed towns were nothing new, but this one was personal. He was alive because of the risks Tilly O'Connor had taken, and Jim Horner was dead because he had obviously refused to reveal the secret room in her hotel.

Any way you sit the saddle, Jake Slade, he told himself, you're responsible.

For another hour, the questioning continued.

A handful of citizens were dead, murdered by Tolliver and his men. Many more were injured, whether by gunfire or beatings. Many left town. In addition to the hotel, the church was burned.

"Where do you go from here?" Right Hand asked the old Navaho.

Altsoba nodded north. "Beyond the mountains is a valley hidden from those who are not Human Beings. We will live there. Much water and game. We will be safe there."

Later that night as the fire burned low, Paleto muttered, "I am glad the Creator look over the woman at the hotel."

"Yeah," Slade muttered, his head filled with the turmoil of unanswered questions. Part of him wanted to return to Juniper Pass and help the citizens take the town back. Another part of him wanted to continue his journey to his brother and give him the everlasting peace and joy with his family in the world beyond.

After several minutes of silence, Paleto spoke up. "Will you return?"

Slade snorted. "What are you talking about?"

With a chuckle, Paleto replied, "Do not deny that you wish to return to the town of Juniper Pass."

Another few moments of silence passed before Slade responded. "Maybe so. I haven't decided." He rolled over on his side and closed his eyes. In the back of his head, the *sentir perdido* persisted. What if he waited so long there were no remains of his brother to be found?

If such happened, he would carry to his grave the shame of being responsible for his brother forever wandering the World Beyond without the pride of a warrior's funeral celebration.

He was well aware of the methodical process the Creator, the One-Who-Lives-Above, used to maintain the balance of nature. The birds pick the flesh from the bones; the animals break them apart for the marrow within; the weather deteriorates the shards; and the ants carry off what little remains.

As the white man proclaimed, ashes to ashes, dust to dust.

# Chapter Thirteen

The stars glittered brightly in the dark skies when the Navahos mounted their ponies next morning.

Slade looked up into the ancient face of Altsoba. "Ride with *El Dios*."

The old Navaho studied the rock-hard face of the young half-breed looking up at him. "And you. Be wise as the owl and silent as the fox when you return. Men like those kill without thought."

Lifting a quizzical eyebrow, Slade said, "I haven't decided to go back."

A knowing smile cracked the old man's dark face. "You have decided. I saw it in your eyes last night."

Slade watched as the small party of Navahos melted into the shadows cast by false dawn among the pine and piñon. A sense of loss washed over him, for he realized with Apache stoicism that he would never again in this lifetime visit with the old chief and his family. They were going into the wilderness to end their lives in grace and dignity as the One-Who-Lives-Above intended, not the violent and bloody death awaiting them back in Juniper Pass.

Paleto came to stand by his brother's side, his black eyes focused on the patches of shadows into which the

Navahos had vanished. "The ponies are saddled. Right Hand wishes to return with us."

Slade looked around at the impassive face of his brother. "I haven't decided yet."

A faint smile played over Paleto's lips. He grunted. "Such was decided when you became our brother many moons in the past. Our brother will understand. And he will be waiting for us when we reach him."

At that moment, Right Hand led the three ponies from the cave.

With a grin, Slade buttoned his mackinaw. "Well then, since you got it all figured out, I don't reckon we need to be wasting any time. Let's ride."

Although Right Hand knew the eastern foothills of the Sangre de Cristos as well as the inside of his own wickiup, travel was slow because of the drifts of snow.

As dusk settled over their second night's camp, Right Hand abruptly looked around, then rose quickly to his feet, hurrying to the mouth of the cave. He peered into the forest below. Moments later, Slade heard the soft whinnying of ponies.

"Young Fox," the Arapaho muttered when Slade and Paleto came to stand by his side. "With his brother, Horsebreaker. They are Northern Cheyenne."

"Why do they come here?" Slade whispered.

Right Hand shrugged.

Suddenly the two warriors reined up, squinting into the forest in the direction of the cave. For several moments, they studied the pine- and piñon-blanketed foothills.

The Arapaho explained, "They work for the old man at the freight line. He is called Leighton. They take care of the horses. The old one, Horsebreaker, cannot speak. He has no tongue."

Shadows from the setting sun crept across the snow-covered valley to the east, engulfing the two Cheyennes. Without taking his eyes off the two, Slade muttered, "Offer them our camp."

Later, seated around the fire and sharing their venison with the newcomers, they listened intently as Young Fox told of the trouble back in Juniper Pass. "We fear for our lives, so we leave. The *proscritos*, the outlaws, they drink much whiskey. Two or three of the Lipan Apache near the river—"

Right Hand nodded emphatically. "Mocha and his brother, Yolcna. Yes, I know them."

Young Fox smiled sadly. "They are dead. Two nights back, *tres asesinos*, three killers, ride upon their lodge and kill them."

His voice choked with emotion, Right Hand asked, "Why?"

"The white men were drunk. That was all the reason they need to kill the Indian."

Slade grimaced. "What about the woman of the hotel?"

The Cheyenne studied the half-breed, noting the gray eyes and the short-cut hair. "I have heard of you. Busca. And your brother, Paleto. You go to put your brother into the Spirit World with his family."

"Yes. Now, the woman."

"She lives. The woman, Rose, who owns the café, makes her well."

Later, as the small fire burned low, barely illuminating the roof of the cave, Right Hand heard Paleto whisper, "What will the three of us do?"

Hot blood surged through the Arapaho's veins when he heard Slade's reply. "We are Apache. We will kill as the Apache. When the white-eyes least expect it."

From the window of the general store, Abner Reed and Mayor Homer Akins peered through the frosted glass as Burl Henry sat behind his team of eight massive draft horses pulling a snowplow down the street and out the north road. Abner chuckled. "Looks like old Burl is keeping the road to the mine open."

Akins spotted two riders ambling in on the freshly plowed street. "Take a look," he muttered. "Looks like some more of Tolliver's killers."

The smaller man gulped. "It's a good thing we sent the women and kids away. To tell the truth, Abner, I'm thinking on following. I don't know what these jaspers got in mind, but it ain't good." He paused and nodded to the frozen body of Jimmy Horner still tied to the hanging tree. "Trouble is right here, now, and it ain't going to get no better."

"What about your store, all your guns and ammunition? You can't just go off and leave them."

The smaller man snorted. "The biggest gun shop in New Mexico Territory ain't no good to me if I'm dead."

Reed ran his slender fingers through his thinning hair. "It's a wonder they didn't kill Tilly. How's she doing?"

Keeping his eyes on the two gunnies as Hatch went out to meet them, Akins replied, "Rose over to the café is tending her. She ain't in no danger of dying or nothing, but she's bad hurt. Rose said she's got a busted arm and lost a couple teeth."

The rail-thin grocery man clenched his fist. "Damn. I wish there was something we could do."

Akins looked up at him in dismay. "Don't be an idiot, Abner. There ain't nothing we can do. Ever since Tolliver rode in, we been losing people. No question in my mind, he had Sheriff Townsend kilt."

Abner grimaced. "We could all get guns."

The smaller man snorted. He nodded to the two gunnies following Hatch into the Golden Queen. "And what? Why, he's got more than a dozen gunfighters over there. More counting them two."

"We can't just sit here and let them do what they want."

"We can't stop them. Look who we got to count on. You, me, Rose, Tilly, and Matthew Leighton at the freight line. C.T. and Hank won't help. They got their saloons to run. Pate at the tax office I wouldn't ask. Oh, I forgot about Burl out there," he added, glancing at the snowplow as it disappeared around the bend in the south road. He paused and turned from the window, his narrow shoulders slumped wearily. "I ain't a brave man, Abner. Not when it comes to dying. I honest to God don't know what to do."

Abner shuffled back to the counter and stuck a couple of tin cups under the spout of a wooden barrel. "We need a drink. Might as well have the best. Old Grand Dad. Hauled in last month and opened it last night."

# Chapter Fourteen

Inside the saloon next door, Frank Tolliver looked up at the two newcomers. "Wingate send you?"

His eyes cool, the young gun hand glanced at the older one and grinned crookedly. "You could say that. My name's Jess Cooper. This here ugly galoot is Arch Simmons."

Tolliver's brows knit. "I asked about Wingate."

Cooper grinned lazily, his cold eyes half lidded, his motionless fingers near the worn butt of his six-gun. "Yeah, you did."

The hulking killer grew impatient. "Did he send any word with you two?"

Arch Simmons stepped forward and loosed a stream of tobacco juice on the floor. "Can't say he did, seeing that he got hisself kilt."

The words hit Frank Tolliver in the face like a bucket of cold water. "What's that you say?"

Cooper nodded. "He hired us over in Fort Union to come here to Juniper Pass and join up with you. He was going to ride with us, but the night before we left, a burglar broke in his room. According to the sheriff, Wingate got a knife run through his brisket during the fight." He paused, drew a deep breath, and then with a taunting grin, added, "Now you know as much as we do."

A flash of anger swept over Frank Tolliver, but he pushed it aside, stunned by the revelation brought him by the two. Now what? All he knew was that Wingate wanted to buy up local property because of the gold strike.

A frown wrinkled the swarthy man's forehead. He cared nothing about property. He wanted money, as much as he could put his hands on, but now such a desire seemed suddenly out of reach.

Simmons interrupted him. "My tapeworm is about to starve. Where can Jess and me find some grub?"

The question jerked Frank Tolliver back to the present. He looked up into the face of the older gunman. "Huh? Oh, over to the bar. All the food and drink you want."

Through narrowed eyes, Frank Tolliver watched the two amble to the bar. He had taken an immediate dislike to Jess Cooper, the younger one, but at the same time, he recognized an intelligence in the man that was not present in any of his other gun hands.

Later Tolliver stared across the table at the amiable face of Jess Cooper. "So, you got no idea what Wingate had in mind?"

Jess glanced at his partner, Arch, and shook his head. "He never told us. Don't you know?"

Pouring a drink, Tolliver said, "All I know is it has something to do with the gold strike back West. He wanted us to convince property owners around here to sell their land and mineral rights at dirt-cheap prices."

Jess Cooper lifted the glass of whiskey to his lips. "And if they refused to sell?"

A cruel gleam filled Tolliver's eyes. "They wasn't going to have the chance to refuse."

The young gun hand tossed the whiskey down and drew the back of his hand across his lips. "Sounds like my kind of man."

Arch shot a puzzled glance at his young partner.

From across the room, Joe Lazlo leaned across the bar and grabbed the owner of the saloon, C. T. Henley, by the lapel and jerked him forward. "I said whiskey. And now."

The frightened saloon owner shook his head. "We're out, mister. Ever' last drop."

Lazlo sneered and shoved Henley back. He strode around the bar and searched the shelves. "What about the back room?"

Henley gulped, the dim lamplight shining off the sweaty sheen on his bald head. "It's all empty, Mr. Lazlo. Honest. I ain't got no more."

For several moments, the killer eyed the saloon owner threateningly. Then he called out, "Tolliver! The bar's gone dry here."

Irritated by the interruption, Tolliver growled, "Hell, there's another saloon in this here town. Get drunk over there." He glanced at Henley. "Go over to the Nugget and bring some of that whiskey back over here."

Within minutes, the Golden Queen began to empty except for the three owl-hoots seated around the poker table.

Cooper nodded to the men pushing out the door. "Wingate hire 'em all?"

Tolliver nodded.

Arch Simmons spoke up. "They know Wingate's dead?"

Tolliver shook his head and leaned forward. "I wanted to talk to you two first." Cooper arched an eyebrow, and Tolliver continued. "There's money to be made up here or else Wingate wouldn't have spent what he did. I got no idea what his plans was after he bought up the land and mineral rights." He paused. "I figured you might have an idea."

Jess and Arch looked at each other. A smug grin played over the older man's lips. "If Wingate could pull it off, so can we."

Tolliver arched a skeptical eyebrow. "What would you know about land titles and such?"

Jess laughed. "Don't sell old Arch short, Tolliver. Why, he's probably the only jasper who escaped the hangman who went to college at Harvard."

Tolliver's skepticism turned into a puzzled frown. He had heard the word *college*, but not the other one. "What's a Harvard?"

Arch grinned at his younger partner. "Nothing to worry about, Tolliver. Nothing to worry about." He paused and rolled a cigarette. "So, what do you say?"

Rolling his massive shoulders, Tolliver studied the grinning man. He had the feeling the control he had maintained over the scheme, whatever it was, was quickly unraveling before him. "I don't know. What do you have in mind?"

Arch scooted forward. "Here's the way I see it. Wingate must have figured there was a heap of gold in these hills. So we do the same thing he was going to do. We buy up the properties at dirt-cheap prices."

Tolliver's frown deepened. "So, where's the money in that?"

Arch glanced at Jess and shrugged. In a patient voice, he continued. "There is such a thing called mineral rights. That means you own anything beneath the ground on all of your properties. Someone takes it out, they must pay you." He paused. "Understand?"

Tolliver understood, but it didn't make sense. "But they ain't digging around here. They digging back West. How long we got to wait on them? Why can't we just get them what has the mine to sign over their title or whatever you call it?"

Arch lifted an eyebrow. "Impossible. That kind of operation has its own lawyers and such. That's one cat we couldn't even begin to skin."

"So," Tolliver growled, "what did Wingate have in mind?"

Jess glanced at his older partner. "What do you think, Arch?"

Scratching his beard, Arch shook his head. "I don't know. Tell you what. Jess and me will ride over and see what we can find out about the company."

Tolliver eyed him suspiciously. "While you're doing that, what do we do here?"

A faint grin curled one side of Jess's lips. "Wait."

Disgusted, Tolliver rolled his shoulders. "I reckon we got no choice, damn it."

Jess spoke up. "One other thing. With Wingate gone, there ain't no money to pay all these gunnies."

Tolliver pondered the remark several moments. Then his grizzled face lit up. "They won't need no money. They can take what they want from the town."

Jess arched an eyebrow. "The townfolk won't like that."

A cruel snarl twisted Tolliver's lips. He laid his black-handled six-gun on the poker table. "Let 'em argue with this."

Later, Jess and Arch hunkered over a poker table, sipping whiskey and plotting. "I figure we've been dealt a losing hand here, Jess."

The younger gunfighter frowned. "I don't follow you."

Arch downed his whiskey and grinned. "I don't know what Wingate had in mind, but I don't see any way he could have figured on buying out the town and making a profit from the gold mining operation. None at all."

The younger gunman studied his partner a few moments. "So why did you suggest riding up to the mine tomorrow?"

A sly grin curled Arch's lips. Like a father talking to his son, the older man patiently explained, "Gives us time to find our own angle. There has to be money up here, or Wingate wouldn't have spent so much on it. Who knows, maybe we'll stumble onto his angle tomorrow. Or one of our own," he added with a grin.

Jess stared at the older gunfighter a moment, and then a sly grin played over his face. He muttered, "You're mighty damned sneaky, Arch. You know that?"

"Not sneaky enough, or I wouldn't have spent five years at Yuma."

North of Juniper Pass, Right Hand reined up. He studied the mountains above. "There is cave high on the slopes. From it, you can see the village. We camp there."

Without hesitation, the Arapaho led them through a labyrinth of narrow passages under a series of low-hanging walls in a rugged area of faulted rock and slabs created millenniums past by sheared tectonic plates when the Sangre de Cristos were being formed.

Slade continually glanced over his shoulder as they wound upward, marking each new branch in the trail. Every Apache youth learned to instinctively familiarize himself with his back trail.

The trail opened into a small clearing with three forks. Around the bend of the left fork gaped the mouth of the cave.

The young half-breed pursed his lips and grunted in appreciation. "This is one cave no one will stumble onto." He grinned at Right Hand.

Dismounting, the Arapaho explained, "When I fought the white soldiers with the Cheyenne, we meet in cave. The soldiers and their Ute scouts never find us." He paused, and a smug grin flickered over his lips. "They never come close."

Looking around, Slade drawled, "I can see why."

Right Hand motioned them to follow. "Come. I show you village." On foot he eased up the right-hand trail to a narrow granite ledge. "There," he announced, pointing to Juniper Pass a mile or so to the southeast.

Scratching at the bristle on his square jaw, Slade studied the small town on the edge of a canyon, feeling anger surging in him when his eyes settled on the snow covering the charred remains of the church and the O'Connor Hotel. Across the street was the Nugget Saloon, the rear portion in ruins.

Back at their ponies, Paleto gestured to the third trail leading off from the clearing. "Where that go?"

With a sly grin, Right Hand curled his finger to them. "Come, but come slow. You see."

Around the bend, Slade jerked to a halt, staring at the forest two hundred feet below. He whistled. "Wouldn't do for a jasper to be a sleepwalker."

Dust lay thick on the floor of the cave, marked only by the sinuous S-curves of snakes. Paleto grunted and nodded to a set of undulating impressions.

Right Hand shrugged. "*Las serpientes de cascabel.*

They winter deep in cave. They not worry us." He paused and patted his belly. "Good to eat."

Slade had spent his life around rattlesnakes. Once he caught some fangs on the calf of his left leg, but the poultice old Haa-Tay, the medicine man, plastered on it sucked the poison out, leaving him weak for a few days with no other ill effects, but with a renewed respect for the rattlesnake.

Quickly, they made their camp, tethering the ponies in an adjoining chamber. While Right Hand gathered browse for the animals, Slade and Paleto laid a fire and put on venison and coffee.

After filling his belly, Slade glanced out the mouth of the cave, then spread his soogan and lay down for a nap. "Tonight," he announced, "we'll slip into town and see where we stand. I'll try to get to the café and see Tilly while you get a handle on how many jaspers Tolliver has got with him." He paused, still puzzling over what Tolliver had in mind for the town.

The cold night was clear and bright. The handle of the Big Dipper pointed almost due west, telling Slade it was about two A.M., which gave them a good five hours of darkness. From the ledge on which they stood, laughter and shouting rolled up the slopes from the Golden Queen Saloon.

Only one or two lights burned in the remainder of the small village.

Right Hand moved quickly, leading them through the jumble of faults and fractures to the outskirts of town, pausing behind the charred ruins of the church.

Across the street, the only light in the Longhorn Saloon was upstairs. Rose's Café next door was dark.

Moving with the stealth of a fox, Slade glided through

the piñon and pines to the rear of the café where Rose lived. He crouched at a window and peered into the darkness. He could see nothing. At the next window, a tiny flame flickered in a coal-oil lantern on the floor beside a small bunk on which lay a figure covered with heavy blankets.

Beyond the bunk, someone dozed in a rocking chair. Rose Perry, Slade guessed. He tapped on the window.

The figure on the bunk remained motionless.

The young half-breed tapped again, harder.

The figure stirred and turned to peer at the window.

Slade grimaced when he saw the swollen and bruised face of Tilly O'Connor.

# Chapter Fifteen

Tilly called out. Moments later, the figure in the rocking chair jerked awake. Within another few seconds, Rose Perry opened the window. "Quick, inside."

Slade slipped through the window. He swallowed the anger flooding through his veins when he looked at Tilly's battered face in the light of the flickering lantern. Softly, he asked, "You hurt bad?"

Her head on the pillow, Tilly grinned, revealing a couple of gaps where Tolliver's men had knocked teeth out. "Those varmints is going to find out what hurt is when I get out of here."

Rose spoke up. "She's better. Sore. I don't think nothing's bad hurt inside. Worse thing is a busted arm, just below the elbow."

Tilly frowned. "What are you doing back here? I figured you was way up north."

"The Navaho, Altsoba, and his family. He told us what happened, so we decided to come back."

Rose pulled her shawl tighter around her plump shoulders. "There's too many of them. You won't have a chance."

He gave her a boyish grin. "Maybe, maybe not. How many you reckon he has?"

She shrugged. "I'd guess twenty or so. They've taken

over the town. A bunch of families have up and gone over to Las Vegas despite the weather. That's how bad it is."

Tilly nodded. "She's right. Those damned owl-hoots is trashing the whole town, taking everything and paying nothing. Why, Rose here couldn't fry up a egg if you offered her a twenty-dollar gold piece."

Slade pursed his lips. "You still reckon the gold strike is what it's all about? They still want the local property around here?"

"What else?"

Rose nodded emphatically, the roll of flesh under her chin flopping back and forth. "Has to be. Just before they cleaned me out, I overheard a couple of them at my counter talking about the strike and wondering if it was moving this way."

The young half-breed studied the two women several moments, seeing in them the same grit and determination he had often seen in the dark eyes of Big Calf, his Apache mother. The only way to stop such women was to kill them, for they possessed the will and fortitude to persevere despite all odds.

"Well, I reckon we'll have to figure out some way to help those jaspers get over that gold fever." A sly grin played over his rugged face.

Tilly and Rose smiled at each other.

Slade glanced around the room. "Bags. Pillowcases. You have any to spare?"

Frowning, Rose nodded. "I got a pile of flour sacks. Why?"

"Give me some, five or six."

With a shrug, Rose disappeared into the next room and returned with several flour bags. "These all right?"

"Perfect."

"What do you have in mind?" Tilly asked.

He winked at her. "Something that'll make some of those cowpokes forget about gold."

Rose leaned forward. "What can we do?"

Shaking his head, Slade replied, "Nothing. We'll be around, and if we're not, we'll be watching. Leave it up to us."

"Us?" A frown knit the plump woman's brows.

Tilly replied, "He has an Apache with him. They're brothers."

Rose's eyes grew wide.

"Don't worry," he said with a mischievous flash in his eyes as he rose to his feet. "We don't take scalps."

Outside, he slipped around behind the jail. A blanket filled the window, but using the muzzle of his Colt, he eased it aside and peered inside. A coal-oil lantern sat on the table, emitting a dim glow. Several hombres had rolled out their soogans on the floor around the potbellied stove.

A devious grin curled his lips.

Back at the cave, the three discussed what they had learned.

Right Hand said, "Many of the men stay at the Golden Queen Saloon. There are rooms upstairs."

Paleto nodded. "Some at the white man's store. Where his family lived before leaving."

"I spotted half a dozen bunking in the jail," Slade replied.

"The one who try to hang you . . ." Paleto hesitated.

"Tolliver."

"Yes. He speak of buying property in town."

Slade frowned. "Buying property? That's what Tilly said." He glanced at Right Hand. "The gold strike is at a place called Cimarron Gorge. You know it?"

"Yes." He gestured west. "Not far." He gestured to the ground. "The Spanish, they mine the mountain many years. After they leave, others come, then mines close down, but many remained behind, building town on top of closed tunnels."

Slade glanced around at Right Hand. "You're saying there're mines beneath Juniper Pass?"

The Arapaho grunted. "Many, but no gold. When I fight the soldiers with Cheyenne, we stay in mines."

"Interesting."

Paleto glanced at his brother, noting the amused look in Slade's eyes.

"You know," Slade said, "I wouldn't mind seeing those tunnels. How about taking us on a tour of them?"

Right Hand frowned. "Tour?"

"Show them to us. Can you?"

"It has been four years. Some may have fallen in."

"Let's look anyway."

After emerging from the field of faults and fractures guarding the entrance to their cave, Right Hand led them back west and a quarter mile down a steep slope to a bed of talus spreading clear to the bottom of the slope like a fan.

"There is mine." He nodded to a tangle of vines covering the mouth of the tunnel. Pushing through the vines, they paused to light the torches they had fashioned.

The smell of mold and must filled Slade's nostrils. A crooked grin curled his lips as he peered into the darkness before them. "I reckon rattlers use this mine, too."

Right Hand grinned. "Still want to look?"

Slade chuckled at the good-natured taunt in the Arapaho's voice. "If you still want to show us."

With a grunt, the diminutive Indian led the way.

The mine twisted and turned, forking often. When Paleto asked of the forks, Right Hand explained they led to other tunnels.

"So, what you're saying is that a jasper could end up wandering around down here a mighty long time."

"As long as he has light."

Slade grinned at Paleto, each of the brothers having the same thought that with the darkness came the rattlesnakes.

Well before dawn, the trio emerged from the mine on a slope east of Juniper Pass. From there, Right Hand took them through a mine running south. In a few hours, he had pointed out six entrances to the labyrinth of mines beneath the town.

Standing on the crest of a granite ridge, Slade studied the village lying to the north. "Who knows of these mines?"

Right Hand shrugged. "Not many. Some of the old ones, perhaps. The town is only a few winters old. Who knows?"

With a chuckle, Slade ran his fingers through his hair. "Well, we might end up making good use of them. Now let's get back to the cave. We're going to be busy tonight."

Seated at the fire in the cave sipping six-shooter coffee, so called because an hombre could float his six-gun in it, the young half-breed grinned wickedly. "Right Hand, how many rattlers can we get from down in the cave?"

The Arapaho frowned. *"Zumbe serpiente?* I do not understand."

Slade pointed to the pile of flour sacks. "We going to give Mr. Tolliver's gunnies some presents they won't forget. So, how many are down there?"

Then Right Hand understood. He glanced at Paleto, and the two Indians' eyes glittered with amusement.

The Arapaho's grin grew wider. "More than you want. As many as you wish."

Slade counted out three sacks. "One for each of us," he announced, checking the bags for holes.

Paleto built the torches. "How many in each bag?"

Holding up five fingers, the young half-breed replied in the Western Apache vernacular, *"Ashdla'i."*

The diminutive Arapaho glanced around. "What do you mean?"

"Five," said Paleto with a sly grin. "My brother sometimes forgets to think and speaks the Apache instead of the American."

Slade shrugged.

With a short nod, Right Hand disappeared out the mouth of the cave only to return moments later carrying a sturdy limb with a forked branch. He cut off some of the fork, leaving a few inches attached to the limb in the shape of a hook.

Slade nodded, recognizing the implement they would use to catch the rattlers. He lay back on his soogan. "Let's get some sleep. We're going to need all our energy tonight."

After awakening around noon, the trio downed a belly-filling meal of venison and fried johnnycakes, washed down by thick black coffee.

Later, Slade ambled out on the ledge and built a cigarette. Paleto and Right Hand came to stand by him. Idly they studied the village far below, noting several gunnies going from business to business.

As they watched, two cowpokes strode into Rose's Café. Moments later, they burst out through the door with Rose in pursuit, wielding a broom. She stopped on the boardwalk and peered up the mountain slopes. Then with a disgusted shake of her head, she stormed back inside.

"She is angry like the wolf standing over her cubs."

"Reckon tonight before we go in, I'll find out what's up. In the meantime, let's get back inside and pick up our little friends." He glanced at the sun. "I figure a few hours in the bag close to the fire will help warm them up." A cruel grin curled his lips.

Paleto and Right Hand chuckled.

Slade nodded to his brother's bear-claw necklace. "Give it an extra rub for me."

Paleto laughed.

Their torches cast a dim, yellow glow on the granite walls as they wound deeper into the cave. Right Hand paused from time to time, holding the torch over crevices and fissures in the wall and floor.

Finally, he peered into a crevice along the wall and turned back with a grin. "Here."

A few feet below the floor of the cave lay a tangled ball of rattlesnakes. Slade chuckled when he looked upon them. The cool air suppressed the musty odor. "Just what we need."

Paleto held the torch while Right Hand slid the forked hook under a three-footer and gently lifted the somnolent serpent from the tangle. It appeared dead, but beneath the scaly skin, muscles rippled, and the spade-shaped head slowly lifted. Gently, but swiftly, the Arapaho deposited the serpent in the sack Slade held.

The three worked quickly and gently. While they knew nothing of how the metabolic processes within the serpent regenerated, they were well aware that stress or heat could bring the rattlesnake from its hibernation.

Within ten minutes, the three bags were filled, each with five stirring rattlers.

"Don't bounce them about too much," Slade cautioned. "They're going to get jostled around enough when we toss them in those nice warm rooms down in Juniper Pass."

# Chapter Sixteen

Not long after dark, the wiry young half-breed tapped on the window at Rose's Café. Moments later, unseen hands raised a single-paned window, and Slade slipped inside. Two shadows knelt before him in the darkness. He whispered, "How do you feel today?"

Tilly spat out her reply. "Mad. Oh, I'm healing up just fine. I'm too damn ornery to stay sick, but I'm madder than a rained-on cat."

"What happened? Something to do with those two owl-hoots who came here today?"

Rose spoke up. "You saw them, huh?"

"We was watching."

Her voice trembled with rage. "Can you believe them sons a' bitches had the nerve to want me to sleep with them? Why, he even offered me a hundred dollars. I told them if they was the last male animal on God's green earth, I wouldn't sleep with them."

Slade turned to Tilly.

She snorted. "They knew better than to ask me."

For a moment, Slade considered the latest turn of events. "How many of you left in town?"

Tilly shook her head. "Hard to say. Me and Rose. Abner, Homer Akins, Jonah, Leighton, and Burl Henry—he's got to keep the road open. Of course there's C. T.

Henley at the Golden Queen Saloon. From what I heard, Hank Cullens at the Longhorn Saloon snuck out last night."

Slade leaned forward. "All right, listen close. After what we got planned for Frank Tolliver and his gunnies, they're going to be mad enough to stomp a greaser into dust. They could take it out on you."

Rose gasped. "They wouldn't dare."

"Who's to stop them? A jasper can hide bodies anywhere around here, and all that will find them are the animals. No, best you leave. There's a cave over the south ridge about a mile from here. You know it?"

"I do," Tilly replied.

"If you want us to take you to Las Vegas, be there in the morning before the sun. After I leave tonight, go see the others. Tell them the same thing."

"All right."

"I mean it, ladies. Go see them as soon as I leave. In a few hours, there's going to be a heap of confusion hereabouts. Those jaspers won't be paying attention to anyone except themselves. They'll never know you lit a shuck out of town."

Excitement filled Tilly's voice. "What are you going to do?"

Slade chuckled. "Just do what I said. Anyone who's at the cave in the morning, we'll get to Las Vegas. Them that stays here, well . . ." He paused and shrugged. "I figure there's going to be a heap of trouble, and someone might catch a stray slug."

Rose whispered, "We understand. Don't worry."

He rose to leave. Rose stayed him. "Wait. Come this way."

Slade followed her through the darkness to the adjoining room, where she opened a trapdoor in a closet.

"I didn't think about this when you were here last. My husband built it to escape Utes and Kiowas. It drops into a tunnel that leads to an arroyo out back." She handed him a candle. "Be careful. The trail at the end of the arroyo goes along the rim of the canyon. It's slippery."

Back at the cave, Slade nodded to the three lumpy bags on the floor. He grinned crookedly at Paleto and Right Hand. "Let's go."

While the stealthy trio carried out their plot, Rose and Tilly hurried to contact the remaining townsfolk. After Akins and Reed sent their families to Las Vegas, they'd been batching in the rear of Akins's gun shop.

Abner Reed ran his fingers through his thinning hair. "I ain't much on running." He gestured to the front of the shop. "Homer here has got plenty ammunition them old boys didn't find in the tunnel below the shop."

"None of us want to run, Abner," Tilly said. "I got no idea what's going to happen later tonight, but according to Mr. Slade, we might get the worst of it from them damned owl-hoots if we stay."

"She's right, Abner," muttered Homer Akins.

For a moment, the lanky grocery man hesitated, then nodded. "All right. Someone needs to tell Burl and Matthew. They're at Burl's livery."

"Matthew's there?"

"He rode in last night."

"What about Jonah?"

Abner frowned. "Jonah Pate? Why, you know you can't trust that little sneak no farther than you can throw this mountain. He'd sell his own mother out for a quarter."

Tilly grimaced. "Still, I hate to run out on him like this."

Abner stepped forward. "I'm telling you, Tilly. Let him know what we're up to and come morning, Toll-iver will have a dozen men at the cave." He shook his head. "No. Just tell Burl and Matthew, that's all."

Rose nodded and pulled her shawl around her shoulders. "We'll tell them. Remember, Mr. Slade said to move when the commotion starts."

After the two women departed, the two men dressed quickly. Homer Akins shook his head. "I feel guilty not telling Jonah."

Abner snorted. "Don't. Give him half a chance, and Jonah Pate would cut the gold out of them teeth of yours."

Pausing outside the small village, Slade nodded to Right Hand. "You do the jail. They stuffed a blanket in the window. Push it aside and empty the bag through the window. Paleto, you take yours to the mercantile store. The back room."

The Mimbre Apache grunted.

"I'll take the saloon. After we separate, give the call of the owl when you are ready. We all will wait until each has given the call."

Paleto and Right Hand nodded.

Like ghosts, they glided down the slope and vanished into the town.

At the rear of the Golden Queen, Slade paused at the base of a flight of stairs leading to the second floor. In the distance, the *hoo-hoo* of a courting male owl broke the silence. The young half-breed grinned. Right Hand was in place.

Quickly, he climbed the stairs, his feet as light on

the treads as a spider on its web. He tried the knob. It turned. At the same time, he felt movement in the bag.

Turning from the building, he cupped his hand and uttered the call.

Seconds later from inside, a guttural voice exclaimed, "Damned owl. Sounds like he's right outside the window. "I'll show that damned—"

A rear window scraped open.

Slade pressed up against the door, trying to melt into it.

A voice came from inside, "Damn it, Sal. Get back in here and close the window. You're freezing my butt off."

"Go to hell, Dutch," Sal shouted, but he closed the window.

Breathing a sigh of relief, Slade relaxed just as the third call echoed from next door at the mercantile.

Untying the knot at the throat of the bag, Slade palmed his Colt and opened the door. He paused, staring down the gloomy hall. The rising heat from the wood-burning stoves below swept over him and his little friends.

He stepped inside and closed the door behind him. Moving quickly to the end of the hall, he backed to the rear door, dumping a rattler in front of each door, then opening the door a crack and using the muzzle of his Colt to nudge the awakening serpent inside before moving on.

Although his furtive moments seemed to take hours, within a minute, he was descending the back stairs.

Paleto slipped up to the rear of the store and opened the back door a few inches. Warm air swept over his face. Inside, all was dark. He listened intently. He heard restless moans of drunken cowpokes tossing in their bedrolls interspersed with the rumble of snores. Loosening the top of his bag, he laid it just inside on the floor and just as silently as he had opened the door, closed it.

Right Hand pushed the blanket from the single window in the jail, noting a lantern burned softly on the desk. He poured the snakes inside. They hit the blanket, muffling the sound of their fall.

By the stove, Joe Lazlo awakened and stared into the shadows on the ceiling. He blinked his eyes against the searing whiskey headache and tried to work up enough saliva to wet his dry lips and throat. After a few moments, he rolled over and fell back asleep.

Below the window, the aggravated rattlers slowly came back to life and headed for the irresistible source of the warmth put out by the stove.

Deep in the slumber into which he had drifted, Lazlo felt movement across his leg. Slowly, he opened his eyes and stared at the spade-shaped head of a rattlesnake swaying back and forth only inches from his face.

The grizzled gunfighter exploded from his blankets, a shrill scream ripping from his throat. "Snake, snake, snake."

As if his screams were a signal, pandemonium erupted in the Juniper Pass Mercantile and Market and the second floor of the Golden Queen Saloon.

In the living quarters of the mercantile, a sleepy cowpoke stumbled from bed and opened the door on the potbellied stove. Without looking, he reached for a piece of split firewood in the firebox.

Two blazing needles punctured his arm. For a moment, he stood transfixed in shock, staring at the rattlesnake hanging from his arm.

When his numbed brain realized what had happened, he screamed and waved his arm frantically, throwing the rattler against the wall.

The other gunnies rolled out of bed, their hands filled with six-guns. "What the hell?" shouted Bull Gutierrez.

"Snake, snake, snake!"

The living quarters exploded with gunfire.

On the second floor of the saloon, Sal rolled out of bed at the commotion. "What the hell is going on?" He growled, stomping to the door in his long johns.

Behind him, his roommate, Wyoming Dutch, muttered, "What is it now?"

Rubbing his sleepy eyes, Sal mumbled, "I got no idea." He stumbled over an object on the floor. "Damn it, Dutch. Why don't you keep your damned boots where they belong? I ought—" He had bent down to grab the boot and throw it at Dutch when he saw the rattlesnake slowly wrapping itself into a striking coil.

He screamed maniacally and in one giant bound leaped on Dutch's bed. His added weight was too much for the flimsy slats, and the bed collapsed to the floor, leaving the two owl-hoots in a tangle of arms and legs.

Sal scrambled to his feet like a madman, screaming, "Snake, snake, snake!" Backing frantically away from the snake, he backed out the window, smashing it and tumbling backward into the snow below, snapping his neck.

Dutch fumbled for his six-gun. He missed the rattler four times before blowing its head off. He slumped back on the shattered bed, suddenly feeling something

warm in his lap. To his embarrassment, he had uri-
nated in his long johns.

Rose and Tilly smiled at each other as the sound of
gunfire and screams echoed across the village. "I don't
know what's going on, but it looks like Mr. Slade and
his Apache brother are stirring up some trouble."

After spending the night, Jess Cooper and Arch Simmons left the Boles Mine early. They had learned a
shipment of gold was pulling out for Las Vegas Friday. As they rode along the snow-covered road, they
put together a scheme to bilk Tolliver out of half the
gold.

"It's simple, Arch. The gold is in a false bottom of
the wagon. I'll hop up in the wagon and hand the gold
out. I'll leave half of it in there. You tell Tolliver that
we're going to pull the wagon off the road and hide it
in the forest. For them to ride on. We'll catch up for the
split."

Arch's weathered face crinkled in laughter. "Tolliver
will be right tickled to do that. He'll figure he'll get our
share, too."

Jess chuckled. "The joke's on him. We'll have fifty
thousand of our own."

Arch grew serious. "It's risky. If he should tumble to
our scheme—"

The younger gunfighter's eyes grew cold. "Fifty
thousand is worth the risk."

Later, Frank Tolliver stood in front of the potbellied
stove in the Golden Queen, a mug of steaming coffee
gripped in his massive hand. He glared at Joe Lazlo.
"How many snakes?"

"We kilt three. There might be more. Hymie Klarner got bit in the neck. He croaked real fast."

"Any others?"

"I ain't sure. Red Sweet gut-shot Bob Penny. I reckon he ain't going to hang on much longer. Sal fell out the window and busted his neck."

"Damn it." Tolliver's blue eyes turned black as ice. "Now, who in the hell would try to pull off a stunt like that?" He shook his head and glowered at his men before him. "None of this lily-livered townfolk would have the guts to try something like that."

Hatch cleared his throat. "You reckon they hired someone to come in? A heap of them have up and run off to Las Vegas. They've done had plenty time to fetch some gunfighters in here."

"That's right, Frank," Fats put in, looking up from his platter of cold venison. "I don't reckon there's more than a dozen of them left in town. A bunch of them could have hired someone."

Lazlo spoke up. "Naw. Gotta be Injuns, Frank."

Tolliver lifted a bushy brow. "Injuns! That's the dumbest thing I ever heard. Why in the hell would redskins pull a stunt like that?"

The smaller gunfighter stared up at Tolliver. "Who knows why Injuns do anything? But now, you stop and think about it. They had to know how to get them rattlers, and then they had to move as quiet as death to put them where they did. Why, one of them dropped off a single snake at every door upstairs here, and no one heard a sound."

Wyoming Dutch broke in hopefully, "Sal heard an owl."

Tolliver snorted. "An owl?" He shook his head in disgust. "A damned owl don't mean nothing."

"Remember, there was a bunch of them Navahos here. And then they just up and took off just a few days after we rode in."

Fats paused in gulping down a mouthful of fried venison. "Yeah. They're Injuns. They could find rattlers during the winter. They could have done it."

Hatch's eyes lit up. "Hey, what about that drifter what kilt Kansas Jack? He was dressed like an Injun, knee-high moccasins and all. Remember?"

"Yeah," Fats chimed in. "The one that broke out of jail."

Tolliver studied them a few moments longer. "How many of our boys did the rattlers get?"

Bull Gutierrez replied, "Charlie Call. Snakebit. Got 'm on the arm."

Wyoming Dutch said, "Sal Gooden."

"Then there's Hymie Klarner. He got snakebit too. Then old Red Sweet shot Bob Penny. That makes four."

"What about them rattlers? You get 'em all?"

Lazlo and Bull Gutierrez looked at each other.

Wyoming Dutch said, "We kilt four upstairs here."

"We got three at the jail," Lazlo said.

Gutierrez lifted an eyebrow. "We found three at the store."

Tolliver grimaced. "Watch yourselves. We don't know how many rattlers them jaspers snuck in on us. Smart thing to do is scout out your room and then seal it off."

Bull Gutierrez chuckled. "Best thing is ain't go to sleep."

# Chapter Seventeen

Tolliver snorted. "Ain't no snakes going to stop me. We're squatting on a chance of a lifetime. Jess Cooper and Arch Simmons is due back in today. We'll have a better handle on just where we stand."

Wyoming Dutch frowned. "I'm ready to get it done and get out of here. I sure miss female companionship."

Slapping his thigh, Joe Lazlo laughed. "Yeah, you should have seen him yesterday. He offered the old woman at the café a hundred dollars, and she come boiling out of the café swinging a broom like she was riding a bronco. Old Dutch there was churning snow like a spooked calf."

The crowd of gun hands roared.

Wyoming Dutch turned red. "It wasn't like that," he replied defensively.

"Oh no," shouted the bearded gunman. "How was it, then?"

At that moment, Arch Simmons and Jess Cooper pushed through the batwing doors.

Cooper shivered and slapped his hands against his arms to warm them. "Damn, it's cold. Why, my spit almost froze before it hit the ground." He grinned broadly as he sauntered to the potbellied stove. "Howdy, boys.

You're all up mighty early. What happened, run out of that rotgut you call whiskey?"

Arch cursed, "Son of a bitch." His six-gun boomed twice, filling the saloon with thunder.

Every gun hand slapped leather and spun just in time to see a five-foot rattlesnake slam against the balusters in the stair railings.

Hammer cocked, Arch approached the writhing serpent warily. "Where in the hell did that monster come from?"

"Damn," muttered Wyoming Dutch, eyeing the top of the stairs apprehensively. "Another one. That makes five."

Hatch gulped, the Adams' apple in his thin throat popping up and down like a cork. "I wonder how many more's up there."

"I don't care," a voice sounded. "I ain't sleeping up there no more."

"Me, neither," a second one chimed in.

Unperturbed by the sudden gunfire, Cooper poured himself a cup of coffee from the pot on the stove and glanced at the still-squirming rattler. "Looks like you old boys had some excitement around here."

Tolliver briefly brought the young gun hand up to date. "Now, forget about what happened last night. What did you find out over to the mine?"

The curious men crowded in.

Tolliver glared at them. "Back away. Get out there and bring in every citizen in town. I want them all here."

"What about the mine, Frank?" Joe Lazlo jutted out his jaw in defiance.

"When I figure it's time for you to know about the mine, I'll tell you. Understand?" His eyes grew hard, and his thick fingers lingered over the butt of his six-gun. "Anyone want to argue the point?"

As one they backed away. Tolliver jabbed a meaty finger at a rear table and nodded to Cooper. "Over there."

Blinking his good eye, Hatch stepped back into the stairwell, then slipped into the storage room. He knew Tolliver well enough to know the big man had something up his sleeve. Just what, he wasn't sure, but he damned well planned on finding out.

Besides, he owed the grizzled killer something for the black eye.

Cooper and Simmons plopped down at the table. Tolliver signaled to the bartender for whiskey. He glowered at the two gun hands. "So? Let's hear it."

The younger gunfighter lifted an eyebrow. "It ain't good."

Tolliver's brow furrowed. "What the hell you talking about? Ain't they mining gold up there?"

"Yeah, but we ain't going to get any of it."

The big outlaw's eyes blazed with suspicion. He eyed the two across the table from him narrowly. "Why not?"

Arch spoke up. "Not what you're thinking, Tolliver. We're not trying to snooker you. It's just that for the land titles around here to be worth anything, they'd have to dig for gold over here. That's already been done. All the gold around Juniper Pass has been taken. Wingate should have known that."

Holding rein on his temper, Frank Tolliver studied the two gunfighters for several moments.

Cooper read the large man's emotions. "He's telling

it right, Frank. We're just as disgusted as you, but that don't help none."

"Then what in the hell did Wingate have in mind?" He eyed Arch. "You tell me. You're the jasper from Harvard."

Scratching his grizzled jaw, Arch chuckled. "I got no idea, Tolliver. None at all."

Rage seethed under Frank Tolliver's collar. He clenched and unclenched fists the size of hams. He wanted to lash out, but at whom? The ones who brought the bad news? Were they trying to hoodwink him? Well, he told himself, they wouldn't get away with it if they tried. First time either one made a false move, he'd blow his damned head off.

Cooper reached for the bottle of whiskey and poured a drink. He leaned back in his chair and grinned at Tolliver. "But we might have some news that'll make you feel better." He glanced at Arch, who was pouring his own whiskey.

"Yeah? Like what?"

"Those jaspers over at Cimarron Gorge at Boles Mining are mighty hospitable. They invited us in for supper and put us up for the night." He sipped his whiskey. "Mighty surprising what you can learn in a bunkhouse at night if you keep your ears open."

Tolliver glared impatiently at the younger gunfighter, then at Arch Simmons.

Arch nodded. "Be patient, Frank. You'll like what you hear."

"All right, then, damn it. What?"

"You ever paid any attention to that jasper plowing the road after a heavy snow?"

Tolliver nodded. "Yeah. So?"

"Well, he keeps it open for two reasons. First, for the stage."

"Stage? I ain't seen no stage."

Back in the storeroom, Hatch Ahearn had left the door open a crack. He listened silently as the hushed conversation continued.

"Oh, there is a stage," said the young gunfighter. "During the winter, they say it only comes through twice a month from Santa Fe to Las Vegas. I reckon it's due anytime." He paused and a sly grin played over his lips. "But the other reason is so Boles Mining can make its shipment of gold to the bank in Las Vegas."

Tolliver's eyes grew wide. "Gold?"

Simmons spoke up. "Gold. They send a wagon to Las Vegas for supplies. The gold is hidden in a false floor beneath the wagon bed so if anyone stops them, there's nothing to see." He leaned forward, resting his elbows on the table and glanced at the younger gunfighter. "Fifty thousand."

Jess nodded. "I got a look at the bed. Once you figure out how it works, you can empty it in five minutes." He shot a furtive glance at Arch, who suppressed a sly grin. "I'll hop up and hand the bars down, and then we'll hide the wagon in the forest so no one will find it until we've got a big lead on them, two or three days at least."

For a moment, the grizzled outlaw stared at the two gunfighters. "You mean, the shipment comes through here, through Juniper Pass?"

"Only way to the bank," Arch said, tossing down his drink.

"When?" Tolliver leaned forward expectantly.

"The way they talked in the bunkhouse, at the end of this week," Arch replied.

Jess glanced at his partner. A daring idea flashed in his head. "Yeah. Saturday. That way they can get it to Las Vegas by Sunday night." He hoped Arch would play along with this sudden change.

Arch Simmons shot a puzzled glance at his partner, but just as quickly looked away, wondering what Jess had up his sleeve.

Jess Cooper added, "That's more than Wingate."

A cruel grin twisted the big man's thick lips. "Yeah. Yeah." He hesitated, then narrowed his eyes. "What kinda split you got in mind?"

Cooper shrugged. "We'll leave it up to you, Frank. Whatever you say will be fair."

"Yeah. Okay." An arrogant sneer split Tolliver's grizzled jaw as he leaned back in his chair. He was so smug with his own ego that he failed to see the look of satisfaction pass between Cooper and Simmons.

As soon as Hatch heard the value of the shipment, he silently closed the door and slipped out the back. He wasn't certain what he had stumbled onto, but the last thing he wanted was to get on Frank Tolliver's bad side. Still, he had some choice information, but just how to use it, he wasn't sure.

Meeting the townsfolk at the cave, Slade told them that Right Hand would guide them to Las Vegas.

For a few moments, there was some protest over a redskin leading the way, especially from Matthew Leighton, whose brother had been murdered and scalped by Utes, but when Tilly insisted she was going, the others, embarrassed by her scathing denunciation of their ancestry, conceded and followed the diminutive Arapaho.

"It's for your own good, folks," Slade explained.

Leighton tugged his gun belt up over his protruding belly. He eyed the wiry half-breed suspiciously. "How do you figure that?"

Slade studied the older man. "I don't know Tolliver personal-like, but I know his kind. They understand one thing." He patted his Colt. "There's going to be a heap of trouble in Juniper Pass. When it starts, those old boys are going to be desperate for a way to stop it. If any of you are around, they'd probably take you hostage." He nodded to Paleto. "Me and my brother can't do what we've got to do if we're worried about you."

Burl Henry spoke up. "I fed my horses before I left. I couldn't turn them out because they'd just starve."

Leighton grunted. "Well, at least my wagons is over to Las Vegas getting supplies. We'll run across them later, and I'll give them the word to go back with us."

"Don't worry about your horses," Slade told Burl Henry. "They'll be fine." He glanced at Paleto, who nodded.

Homer Akins cleared his throat. "Those bastards have just about stripped the town of everything. They took all my guns and ammunition." He paused and winked at Abner Reed. "But they don't know about the storage room under my shop. I've got a little bit of everything down there, kegs of black powder, cases of .36 and .44 caliber cartridges, and a dozen or so Winchester Yellow Boys."

Slade and Paleto grinned at each other.

The slight mayor added, "The trapdoor is in the

storeroom. I got a rug covering it and a table on top of the rug."

As they mounted to ride out, Slade asked, "Is this everyone?"

The locals exchanged embarrassed glances, all except Tilly. "C.T. at the saloon. Jonah Pate at the tax office. Pate thinks of nobody but himself. If we'd told him we was riding out, he'd have run across the street to Tolliver faster than you could spit."

Abner looked at Tilly. "You didn't tell C.T.?"

She shook her head. "I couldn't get to him. Not in the saloon."

Later, perched in a tall pine outside Juniper Pass, Slade and Paleto watched the village as cowpokes wandered from one deserted building to the other.

Once a terrified scream broke the stillness of the crisp mountain air and a cowpoke came hobbling out of the mercantile, holding the calf of his leg. His frantic words carried to the two brothers. "Snake!"

Paleto grinned. "I think they not sleep much tonight."

Then Slade remembered the tunnel beneath Rose's Café. "Wait here."

A frown knit Paleto's forehead. "Where you go?"

A wicked grin curled his lips, and he tapped a finger against his temple. "To play some games with their minds."

Down in the Golden Queen Saloon, one owl-hoot after another hurried in to report he could find no citizens in town. "I looked everywhere, Frank," one said. "They're all gone except the old man at the tax office and the barkeep here."

Another chimed in, "Two of them, the old man who owns the store and the one who owns the gun shop, was staying at the shop. But they're gone."

"What about them two over at the livery?"

"Them, too," said Bull Gutierrez.

"Damn." Tolliver slammed his fist down on the table, upsetting the bottle of whiskey and spilling it on the floor. He looked up suddenly. "What about the hombre what keeps the road open? You know, the one who runs the snowplow?"

Gutierrez shook his head. "I told you. He's gone."

Tolliver grimaced. "That means we got to keep the road open for the next week."

Jess Cooper and Arch Simmons exchanged knowing looks.

Ten minutes later, moving as silently as a soft breeze, Slade slipped into the tunnel running beneath Rose Perry's café. He paused beneath the wooden hatch, listening for the slightest sound. He heard nothing. He placed the burning candle on the floor of the cave and, lifting the trapdoor, slipped up into the kitchen closet and paused.

Still hearing nothing, Slade sneaked into the dining area and crouched behind the counter. He peered out the window, spotting three cowpokes outside going from building to building.

He grinned and strode across the floor and stopped in the window in full view of the owl-hoots outside.

Suddenly one spotted him and shouted. The others spun and raced for the café.

Within half a dozen steps, Slade had slipped back down the opening, closed the door, blown out the candle, and now he waited.

He heard the café door open.

Moments later, the thump of boots echoed throughout the small café. "You see anything, Hatch?"

"Naw, Red. Nothing."

Slade could hear their voices, but their words were soft and garbled.

The steps came closer until they were above and to the right of the tense half-breed. "Me, neither," muttered a voice. The steps turned and moved away. "Speck was seeing ghosts."

"I was not. I saw someone."

Hatch chuckled. "Hey, boys, you hear anything about a shipment of gold coming through here?"

Slade stiffened. He heard the word *gold*, but the rest of the conversation faded as the three moved to the front of the café.

Red muttered, "Gold?"

Speck called back, "What do you mean?"

"I don't know for sure. Don't say nothing, but I figure why we're all here is to take a shipment of gold."

Red laughed. "I'll go for that."

"Yeah." Speck laughed. "Well, I don't see nothing in here."

"Me, neither."

"You must've been seeing things," Hatch shouted.

"Go to hell."

Without a whisper, Slade slid the trapdoor aside and eased up into the closet. He could hear clearly now, but the mention of gold never came up again. He spotted one of the gunnies prowling through the kitchen. He glanced into the dining area where a second jasper was searching.

He shucked his Colt and had started toward the gun hand when Hatch's voice sounded just around the corner of the kitchen door. "I don't see nothing, either."

Slade started to back away, but Hatch suddenly exclaimed, "Hey, Red. Come take a look at this."

At that moment, Speck turned and spotted Slade.

Leaping forward on the soundless soles of his leather moccasins, the wiry half-breed cold-cocked the slight cowpoke with the muzzle of his Colt. He grabbed the unconscious outlaw before he hit the floor and hastily dragged him to the opening in the floor and slid him feet first to the tunnel below.

From the dining area, a voice called out, "What was that? Hey, Speck. You find something?"

Glancing over his shoulder, Slade dropped through the hole and quickly closed the door.

He cocked his Colt and waited.

In the faint light given off by the flickering candle, Slade saw that Speck was still unconscious. He grinned to himself as his gray eyes shifted to the door just above his head.

Footsteps and puzzled voices came from above. He heard the clomp of boots in the closet, but the trapdoor was in the shadows to one side of the door. The only way it could be spotted was by lantern light.

"Where in the hell did he go?" Hatch growled.

"Look out back."

"He didn't go out that way. The lock bar is down on the door." Hatch paused. When he spoke, his voice had a quiver in it. "The only way out is the front door, and we was up there. We would have seen him. No. He—he just vanished."

"Don't be crazy," Red snapped. "Nobody vanishes."

"So what happened? You know so much, where'd Speck go?"

"How in the hell should I know? All I know is that nobody can vanish. It takes a ghost or goblin to do something like that, and you know as well as me there ain't no such things as ghosts and goblins." He paused, and gave a worried glance at the rear door.

"Speck said he saw someone in the café, Frank," exclaimed Red Sweet back at the hotel.

"Yeah," Hatch said. "But when we got there he was gone, and then Speck, he up and disappeared into thin air."

Frank Tolliver narrowed his eyes. "Nobody disappears into thin air. He went out the back door."

Sweet shook his head. "He couldn't have. The lock bar was on the door." He gave his head a shake. "New snow out back. There wasn't no tracks. The door was locked. What else could have happened? He just disappeared."

Jess Cooper glanced at his partner, Arch Simmons. The older man shook his head as if to say Hatch and Sweet had either chugged too much whiskey or eaten a bushel of loco weed.

Tolliver tossed down a tumbler of Old Grand Dad whiskey. "Nobody just disappears."

"Speck did, Frank. Honest," Hatch said.

"All right. Forget about Speck right now. This moving thing you saw in the window. What did he look like?"

Hatch and Red glanced at each other.

"Well, truth is, I ain't sure. Speck said he saw him. I ain't sure if I saw anyone. The sun reflecting off the snow kinda blinded me."

Hatch nodded. "The sun was awful bright."

Tolliver splashed more whiskey into the tumbler before him. "You know what I think? I think both of you had too much to drink. You was seeing things."

# Chapter Eighteen

When the front door slammed shut behind Hatch and Red, Slade quickly slipped back into the kitchen and removed the lock bar from the door, then returned to the tunnel.

Speck remained motionless.

Slade stirred him awake. Groggily, the gunnie staggered forward.

They emerged from the tunnel a hundred yards behind the café. In the arroyo beyond the mouth of the cave, Slade indicated the set of tracks he'd made coming in. "Follow them. There's a dropoff to your left, so watch out that you don't slip. I—?"

Without warning, his teeth bared in a snarl, the slight gunslinger spun and lunged at Slade with a knife raised above his head. Just as abruptly, the anger fled the gunnie's face, replaced with alarm, then fear as his foot slipped. The momentum of his spin carried him over the precipice. A scream tore from his lips.

Slade grabbed for the falling cowpoke, but his fingers clutched only air.

Hatch froze, his startled eyes fixed on Frank Tolliver's as a terrified scream echoed through the frigid air. He jerked around. "What was that?"

Every eye in the saloon turned toward the door.

"Someone screamed," Joe Lazlo said.

Frank Tolliver guffawed. "That wasn't no scream. It was a mountain lion. I saw tracks yesterday."

Red Sweet ran his tongue across his dried lips and turned to Tolliver. "So, what about Speck?"

With an angry shake of his head, the large-boned killer shoved to his feet and cursed. "All right, damn it. Let's go over to that café and take a look."

Before he could take a step, Wyoming Dutch shoved Jonah Pate through the batwing doors. "This here jasper is the only one we could find in town, Frank. All the others has done run out except him and the barkeep."

The diminutive man trembled. "Please don't hurt me."

Tolliver snorted. "What in the hell is a mama's boy like you doing out here?"

Back in the cave, Paleto grinned at Slade upon the latter's return. "I hear scream."

He held up a single finger. "One less."

The Mimbre Apache lifted an eyebrow and held up two fingers. "Two. The one from the store—the one the snake bite. He is dead. I see two white men carry him into the pines."

A crooked grin twisted Slade's sun-browned face. "That whittles the number down to about twelve or thirteen. We . . ." He paused, his gray eyes on the cowpoke at the end of the street herding a small man in a business suit to the Golden Queen Saloon.

Slade looked at Paleto, puzzled. "That must be Pate, the one Tilly talked about."

Paleto shrugged.

For several moments, Slade considered the situation. He knew Pate and the bartender remained, but there was nothing he could do about it. With Apache fatalism, he told himself they'd just have to take their chances. "We can't worry about him now," said Slade. "We best grab some sleep. We'll be mighty busy tonight."

Tolliver eyed Jonah Pate malevolently. "How is it you're the only one left in town?"

The frightened little man shrugged. "I didn't know everyone had left." Fearful for his life, he glanced around at the eyes glaring at him murderously. "That's the truth."

For a moment, Tolliver studied the small man, then gestured to the batwing doors. "Get out of here, but hang around in case I want you, understand?"

The small man nodded fearfully.

Tolliver poured a tumbler of whiskey, tossed it down, drew the back of a gnarled hand over his lips, and headed for the door. "Now, let's go see about Speck."

Hatch and Red stared incredulously at the unlocked rear door in the café. "I tell you, Frank," Hatch babbled, pointing to the wooden lock bar leaning against the wall by the door. "That bar was across the door when we was here. Ain't that right, Red?"

"The gospel, Frank. We both saw it."

The massive killer narrowed his cold blue eyes. He opened the door and stared out at the layer of snow on the ground, unblemished except for animal sign. There were no boot tracks. He shook his head and closed the door. "I reckon you'll probably find him waiting for you over to the saloon and laughing his head off at fooling you like he did."

Hatch pursed his lips. "What do you mean, Frank?"

Tolliver gestured to the door. "He hid out here somewhere. After you left, he took the bar off the door and went out the front. He's just been making a game with you."

Red started to protest, but Tolliver snorted and pushed through the crowd of cowpokes that had followed them to the café.

Cooper and Simmons had remained behind, discussing the sudden disappearance of the townsfolk. Arch leaned forward. "All right now, Jess. What's up your sleeve? Why did you give Tolliver the wrong day?"

The younger gunfighter grinned slyly as he reached for a bottle of Old Grand Dad. "To tell the truth, I didn't know he'd take our word that the false bed was empty or not."

The older gunfighter nodded. "So?"

"So it suddenly dawned on me that we could take it all."

Arch studied his young partner with pride. A knowing grin spread over his grizzled face. "So that's it. I always thought I was the sneakiest of the two of us, but I was mistaken. You're sneakier than a preacher in a whorehouse." In one quick move, he tossed down his drink. "So that's why you told the dumb ape it was coming on Saturday, huh?"

Cooper leaned forward, a sly grin on his face. "Yeah. We can get the whole hundred thousand like this. You know me, Arch. I'm always looking out for the two of us."

The older gunfighter ignored the icy chill in Cooper's eyes. "So, what do you have in mind?"

Jess glanced around. "Back in the bunkhouse, I was listening to a bunch of the old boys talking around the stove when that old-timer they called Pickax said something mighty interesting."

"Yeah. I remember him."

"Well, the road goes from Santa Fe to Juniper Pass and then on to Las Vegas."

Arch frowned. "So, what's your point?"

"So, you heard Tolliver say his boys had to keep the road open to the mine. When the time comes, I think we should volunteer to do that very thing."

"What? Are you crazy? You know just how hard—" He cut off his protest in midsentence when he spotted the sly grin on his young partner's face. Suddenly he realized what young Jess was suggesting. He laughed. "When I said you was sneaky, I didn't know how sneaky. Why, I reckon you could peel the skin from a rattlesnake, and he wouldn't even notice it 'til the meat fell off his bones."

Cooper's grin broadened. "A hundred thousand. And it goes out this Friday. We hit it, skirt the mine, and then take the road to Santa Fe, and Tolliver won't know nothing for another twenty-four hours. By the time that dumb galoot figures out what's happening, we'll be lost out there somewhere," he added, gesturing to all of the Southwest. His grin grew wider, and he winked at his young partner. "I always figured you was smarter than me, son. Now there ain't no doubt." He hesitated, a frown wrinkling his brow. "Still, it'd be easier getting rid of the gold in Fort Union than Santa Fe."

Jess shrugged. "If we do that, we'd have to come back through Juniper Pass and Tolliver."

"That wouldn't be too smart," Arch drawled.

* * *

On the outskirts of Juniper Pass, Paleto and Slade ghosted through the forest and came in behind the gun shop next to the jail, from which came laughing voices.

While the starlight cast a dim glow over the snow-covered landscape, inside the shop was dark as a raven's wing. Slade didn't dare strike a lucifer, so the two felt along the puncheon floor for a table.

"Here," Paleto grunted, dropping to his knees and pulling the rug and table from the trapdoor. He popped it open and felt inside for a flight of stairs. "Steep," he said as he started down. "Make sure you not fall," he muttered, his tone carrying light sarcasm.

"If you can make it down, I can make it down," Slade shot back. He paused halfway down the ladder, and by feel, closed the trapdoor so as not to permit any light to escape.

At the base of the stairs, he struck a match and surveyed the hidden room. A grin played over his lips. There was enough firepower here to wage a small war, and the young half-breed reminded himself, that might be exactly what they would find themselves in.

Working quickly, in the next hour they cached saddle rifles, ammunition, black powder, and a spool of hemp rope a few yards deep into the forest.

By midnight, they had carried it all to the cave, where, to their surprise, they found Right Hand waiting for them. The weariness in his thin face told them he had traveled hard.

"They are all safe," he said.

"No problems?"

"None."

Slade nodded. "Good. Now let's get busy and set up

a few tricks to whittle that bunch down a bit. We'll do it at either end of town." He winked at Paleto. "Remember the snares we set for rabbits when we were children?"

The twinkle in Paleto's eyes gave Slade his answer.

"I'll rig up a snare or deadfall north of town. You go south. Near a tunnel entrance should they get too close." He gestured to the four kegs of black powder. "Right Hand, I reckon you're tired from the long trip, but you must place one of those under the Golden Queen Saloon." Slade hesitated. A twinkle gleamed in his eyes. "And you might as well turn their ponies from the corral after your blow up the saloon."

The usually dour expression of the diminutive Arapaho's face turned into a broad grin. "I will do so."

A rush of adrenaline flooded Slade's veins, the surge of exultation an Apache warrior always experienced when he was going into battle.

He turned to Paleto and Right Hand. "Signal like the owl when you are ready. I will do the same. Then I will call them out. Their ponies are in the barn. They will not take time to saddle up when they see us on foot. When they start after me, fire your six-gun. Some will pursue you. Right Hand, when the men disappear into the forest, fire the powder and turn the ponies loose."

With a solemn expression, Right Hand nodded. "As you say."

# Chapter Nineteen

Right Hand waited at the edge of the forest as the clouds scudded overhead, small patchy puffs of condensation that threw fleeting shadows over the pristine snow like racing mustangs. After several anxious minutes, he spotted heavier clouds, and as they pushed in, he hurried across the clearing to the shadows of the Golden Queen Saloon.

Without hesitation, he placed the keg of black powder under one corner of the saloon, and with the next passing shadows, fled back to the safety of the forest.

Inside the saloon, eight or nine gunfighters slept on poker tables, the bar, and the roulette table, leaving the entire second floor to any rattlesnakes that might still be claiming the territory.

One of them, Bull Gutierrez, had awakened and stepped out the front and around the corner to relieve himself. From the corner of his eye, he caught movement at the edge of the forest, but when he looked, he saw nothing. He shrugged and went back inside.

Upon reaching the forest, Right Hand glanced back. His heart leaped into his throat when he spotted the shadow of a white man at the corner of the saloon. For long seconds, he remained frozen, knowing the shadows hid him, but fearful any movement might reveal his presence.

As the gray fingers of false dawn shoved the darkness of the night back to the west, Slade studied his handiwork. The trail down which he planned to lead the owl-hoots curved beneath a granite ledge under which he had placed a keg of black powder. He found a spot to hide so that as soon as they came in sight, he could touch off the keg.

He made his way to the edge of the forest near Burl Henry's livery and waited for the signal. He heard a horse whinny, reminding him of his promise to Henry. Quickly, he slipped into the barn and dipped feed into the troughs. Within minutes, he was crouched back in the forest.

The sky grew lighter.

And then, a faint *hoo-hoo* sounded, followed almost immediately by a second. Slade grinned and replied. He clacked a cartridge into the chamber of the Winchester and drew down on the front windows of the Golden Queen Saloon.

Inside the hotel, Bull Gutierrez had not gone back to sleep, instead putting a pot of coffee on the potbellied stove. He looked around at the call of the owls and shook his head.

Without warning, there came a sharp crack of a rifle and one of the front windows of the saloon exploded. The racketing gunfire continued.

Windows shattered; oil lamps exploded; startled cowpokes ducked under poker tables; stovepipes ripped open, spreading a billowing cloud of black soot over the room.

When the firing ceased, Frank Tolliver bellowed like an angry longhorn bull and stormed toward the batwing doors, six-gun in hand. "Kill them sons a' bitches."

Jess Cooper started to follow, but Arch Simmons held him back, muttering, "Let them go and get themselves killed. We got other plans, remember?"

Cooper looked around at his partner with a crooked grin. "Yeah, yeah. Thanks for reminding me."

As soon as Slade saw the angry gun hands burst onto the porch, he deliberately fired once again, then raced down the trail.

Tolliver recognized Slade. "There he is. It's that drifter," he shouted. Like a herd of wild horses, the hired guns ran through the snow. Behind them came more shots. When they looked back, they saw Paleto disappear into the forest. "Red, some of you get than Injun," Tolliver ordered. "The rest of you come with me."

Bull Gutierrez hesitated, remembering the movement he had seen earlier. He glanced at the forest behind the saloon just as the barrel of a rifle pointed toward the saloon. Instantly, he snapped off three slugs. "There's another back behind the saloon," he cried out, charging the forest.

Right Hand jerked back as slugs tore through the treetops above his head. When he saw two gunfighters racing toward him, he turned and disappeared into the forest.

Slade sprinted down the trail, careful to leave tracks in the snow. He passed under the granite ledge and, around the next bend, cut off the trail and clambered over the rocky slope and nestled into a niche overlooking the trail. He chambered a cartridge and waited, his eyes on his back trail.

Tolliver and two others came into view. Just before they reached the ledge, Slade fired. The black powder exploded, sending tons of rock cascading down the slope in a cacophony of cracking rocks, snapping tree trunks, and frantic screams.

Finally, the last boulder settled, and an ominous silence settled over the forest.

Paleto led four gunfighters along the south road, taking a trail between several tall pines around the first bend. The four followed with Red in the lead. Without warning, a supple tree whipped up, snapping Red off his feet and sending him flying ten feet up in the air to hang by one foot.

The other three slid to a halt.

"Get me down," the dangling outlaw shouted.

The other three looked around at each other.

At that moment, the sharp crack of a rifle broke the silence, and the dangling cowpoke fell to the ground, the slug having sliced through the rope.

As Red climbed to his feet, the sound of underbrush crashing reached their ears. "There he goes," shouted one.

Red snorted, "I ain't going after him."

The others looked at each other and nodded agreement.

When Tolliver saw the ledge start to fall, he leaped behind the thick bole of an ancient pine and pressed up against it as hard as he could. To his horror, he felt the huge pine tremble and shake as boulders weighing up to two thousand pounds bounced off it, stacking up almost shoulder deep around him. After what seemed like hours, the forest grew silent. He remained motionless, knowing whoever was responsible for the insidious trap was still out there.

He lost track of time. Later, he heard movement above. Cautiously, he peered around the forest, but saw nothing. Then, far off in the pine and piñons, he thought he spotted a fleeting figure ghosting through the forest, but when he blinked, it had disappeared.

Bull Gutierrez snorted, "I don't know who the jasper was, but he had planted a keg of black powder under the saloon here. We dumped it in the snow. It would have caused a heap of damage here."

Eyeing the destruction in the Golden Queen Saloon, Tolliver replied sarcastically, "Couldn't have done much more damage than what I see here." He glanced around and added, "Reckon we'll have to move down to the Longhorn at the end of the street."

The doors swung open and Red and his three compadres came in. Red shook his head. "The Injun got away, Frank."

Tolliver cursed.

Cooper spoke up. "Any idea who's behind it, Frank?"

"Yeah," the grizzled outlaw growled. "I know who's behind it. That drifter we shoulda hung." He looked at Hatch. "What's his name? The one that plugged Kansas Jack?"

"Slade. Jake Slade."

Jess and Arch exchanged surprised looks.

"Yeah, that's it, Slade. I recognized him out there. I

figured when he broke jail, he'd hightail it out of the country."

Lazlo stepped forward. "Frank, you and me have knowed each other a long time. You know me for a straight-spoken hombre. I want to know what's going on or I'm riding out." He hastened to add, "That's no threat to you or anyone. I just don't like the idea of some stranger playing games with me. A few days back, we lost four or five to those damned rattlesnakes. Then Speck up and disappears. Today, my two boys got kilt in that landslide." He looked around the room. "There's ten of us left, and we got no idea what's taking place."

Bull Gutierrez stepped up beside Lazlo. "No offense, Frank, but that goes for me and my boys, too."

Tolliver eyed them warily, his feverish brain quickly calculating his options. He had three men, Hatch, Fats, and Wyoming Dutch. He glanced at Cooper and Simmons. With them, it was six to four. He grimaced and backed way. The odds weren't good enough. With a broad grin, Tolliver replied, "I don't blame you boys. So I'll be honest with you. After you hear what I got to say and you still want to ride out, I won't try to stop you. You okay with that?"

The two gunfighters looked at each other. Lazlo shrugged. "Why not?"

# Chapter Twenty

Tolliver glanced at Cooper and Simmons, who eyed him coolly. He grabbed a bottle of whiskey and chugged a couple of slugs straight from the bottle. Wiping the back of his gnarled hand across his thick lips, he glared at the men around him and said, "In case you ain't heard, Wingate's dead along with whatever reason he paid us to come here."

Several of the gunfighters glanced at each other.

Tolliver continued. "But Jess and Arch here found out that sometime this week, the mine up at Cimarron Gorge is sending out a shipment of gold, ten thousand dollars' worth." He paused, shooting Jess and Arch a warning look. He continued. "Now, that ain't nothing like we first figured, but looking at our numbers, if we split it in equal shares, we'll come away with about a thousand a head. As far as I'm concerned, a thousand is a hell of a lot better than nothing."

A murmur of approval sounded from all of the gunfighters except Hatch. When he had overheard the discussion between Tolliver and Cooper, the sum was fifty thousand. His one eye narrowed, and his brain began working feverishly.

Cooper smiled knowingly at Arch Simmons. Both recognized the scam Tolliver was pulling on his men.

Arch returned the grin, imagining Frank Tolliver's rage when the gold failed to reach Juniper Pass.

Outside, snow began to fall. Tolliver continued. "Now, I don't know if none of you noticed, but a local jasper keeps the roads plowed. That's the only way the mine can move its goods. Well, that old boy has lit a shuck out of here for Las Vegas. It's up to us to keep the road clear if we want to get that shipment of gold."

A groan of protest rose from the grizzled killers.

Jess Cooper winked at Arch and spoke up. "We'll do it, Tolliver. Me and Arch."

Simmons nodded. "Jess is right." He glanced around at the gun hands staring at him. "No sense in you fellers getting out there, unless you want to."

A chorus of negative replies filled the air.

Tolliver shrugged. "I ain't going to argue with you."

Jess grinned. "Come on, Arch. Let's get over to the barn and see what we can find."

"All right," said Tolliver. "Let's the rest of us grab our gear and move down to the Longhorn. Save having to haul whiskey back up here like we did before."

"The old boy who owns this livery is particular with his tools," Arch said, nodding to the snowplow in the corner of the barn. "Most jaspers let 'em sit out in the weather."

Jess grinned, surveying the large barn with the aid of a coal-oil lantern. He shivered. "Cold in here."

Arch laughed. "What do you expect? It's a barn."

The younger gunman gave him a go-to-hell look. He led the way into Burl Henry's quarters. "Not bad," Jess muttered, setting the lantern on the potbellied stove in the middle of the room. Along one wall was a bunk and several pegs for clothes. A table that served both for eating and as a desk stood against another wall. Cooper chuckled. "Truth is, I'd just as soon bunk in here as down at the Longhorn. What about you?"

The older gunfighter sneered. "Anything so I don't have to listen to the bellowing of Frank Tolliver."

"Fine. Start us up a fire while I tend the animals."

Arch had a small flame started when Jess hurried back into the living quarters. "Put out the fire, Arch. Quick."

"What?"

Jess jabbed a thin finger at the stove. "I'll tell you, but just do it."

After the older man smothered the fire, he frowned at his partner. "What's tapping at your cork?"

"The stables. How long the townspeople been gone, two, three days?"

"About. Why?"

Somebody's feeding the animals. The feed troughs are almost full."

A frown furrowed Arch's brows; then he grinned. "Probably that one they call Jonah Pate."

Jess laughed. "That spooky little mouse? Don't kid me."

Shaking his head, Arch reminded his younger partner, "Remember, son, it isn't too smart to take things the way they look. Sometimes, usually at the least convenient time, you get the hell surprised out of you. Pate might be one of those things."

Growing serious, Jess agreed. "Tell you what. Let's go about business as usual, but at night, we'll slip in here and see if we have any unwelcome visitors."

Arch studied him a moment. "You think that Slade hombre or his Injun sidekick is the one feeding the horses?"

"You got a better idea?"

The older gunfighter shrugged. "Nope. In fact, it sounds good to me, but we can skip tonight."

"Tonight? Why?"

"Didn't you say the feed trough was full?"

Jess nodded slowly. "Yeah. Yeah. You're right. He won't be back tonight."

In their cave high above Juniper Pass, Slade leaned back against his saddle and pulled out his bag of Bull Durham. Their bellies were full, the chamber was warm, and they were satisfied with the morning's work.

"The rocks kill two?" Paleto held up two fingers.

Smoke drifted up past Slade's eyes. "Yep. I figured I got Tolliver, too, but I spotted him coming out about thirty minutes later. He went to the Golden Queen Saloon, and just after the snow started, they headed up the street to the Longhorn." A sly grin played over his lips. "I reckon the Golden Queen is just a little bit too airy."

Right Hand grimaced. "It would have been much colder if I had not failed."

Slade chuckled. "Two out of three. I'll take those kinds of results anytime."

The Mimbre Apache lifted an eyebrow. "That leaves how many?"

The young half-breed grinned. "Ten. Enough to go around."

All three chuckled.

Slade grew serious. "Two of them went over to Burl Henry's barn for a few minutes, then headed back up to the Longhorn."

Paleto's dark brow wrinkled. "What reason they go to barn?"

The young half-breed met his brother's eyes. "I got no idea, but it worries me." He leaned back and took a drag on his cigarette. He stared at the smoke as it curled upward to the ceiling of the cave. "When we started this, I reckoned on driving Tolliver and his boys out of Juniper Pass, but we don't seem to be doing anything except killing them off." He slid his gaze to Paleto. "What makes them so stubborn?"

For several moments, the two brothers stared at each other. Finally, Paleto said, "Remember the day we left our father, and we saw the fox finally catch the rabbit?"

"I remember. What does that have to do with today?"

"What if the fox had chased a mouse, and the mouse ducked into a hole?"

"The fox would have gone to another hole."

"Yes." Paleto nodded. "A mouse is but a mouthful to the fox, but a rabbit? A rabbit will fill fox's belly for a week."

Slade understood. His eyes narrowed. "Whatever it is, then, is worth more than the trouble we're causing."

"Yes," Paleto replied. "But then, I am only ignorant Apache."

The young half-breed grinned at the taunting amusement in his brother's eyes. "Well, brother of mine, if you hang around with me, some of my smarts might rub off on you."

"If I am lucky." He paused. "What could be so important to men like these?"

A frown knit Slade's brows. "Gold, but I don't see how. When I was hiding in the café, I heard them mention gold, but I couldn't make out the rest of their jabbering." He turned to Right Hand. "Didn't you say all the gold had been mined out below Juniper Pass?"

The diminutive Arapaho nodded. "Many years ago. The one at the Cimarron Gorge not do good. Talk to close it. What owners do, I don't know, but they find more gold in mine."

Slade looked around at Paleto. "Some of this is making a little sense, not much, but a little. From what Tilly said, a stranger wanted to buy mining claims, local property. Maybe he heard that the mine owners had come up with a method to get out more gold. That could be why so many of the gunnies showed up. He hired them to persuade locals to sell out, yet not one of the locals mentioned anything about these jaspers trying to force them to sell." He scratched his head. "But that's as far as I can go. Why are they staying in Juniper Pass if they're not after mining claims?"

Paleto lifted an eyebrow. "There is gold at mine."

Slade chewed on his bottom lip. "Maybe that was the gold I heard those old boys talking about." He nodded sharply. "I'd bet the house you're right. The gold. They're after the mine's gold."

"You think they attack mine?"

His brow knit in concentration, Slade replied, "No. But the mine has to ship the gold out. Maybe that's when they plan to hit it."

The Mimbre Apache lifted an eyebrow. "We not know for sure."

"No. We don't." He looked at Right Hand. "Where do they ship the gold? Any idea?"

The slight Arapaho nodded briefly. "Las Vegas."

Slade nodded thoughtfully, then grimaced as another thought hit him.

"What is wrong?"

"The town and the mine are joined hip to hip. The town supplies the mine most of its goods. The mine goes under, so does the town. At least, that's what Tilly said."

The storm only lasted one day. The second day dawned with a sky as blue as a robin's egg. Jess blew on his coffee and muttered, "Let's don't run the plow today."

"But the storm's past."

"I know, but if that jasper, Slade, spots us with the team, he won't bother to come down tonight and feed them."

Arch's face lit with pride. Arch had no offspring, but had he any, he hoped they'd be like Jess. "You're getting smarter, Jess."

Jess chuckled and sipped his coffee, a sly grin on his lips. "I had a good teacher."

The older gunfighter beamed.

Up above, Slade studied the village. No one was moving about. Probably all in the saloon staying warm. Maybe it was time to take advantage of the catacombs beneath the village and see what they could learn of the gang's plan.

He looked down at the diminutive Arapaho. "Do any of those mines come out near the Longhorn Saloon?"

"No."

"What about near Rose's Café? You know of her tunnel."

A frown wrinkled his dark face. "I know of no tunnel."

"It comes out close to the rim of the canyon."

Nodding slowly, he said, "One mine does open near the rim."

"Good. Show me."

"I go, too."

Slade shook his head at his brother. "They're all at the saloon. Just one of us has a better chance going unseen."

# Chapter Twenty-one

Slade paused behind the snow-covered tangle of dead vines covering the mouth of the mine. He shook snow from the vines and peered outside. A faint grin split his slender face when he spotted the arroyo that led to Rose's tunnel less than twenty yards distant. Back to his left was Juniper Pass.

Easing out of the mine, he lay in the snow behind a tall pine, studying the village. The sun was drawing near the western peaks of the Sangre de Cristos.

Suddenly shouts erupted from the town. Between the buildings, Slade spotted a tangle of arms and legs rolling into the street. Several gun hands boiled from the Longhorn Saloon to gather around them.

Slade took advantage of the distraction and darted into the gully. Ten minutes later, staying back in the shadows behind the counter, he peered out the window of the café.

By now, the two drunken cowpokes were too exhausted to continue their battle, so, arms slung around each other's shoulders, they staggered back to the saloon, followed by a crowd of drunken owl-hoots. Evening shadows fell across the street, soon engulfing the small village.

The wiry, young half-breed slipped out the rear door

and darted under the Longhorn Saloon, staying close to the thick wooden piers supporting the building.

Voices and laughter came through the puncheon floor over his head. He crawled about under the floor, picking up phrases containing the words, *Saturday*, *snowplow*, but not once did he hear any word that suggested exactly what the gang had in mind.

After several minutes crouched beneath the saloon, Slade pinpointed Tolliver. He grinned to himself, wondering what the grizzled outlaw would think if he knew only a two-inch floor separated them.

An hour passed. Finally, cold and disgusted, Slade eased out from beneath the saloon. He started back into Rose's Café, then remembered Burl Henry's horses. He hesitated, not wanting to push his luck. Still, the animals needed to be fed. Overhead, the stars shone brightly, illuminating the village with a bluish glow.

As Slade approached the barn, a horse nickered. Several others joined in and ambled over to rails. He muttered, "Hungry, huh?"

He climbed between the two lower rails and entered the shadows of the barn. Feeling his way through the dark, he had filled a scoop with feed and was turning back to the trough when a voice cut through the darkness. "Don't move, Slade. I got you spotted against the stars." Seconds later, a lucifer burst into flame, and a lantern lit the feed room.

Jess Cooper grinned at the young half-breed. "I figured it was you feeding the horses," he drawled, the muzzle of the .44 on Slade's belly.

Slade nodded to the scoop of feed. "All right if I dump this?"

Jess laughed, but the laughter was without mirth. "Sure. Go ahead. Feed 'em. I hate to see animals go hungry, but don't let that hand wander too close to the butt of that six-gun of yours."

It was Slade's turn to laugh. "Don't worry. I've seen you draw." He began feeding the horses. One animal, a big sorrel with a star and stripe on his forehead, pushed in. Slade shoved his muzzle away. "Just hold on there, horse. There's plenty." He filled the trough. "What are you doing here with the likes of Tolliver, Jess? He's heading for the hangman's noose along with all those with him."

The young gunfighter chuckled, lowered his hammer, and did a reverse spin with his six-gun into his holster. "Not me, Slade. I don't want to kill you. You and your Apache brother saved Arch and my hides back yonder. You keep hanging around here, and that's what's going to happen. In another couple days, me and Arch'll be gone. If you're hell-bent on taking Tolliver, just do me a favor and stay out of town 'til after Friday." The slender gunfighter stared at Slade with a faint grin. "That ain't too much to ask."

"Look, Jess. I don't know what you've got in mind, but I figure Tolliver is going to hit the mine. That mine is what keeps this town going. I can't stand by and watch it go to hell on a shutter." His gray eyes darted to Jess's six-gun.

"Don't try it." Jess took a step back. "You saved my life. Now I'm giving you yours back." He nodded to the wide door behind the wiry half-breed. "Go. The way you came." His eyes turned black as old ice. "Next time I see you, I'll kill you, Slade. That's a promise."

Slade chewed on his bottom lip. "I wish it didn't have to be this way, Jess. If you're looking for a job, come with me. I'm a partner in a stage and freight line from Fort Atkinson all the way to California. We—"

Jess interrupted. "Not me. I ain't no bull-whacker. Never have been, never will be." His eyes softened. "Things happen that can't never be changed, Slade. This is one of them."

For several moments, the two men locked eyes. Finally, Slade nodded and backed away. He paused. "If you change your mind, I—"

"I won't. *Adios, amigo.*"

Slade nodded and stepped into the night, cursing himself for being unable to talk Jess Cooper out of whatever was primed to happen. He was so involved with his own thoughts that he failed to notice the shadow next to Rose's Café when he turned the corner of her building.

"Hey. Is that you, Red?"

The words galvanized Slade into action. He shucked his six-gun as he spun and slammed the barrel across the shadow's forehead. The cowpoke dropped like a poleaxed steer.

Slade disappeared into the café and moments later, dropped down into the tunnel.

Thirty minutes later, he sat by a small fire in the cave with Paleto and Right Hand. "Nothing. I heard talk of the mine and the gold, but nothing to hang a hat on. The only hint I got was that whatever it is, it will be in the next couple days. And that I got from Jess Cooper," he continued, relating the events in the barn.

Paleto frowned. "What do we do?" He nodded toward his Osage orange bow. "You wish me to act?"

"No. I think we just watch. When Tolliver and his men ride out, we'll follow."

Next morning while Slade enjoyed a Bull Durham on the ledge at the mouth of the cave, the snowplow emerged from the barn and headed up the road to the mine. He muttered, "Now, who do you reckon that is?"

At his side, Paleto squinted, but the distance was too great for him to discern the features of the two men even with his eagle eyes. "I cannot make them out."

"Burl Henry is the one who keeps the roads clear. And he's in Las Vegas."

Right Hand mumbled, "Tolliver."

Slade grunted. "Makes sense."

"We should follow?"

Keeping his eyes on the snowplow, Slade replied to the Arapaho, "Might not be a bad idea. Let's see what they got up their sleeve."

Hatch turned from the frosty window and, with his one good eye, stared across the saloon at Frank Tolliver. "Them two is moving out with the snowplow, Frank."

Better them than me, Tolliver told himself as he grunted and reached for the bottle of whiskey, content in the snug warmth of the Longhorn Saloon as well as its lack of rattlesnakes. He dealt out a hand of solitaire while the others drank free whiskey and played poker.

About that time, Bull Gutierrez rushed in. "Tolliver. It's Wyoming Dutch. He's done gone and froze solid."

Tolliver looked up from the cards. "Froze?"

"Just found him out behind the café. He must have fell and hit his head on something. Anyway, he's out there stiff as a board."

The grizzled outlaw suppressed a smile. One less in the split.

"What do you want us to do with him? Ground's too hard for a grave."

Tolliver shrugged. "Drag him out back to the canyon

rim and toss him off. He stays out back there, he'll draw animals."

Bundled in his fur-lined leather coat and his Stetson tied down over his ears, Jess Cooper yelled at his partner from where he was perched on the seat of the snowplow, "This ain't as bad as I thought, Arch."

Simmons nodded, breaking the trail ahead of the brace of eight stout horses. Glancing up at the tree-lined slope above him, he reckoned if a jasper had to fork a snowplow, this was as good a road as any. The narrow trail clung to the south slope of the mountain. Most of the snow had drifted to the south edge of the road and the blade of the plow had no problem in pushing it over the edge. "Looks like we'll reach the mine before noon," he shouted back.

A hundred yards up the slope, Right Hand ghosted through the pine and piñon, his keen eyes on the two gunfighters below.

Just before they rounded the last bend to the mine, Arch rode back to Jess. He nodded to the six-shooters tied down to the younger man's legs. "Hide them." Before Jess could question why, Arch explained, "No plowman wears two guns tied down." While he spoke, he was busy shucking his gun belt and placing it in his saddlebags. He stuck one six-gun under his waistband. "We got to look the part."

Jess followed his example.

When they made their turnaround at the mine, the foreman and his assistant came out to meet them. The bandy-legged foreman waved. "Howdy. Where's old Burl?"

Glibly, Arch replied, "He ran over to Las Vegas to

look at some fresh stock. He hired us to keep the roads clear until he gets back sometime next week."

A frown wrinkled the foreman's brow. "Hey, wasn't you old boys up here a few days back?"

Arch laughed. "You got a good memory, friend. Yep. You put us up for the night. When we left here, we rode on down to Juniper Pass and since we was sorta at loose ends, old Burl hired us."

The foreman grinned and waved them to the cook shack. "Name's Al Grimes. Coffee's hot. Grub's on the stove. Fill your bellies before you head back."

Arch accepted amiably as if they were long-lost relatives. Cooper was reluctant. Inside, Arch kept the conversation going, talking about snow, and plows, and horses until he guided the conversation back around to the most recent storm.

"Naw, that wasn't a bad one," said the foreman, sipping his coffee. "I've seen them where old Burl couldn't get through for two weeks."

Arch shook his head. "That so? What do you do if something serious comes up, like an emergency or something? Just stuck here?"

The foreman grinned at his assistant. "You old boys ain't from around here, huh?"

"Nope. Back south around Tucson."

"Well, sir," he began. "We got us our own private trail. Back down the road at the first bend, a trail leads down the slope and up the far side. Halfway up is an old mine from back in the days of the old-timers. It cuts right through that mountain there and comes out on the east slope a couple miles south of Juniper Pass. At night, if you squint right hard, you can see the lights of Las Vegas to the east." He paused and shook his head.

Arch glanced at Jess and downed the rest of his coffee. "Sounds mighty convenient."

"It is."

The older gunfighter pushed to his feet and extended his hand. "My name's Frank Tolliver and this here young colt goes by the moniker Hatch. Hatch Ahearn. Much obliged for the coffee."

Fifteen minutes after they rounded the bend, Arch pulled off the road. "Keep going. I'm going to find that cave. I got a feeling that old boy at the mine just did us a big favor."

Had Jess Cooper glanced over his shoulder moments later, he would have spotted the lithe figure of Right Hand dash across the road and down the slope in pursuit of Arch.

# Chapter Twenty-two

Hatch hurried up to Tolliver's table when he and Bull returned from disposing of Wyoming Dutch's body. Tolliver grunted, "Get the job done?"

Hatch nodded emphatically. "Yeah, Frank, but I don't figure Dutch fell and hit his head. Ask Bull here. We looked at the wound, and someone whacked him on the head with a six-gun."

Tolliver frowned.

Bull agreed. "That's right, Frank. Someone hit him. You could see the mark of the muzzle."

Tolliver's grizzled face grew hard. "Slade!"

Joe Lazlo eyed Tolliver. "The one what shot up the place?"

"Yeah. Him and that Injun of his," Hatch said.

Tolliver narrowed his eyes. Slade had bitten off more than he could chew. "That mama's boy still down at the tax office?"

"The one named Pate?" Hatch nodded. "Yeah."

"Go get him. And that one," he added, gesturing to C. T. Henley behind the bar. "They'll be our bargaining chips with that Slade hombre."

That afternoon when the snowplow pulled into the livery, Slade frowned, puzzled by the fact that two of

Tolliver's men had ridden out that morning, but only one had returned.

A few minutes later, his frown deepened when he spotted a Tolliver rider coming in on the south road. Moments later, Right Hand emerged from the forest, not from the north, but the south.

Slade suppressed his curiosity and motioned the dark Arapaho into the cave. "Come. Eat and rest."

Inside, the slight Arapaho cupped his coffee with both hands. "They eat with the white-eyes at the mine. When they leave, the old one, he ride into forest. He find old mine. I remember the mine, so I follow." Holding a strip of broiled venison between his fingers, he gestured from north to south. "The mine go through the mountain. No cave-ins." He gestured to the south. "That why I come from back there."

Slade and Paleto exchanged puzzled looks. "That don't make sense," Slade muttered, rolling a Bull Durham. "There's only one road to Las Vegas, and that's through Juniper Pass. If they're after the gold shipment like we guessed, why look for another way in or out?"

Paleto shrugged.

Slade continued. "Something's out of kilter. When I was under the saloon, I heard some of those jaspers talk about Saturday, day after tomorrow. Then Jess Cooper says tomorrow."

A distant gunshot rolled up the mountain slope, followed by two more. The three eased to the rim of the ledge and peered down into the village. Standing in the street in front of the Longhorn Saloon were two men, one wearing a white apron, the other a black suit. The one in the black suit held a white flag. Next to him stood the hulking figure of Bull Gutierrez bundled in his red mackinaw and his black Stetson with the Montana crown.

Gutierrez fired again, then cupped a hand to his lips and shouted four times, once in each direction, but he was too distant to discern his words.

Paleto arched an eyebrow. "They seek you, my brother."

"Looks that way," Slade muttered. "Those two jaspers must be the ones Tilly and them told us about." He stroked his chin thoughtfully. "Wonder what Tolliver's got in mind."

A touch of wry humor edged Paleto's reply. "Only way is to go down and see."

As they watched, Gutierrez returned to the saloon, leaving the two standing in the middle of the street.

To the north, a few clouds blew in.

Slade buttoned his mackinaw. "I'll go down the street to the mercantile with a Winchester in case they try something. Paleto, you go to the rear of the jail across the street from the saloon and call to them."

A knowing grin curled Paleto's lips. "Do not go inside. They might not have found all the rattlers."

Returning his brother's grin, Slade chuckled. "Don't worry about that. Right Hand, you come in at the rear of the Longhorn. If they want me, my brother, tell them I am gone. I will return later." When he saw the puzzled frown on the Mimbre Apache's face, he added, "That'll give us some bargaining time. If we're lucky," he added ruefully.

Night was settling over Juniper Pass by the time the three found their places. Paleto peered into the jail, but it was empty. He nodded with satisfaction. All the gun hands were at the saloon.

He looked around the corner.

The owl-hoots had taken Henley inside to serve drinks, leaving Jonah Pate shivering in the middle of the street, his thin arms hugging himself for warmth and still holding a white flag.

Clutching the bear-claw necklace about his neck, Paleto gave a shrill shout.

Moments later, several gun hands stepped out on the porch.

Tolliver stepped to the front. "Slade! That you?"

"He not here. Return later."

Tolliver snorted. "You that Apache what runs with him?"

Paleto remained silent.

"Well, if you are, you'll do just as good as Slade. Come on in, or we'll shoot Mr. Pate there."

Paleto moved to the other side of the jail. "I hate white-eyes. I shoot him for you, yes?"

A round of guffaws sounded from the porch.

Tolliver shouted. "I mean it, redskin. I'll blow his damned head off if you don't get your stinking carcass over here."

A crooked grin played over Paleto's lips. Quickly, he raised his Osage orange bow and nocked an arrow. He drew back and released the three-foot-long shaft. With a loud thunk, it slammed into the post by Tolliver's head.

The grizzled outlaw didn't move. A grin played over his thick lips. He hated Indians, but he understood the statement the Apache had just made. "Have it your way, redskin. Tell Slade I'll swap this worthless excuse of a man for him. Come morning if I don't hear from Slade, I'll kill the dude. The bartender the next day."

Pate began sobbing.

Tolliver nodded to Fats. "Go get him and put him upstairs. I want him where I can find him." His eyes narrowed. "I'll get Slade in the morning."

Fats looked up at him. "What if Slade won't give hisself up."

A cruel sneer twisted Tolliver's thick lips. "He will. He ain't the kind not to."

"What will you do, my brother?" Paleto studied Slade's face around the small fire back in their cave.

"No idea," he replied, pouring a cup of coffee and reaching for his bag of Bull Durham.

Right Hand held a tin cup of coffee in both his hands. Keeping his eyes on the coffee, he muttered, "The fat white-eye, he put little man in corner room above saloon. We take him from there."

Slade frowned. The suggestion seemed crazier than a blind dog in a meat market.

Paleto asked, "How?"

The slight Arapaho made the motion of climbing. "Stairs behind hotel."

Frowning, the Mimbre Apache looked at Slade. "This Tolliver, you think he watch stairs, my brother?"

The young half-breed grinned, seeing just what Right Hand was suggesting. "I would, but then I don't have a saloon full of free whiskey in front of me, either."

Both Indians smiled.

"We'll give them time to relax and down a few drinks. Right Hand, you stay in the forest at the rear of the saloon. When I bring Pate down, you take him through the mines up to the cave. Paleto, you take the front."

The Mimbre Apache nodded. "What of other white man?"

Slade grimaced. "The bartender?" He shook his head. "I don't know. Let's get Pate out and worry about Henley later."

Just after midnight, snow started falling again.

Slade and Right Hand paused at the edge of the forest, studying the saloon. Downstairs, lights blazed, but every window on the second floor was dark. Right Hand indicated the room on the southeast corner, second floor. "That where they take him."

Moving as lightly as a stalking cougar, Slade slipped wraithlike up the stairs and on past the second-floor landing and crouched at the door, his ear pressed against it for any sound.

He heard no sound, no movement.

Still, leaving nothing to chance, he stood against the clapboard wall next to the door and shucked his six-gun. His pulse was pounding in his ears. With the muzzle, he scratched on the door and waited. Nothing. He drew a deep breath to still his racing pulse and scratched again.

Without warning the door opened.

Slade pressed harder against the wall.

For what seemed like hours, there was no movement until finally, a figure stepped out on the landing.

Before he had a chance to look around, Slade laid the barrel of his .44 across the hardcase's temple. With a sharp grunt, he fell.

# Chapter Twenty-three

Slipping into the dimly lit hall, Slade opened the door to Pate's room and stepped inside, leaving the door cracked so he could see.

Pate lay on the bed, covered with blankets. Slade clapped his hand over the small man's lips, jerking him awake. His eyes wide with terror, he stared up at the half-breed.

"Quiet," Slade whispered. "I'm not going to hurt you. I'm taking you out of here away from Tolliver. It's your only chance to stay alive. Now get up and don't say a word. You understand? If you do, nod."

Pate nodded once.

Slade removed his hand. "Follow me."

Fumbling with his shoes, Jonah Pate managed to jam his feet into them.

"Hurry."

Pate nodded.

Slade peered up and down the hall, then reached for the rear door. He jerked it open and stared into the blurred eyes of the still-groggy jasper he had cold-cocked. Without hesitation, Slade leaped for the door, grasping the overhead jamb and swinging his feet forward, catching the hardcase in the belly and knocking him over the rail to the ground below.

A scream ripped from the man's throat.

Pate froze.

"Come on," Slade whispered harshly.

The small man didn't move.

"Damn it, I said, let's go." He grabbed Pate and jerked him down the stairs even as he heard footsteps pounding up the stairway at the far end of the hall.

Slade pulled the stumbling man down the stairs and into the forest after him. He shoved him at the small Arapaho. "Take care of him."

When Pate saw Right Hand, he stiffened and backed away. "No."

From the landing, a voice shouted, "There. They're going into the woods."

A second voice bellowed, "Get the bastard."

Muttering a curse, Slade spun Pate around and slapped the small man. "Tolliver will kill you if you don't run. Now get the hell out of here." He shot a glance at Right Hand. "Go. If he don't follow, forget about him."

"Where you go?"

Slade glanced back at the clamor of boot heels thumping down wooden stairs. "Lead them away from you." He spun and raced north along the edge of the forest.

"There he is. Out back," someone shouted.

Bursts of orange ripped through the dark night. Slade heard slugs whine through the trees. Chunks of snow exploded at his feet. Six-guns were notoriously inaccurate over thirty feet, doubly so at night, but there was always the chance of someone getting lucky.

Inside, C. T. Henley found himself the only jasper left in the saloon. He lost no time grabbing his coat and vanishing out the front door into the snowy night.

\* \* \*

Ahead, Slade spotted Burl Henry's barn. Smoke rose from the stovepipe chimney. Cooper. A shadow moved in the corral. Slade cut back into the forest. A faint grin curled his lips when he remembered the gully that led to the tunnel to Rose's Café. That was where he would be, all snug and warm while Tolliver and his band of hardcases were freezing their tails off looking for him in the forest.

He doubled back. Five minutes later, he ducked up the gully, and in another five minutes, he was peering out the window of the café.

Chuckling to himself, he crouched on the floor beneath the counter, pulling his knees up to his chest for warmth. He drew a curtain across the opening, concealing himself from view. He'd wait a spell until Tolliver's boys dozed off, and then he'd head back to the cave.

Back in the barn, Arch Simmons propped himself up on an elbow in his bunk when Cooper returned. "What was that all about?"

The young gunfighter crawled back into the warmth of his soogan. "Probably Slade causing trouble again."

Arch lay back and laughed. "You reckon we ought to reward Slade for causing Tolliver so much trouble that the dumb ape doesn't have time to figure out what we're going to do to him?"

Cooper rolled onto his side and pulled the blankets up about his neck. "Do what you want, but he ain't getting none of my share. Now go to sleep. We got important business tomorrow."

The older gunfighter laughed again.

* * *

Back in the saloon, Tolliver glared at the five gunnies staring at him. That another of his men was dead meant nothing to the coldhearted killer. What infuriated him was the fact that Slade was responsible, that he had been responsible for ten or twelve more deaths, and he was still untouched.

"Like a damned ghost, that jasper," he growled.

Joe Lazlo scanned the saloon. "Where in the hell is that barkeep?"

"Hell, he's gone," exclaimed Hatch. "Why, that—"

Tolliver glared at Hatch. "He's what?"

The one-eyed gunnie glared at the front door. "He run out while we was upstairs."

Lazlo poured a drink for himself and one for Tolliver. "Relax, Frank. Forget about the bartender. Just remember that day after tomorrow, we'll be ten thousand dollars richer. We'll leave Slade behind. Let him freeze his butt off up here." He tossed down his drink. "We'll be nice and warm in Santa Fe with some of them smooth-skinned senoritas."

Tolliver picked up his tumbler of Old Grand Dad. His sausagelike fingers tightened about it until his knuckles turned white. "I don't give a damn if it's Friday, Saturday, or Resurrection Day. I want Slade. I want him dead."

Later, Red Sweet sat at a table with Hatch and Fats. He had downed three or four whiskeys, and the warm glow in his belly gave him a sense of invincibility, of wisdom. "Wonder if any of us hit Slade out there."

Fats grunted. "We don't know that it was even Slade. It might have been someone else."

"It was Slade. Couldn't been no one else. And one of us might have hit him."

Hatch and Fats looked around at him. "Naw," replied Hatch, blinking his one eye. "Too dark."

"I know. But one of us might have got lucky."

Fats snorted. "Not likely." He tossed down his whiskey and pushed back from the table. "I'm heading upstairs."

"Me, too," said Hatch, following on unsteady legs.

Red watched them climb the stairs. He poured another drink, unable to shake the thought that a random slug might have caught Slade.

On impulse, he donned his heavy coat and grabbed a lantern.

Only a couple of other hardcases were still up, but they ignored Red as he pushed through the front door.

At the edge of the forest, the dim light from the coal-oil lantern fell over footprints. Red Sweet had no great skill as a tracker, but even he was not so dense that he couldn't make out the difference in moccasin tracks and boot prints. "Slade," he muttered, a sneer curling his lips.

He followed the indistinct tracks into the forest, where he lost it a few times, but always discovered it again. The whiskey was wearing off, and he was beginning to feel the cold. Just when he decided to give up, he stumbled onto the gully.

To his surprise, the trail led up the gully. Five minutes later, he discovered the tunnel.

Slade jerked awake when he heard the trapdoor opening. He shucked his Colt, and waited, expecting footsteps. After a few moments, the trapdoor closed, and an icy silence fell across the café once again.

He measured his time, figuring he had only a few minutes to spare. The tunnel was out of the question.

Someone might be waiting for him. His only choice was the rear door.

Red Sweet banged on Tolliver's door. "Frank, Frank, wake up."

A bleary-eyed Frank Tolliver jerked opened the door. "What the hell do you want?"

"It's Slade. I know where he is."

Tolliver blinked once or twice.

Red continued, his words running over each other. "He's next door, in Rose's Café. There's a secret tunnel. I followed his tracks and they led through the gully out back to a tunnel that opens up inside Rose's Café. I—"

Instantly, Tolliver was awake. "Wake the others. Fast."

Five minutes later, four gun hands surrounded the café while Red showed Tolliver the trail leading up the gully. "He's got to be there. There ain't no tracks coming out except mine."

Tolliver gestured to the trail. "Follow them."

Tolliver looked around the interior of the deserted café. He clenched his teeth in anger. "All right, where in the hell is he? We've looked everywhere, and he ain't around." He glared at Red. "Well?"

The smaller man swallowed hard. "He—he must've slipped out somehow." He glanced at the back door and exclaimed, "Look. The door ain't locked."

Narrowing his eyes, Tolliver glared at Red. "It wasn't locked when Speck disappeared. Remember?"

Not answering Tolliver's question, Red hurried out the door with the lantern. He knelt by a set of tracks in the snow. He looked up in excitement. "Look. Here's his tracks. See? Moccasins, not boots."

A cruel gleam glittered in Tolliver's eyes. "Yeah, yeah, I see."

Even as they stared at the tracks, a light snow began to fall again. To the east, false dawn pushed back the shadows of the night.

Tolliver called his men. He nodded to Hatch. "Get down to the barn and tell Cooper and Simmons to get up here. We're going to track Slade down." He looked around. "Bull, you and Lazlo get over on the other side of the street. Me and Red will track him from here. You two just make sure he don't make a break to the forest."

Knowing any argument would be futile, Lazlo glanced at Bull Gutierrez and shrugged. "Let's go."

Slade crouched in the shadows of Matthew Leighton's freight line. When he peered around the corner, he spotted Hatch coming in his direction. Hastily, he dropped to his knees and rolled under the board and batten office.

The one-eyed gun hand didn't even glance in Slade's direction when he passed, heading for the livery.

The wiry half-breed hurried to the street, pausing at the corner as Gutierrez and Lazlo disappeared behind the blacksmith's on the opposite side of the street.

Taking a deep breath, he dashed across the street and pressed up against the Golden Queen Saloon. He flexed his fingers about the butt of his Colt.

# Chapter Twenty-four

Crouching near the rear of the saloon, Slade spotted Hatch leaving the barn and heading back in the direction from which he had come. At that moment, the livery doors squeaked open and Jess Cooper geehawed the snowplow out, followed by Arch Simmons, who was leading Jess's pony. Slade nodded his understanding. The gang was keeping the road open so they could hit the shipment the next day.

He glanced around. As soon as he got back to the cave, he'd ride over to the mine and warn them. The snow grew heavier. Slade grinned in relief as he saw the falling flakes fill his tracks.

Hatch approached Tolliver reluctantly.

The broad brow of the large outlaw wrinkled in question. He glanced over Hatch's shoulder at the livery. "Where's Jess?"

The one-eyed gun hand dragged the tip of his tongue over his lips. "He—he said he had to plow the road, Frank. What with the snow and all, he wanted to keep it open for the gold shipment tomorrow." He took an inadvertent step back when he saw Tolliver's frown deepen.

After a few strained seconds, Tolliver grunted. "Yeah.

He's right." He jerked his head toward the street. "Let's get moving. The snow's covering Slade's tracks."

Easing to the front of the Golden Queen, Slade spotted Tolliver following his trail down to the freight office. Hatch and Red were right behind him. Muttering a curse, he glanced over his shoulder, wondering just where Lazlo and Bull Gutierrez had gone.

He hurried to the rear of the saloon and peered around the corner. Lazlo and Gutierrez were nowhere in sight. He had started along the back of the saloon and mercantile store when he spotted movement ahead.

Without hesitation, he darted through the first door, only to realize, once he was inside, that he was in the living quarters at the rear of the mercantile in which Paleto had dumped the rattlesnakes.

Though snow fell even heavier from the thick clouds, enough light from the rising sun glowed through the window to chase away the shadows in the small room. Quickly, he scanned the room, seeing no sign of the snakes. His breath was frosty, giving him some assurance that if any serpents were around, they would be almost immobile.

He waited and listened.

Several minutes later, voices came from outside. Six-gun in hand, Slade pressed his ear against the door, straining to hear.

A voice he recognized as Tolliver's cursed. "He's around here somewhere. We found his tracks crossing the street, but this damned snow has gone and covered up all sign. You sure you didn't see him head for the forest?"

Gutierrez's voice replied, "Nope. We ain't seen nothing."

Several moments of silence passed. Slade tried to imagine what was taking place. There was a window beside the door, but he resisted the almost overpowering urge to peer out it.

Finally Tolliver said, "He's here somewhere. We'll tear this town apart stick by stick to find him. Bull, you search the saloon. Hatch, you take the mercantile. Lazlo, you search the blacksmith's, Red, you stay out here in case he makes a run for the forest. I'll take the tonsorial parlor."

An unbidden grin leaped to Slade's lips when he heard Hatch protest. "But, Frank, there might still be some rattlers in the mercantile store."

Bull Gutierrez snorted. "Stop crying. You want your share of the gold, then do the job. There's rattlers in the saloon here. You don't see me whining like a little dogie that's lost her mama, do you?"

Lazlo spoke up. "Hell, I'll go in the mercantile. You take the blacksmith's." He paused, then, his words coated with sarcasm, added, "Watch out for all the anvil in there. It might jump on you."

The three gunfighters laughed as Hatch stormed away.

Tolliver called out, "You find him, bring the bastard to me. I want to kill him."

Just as Lazlo turned the doorknob, Slade ducked through the connecting door into the front of the store and crouched in the shadows beneath a window. His blood ran cold. He smelled the musk of the rattlesnake, and shivered at the chill radiating from the glass panes. He hoped that chill had driven any snakes remaining to find warmth elsewhere.

His keen eyes scanned the room, quickly taking in the piles of clothing stacked on six tables with aisles between them, barrels of flour and beans along the front of the counter, and cloth goods on the shelves behind the counter, all heat-holding refuges for a cold-blooded serpent.

Abruptly, the door opened and the short, stocky silhouette of Joe Lazlo stood in the opening. Slade crouched lower.

Outside, the snow slackened.

Lazlo stood motionless, his eyes studying the room, his breath frosty.

Peering beneath the tables, Slade saw the legs of the hardcase as he slowly made his way up one aisle and down another. He flexed his fingers on the trigger of his Colt as Lazlo grew closer.

When the killer reached the end of one aisle, Slade, moving as silently as a stalking black widow, eased along the end of the tables toward the counter. He paused, peering back under the tables. He caught his breath. Lazlo had disappeared.

Suddenly a rasping voice growled, "Well, well, well. Look what we got here."

Slade looked up into the muzzle of a .44.

Lazlo was standing behind the counter, leering at him. His eyes grew cold. "Just drop that hogleg and stand up nice and easy. I know somebody who's mighty anxious to see you, and he'd be right put out if I had to put a couple lead plums in your gizzard. Now lift them hands and stand up."

Slade rose slowly, every muscle wound tighter than a clock spring. As he did, he spotted a coiled rattlesnake on the cloth goods shelf behind Lazlo. The dark eyes in the spade-shaped head were fixed on the stocky killer, and the serpent's tongue flicked out, searching for the heat given off by the object before it.

The young half-breed's brain raced. Snakebite was a hell of way to die; so was a slug in the belly.

Suddenly a faint rattle broke the icy silence in the room.

Lazlo's eyes grew wide, and he cut them sideways as far as he could without moving his head.

Lowering his hand and grasping the butt of his Colt, Slade whispered, "On the shelf right behind you. He's cold. Just move slow, real slow. Any noise, any sudden movement, he'll strike."

At that moment, the back door slammed open and Red Sweet shouted, "Lazlo! What's taking you so long in there?"

Even before Sweet finished his question, the snake struck, hitting Joe Lazlo in the carotid, that pulsing artery that takes blood to and from the brain.

Lazlo screamed.

Slade ducked into the shadows behind the counter as Sweet rushed in. He spotted the snake on the shelf and blew its head off.

In the meantime, Slade ducked out the rear door and disappeared into the forest.

The snow continued to fall.

Arch Simmons looked back toward Juniper Pass when he heard the pop of gunfire. He grinned at Jess. "Looks like Slade's still giving them trouble."

Jess laughed. "Damned shame Slade's not one of us. No telling how far we could go."

The older gunman shrugged. "He'd never fit in with us."

"Why's that?"

"He's an honest man."

For a moment, Jess studied his partner, then nodded.

"Yeah. I'd forgotten that. He couldn't trust jaspers like us."

Simmons failed to grasp the veiled warning in the younger man's voice. He nodded. "Yeah." He laughed. "Even we can't trust jaspers like us."

You don't know how true that is, old man, Jess said to himself.

Ahead lay the trail down the slope to the deserted mine cutting through the mountain. Arch rode ahead, tying Jess's pony off the road. No sense in arousing anyone's curiosity over an extra pony.

Just before they reached Boles Mine, Jess called out, "Remind me. Am I Hatch or Frank?"

Arch shook his head in mock disgust. "You're Hatch. I'm Frank. You think you can remember that?"

With an amused gleam in his eyes, the younger gunfighter replied, "Are you sure that's how you introduced us? You know, you're getting old. Your memory ain't what it used to be."

"Go to hell." Arch grinned at the young man who had become like a son to him.

At the mine, they sat around a table in the chuck house, sipping coffee. The foreman, Al Grimes, introduced them to the wagon drivers. "This here is Finas Combs. That young one grinning like a possum is Windy Pitchings."

"Howdy," Jess replied.

Arch nodded.

Al grinned at the older gunfighter. "You boys got here early, Frank. Appreciate it. What's the road like?"

Arch shrugged. "You got no problem, Al. Open all the way. We figured you'd want to get an early start."

He spoke to Finas. "Just follow along behind us. That shipment of yours is as good as in Las Vegas already." He nodded to Jess. "Me and old Hatch here have done taken good care of you boys."

Jess suppressed a grin.

Al shook his head. "I ain't been down to Juniper Pass in a spell. How's the town doing? Old Jimmy Horner still drink like he did?"

Jess remembered the old drunk tied to the hanging tree and filled with lead. He shook his head. "Not no more. He gave it up a few days ago."

"Glad to hear that. He's really a good man, just a little weak in the whiskey part. You know?"

With a wry grin, Jess replied, "I think he's got that habit kicked."

Arch grunted and rose. "Reckon it's time to move out. You boys ready?" he said to Finas and Windy.

"Let's go."

Al nodded. "Tell them folks in Juniper Pass hi for me."

A quarter of a mile past the trail to the deserted mine, Jess pulled the snowplow to the side of the road. Windy and Finas frowned as Arch rode back to them. The older driver asked, "What's the trouble, Frank? Plow break down?"

Arch grinned and shucked his six-gun. "Nothing like that, boys. We're just going to relieve you of your shipment."

Windy and Finas looked at each other. They didn't know whether to laugh or not. Jess came up on the other side, his revolver drawn, his face cold. "No joke. Climb down."

Finas sputtered. "But—but—"

Patiently, Arch explained, "Think about it. Ain't no gold worth dying over, Finas. Now climb on down."

Jess growled, "Or else."

Arch saw a look in Jess's eyes that disturbed him. The young man wanted to kill the two. Arch had seen the look too often over the years to mistake it.

"Best do as he says, boys," the older gunfighter drawled. He glanced at Jess. "Easy, son, easy."

Five minutes later, they had been tied, gagged, and blindfolded.

Quickly, Jess and Arch unhitched the two lead horses, draped leather *bolsas* over them, and loaded both with a hundred and eighty pounds of gold bars, each one-pound bar worth a tad over three hundred and fifty dollars.

In ten minutes, they moved off the road and down the slope, where Jess picked up his pony. They headed for the deserted mine, each leading a horse carrying fifty thousand dollars.

"I got to hand it to you, Jess," Arch said over his shoulder. "This plan of your was slicker than calf slobber."

Jess chuckled. "It ain't over yet."

Arch frowned, wondering what the young killer meant.

As they descended the old trail, the snow-laden clouds opened up, dropping heavy, wet flakes.

The older gunfighter grunted. "Lucky we found this mine. Moriaty over in Fort Union will give us more for the gold than we could've got over in Santa Fe."

After tossing Lazlo's corpse off the canyon rim, Red and Hatch gathered in the saloon with the other owlhoots. Outside, the snowfall grew heavier.

"That damned Slade is like a ghost."

"Yeah," Red muttered.

Tolliver glared at the smaller man suspiciously. "You damned sure you never saw him in the store?"

"Honest, Frank. Never did. I heard Lazlo scream. I ran in and kilt the snake, but I never saw hide nor hair of Slade."

Scratching his bearded jaw, Tolliver glanced at Hatch. "Jess and Arch back yet?"

"Nope. They're running late." He looked at the falling snow. "Reckon they'll be running that plow again in the morning if this don't let up. Sure don't want nothing to hold up that gold shipment." He grinned, and a gleam of greed glittered in his single eye.

Tolliver grunted.

Screwing up his courage, Hatch slipped in across the table from Tolliver. He glanced over his shoulder at the others, then whispered, "I figure my split ought to be a tad more than just a thousand, Frank."

Tolliver's brow knit. "Yeah? How do you figure that?"

Hatch swallowed hard, then replied, "Because I know the take is fifty thousand, not ten."

The massive outlaw glowered at Hatch.

The one-eyed killer added, "I ain't greedy, but I figure five thousand is enough to keep me quiet."

For several moments, Tolliver studied the slightly built gunfighter. "Think you pretty smart, huh?"

Swallowing the fear in his throat, Hatch shook his head. "No. I just have information that I know you don't want anyone else to have."

Tolliver chuckled. "You was always the sharp one, Hatch. Looks like you got me over a barrel. It's a deal. Let's drink on it."

"You ain't mad about it, are you, Frank? After all, it's fifty thousand."

"Naw. I ain't mad. There's plenty to go around. Now drink up."

As Hatch turned up his glass, Tolliver smiled to himself. After they got the gold, his first bullet was reserved for Hatch Ahearn.

# Chapter Twenty-five

Slade sipped coffee and chewed on broiled venison as he related the events of that morning.

Wrapped in a blanket, Jonah Pate leaned against the wall away from the fire, staring at Slade and the Indians with fearful eyes. Next to Slade squatted C. T. Henley, whom Paleto had found wandering the forest.

Paleto nodded. "As I count, that leaves six or so. Soon, we can continue our journey to the north."

Glancing toward the mouth of the cave, Slade said, "I figure Jess and Arch should be getting back about now. They moved out early this morning." He paused and stretched his arms over his head. "Soon as we finish here, we best ride over to the mine and tell them my suspicions. Let them put a guard on the shipment. That ought to take care of Tolliver and his boys." He glanced at Pate and Henley. "Then you folks will have your town back."

A weak smile ticked up one edge of the small man's lips.

Henley grunted. "I hope so."

"If we go to mine, we go now. Snow will come before night."

Slade never argued with his brother's predictions about the weather. As a youth, he had learned all of nature's tricks, the moss on a tree, halos around the moon, wet moss, dry moss, heavier coats on animals, the same as Paleto, but his brother possessed an extra sense about the weather, one Slade could not fathom, only follow. "Let's ride."

Right Hand led Paleto and Slade across the mountain to intersect the road to Boles Mine.

As they climbed the slope to the road above, the slight Arapaho reined up. He stiffened in his saddle. The pounding of hooves and the grunting of straining horses rolled down the slope to their ears.

Slade and Paleto frowned at each other. "What do you reckon is going on?"

With a wry grin, Paleto shrugged. "The white-eye is too hard for the Apache to understand."

With a chuckle, Slade replied, "Sometimes the white man can't understand himself, either."

With a click of his tongue, Right Hand continued up the slope, but the leather-tough young half-breed stopped him. "No." He scratched the back of his neck. "I got a strange feeling we'd be walking into a heap of trouble if we rode up to the mine. For that many riders to be stampeding down the road to Juniper Pass like that, something's put a burr under their saddle." He reined around. "Let's get back and see what's going on."

Paleto frowned. "What of gold?"

Slade laughed softly. "Tolliver would be a fool to try for the gold with that many miners in town. And one thing about Tolliver, he's no fool."

Later, Al Grimes reined up at the edge of Juniper Pass. His riders milled about him as they all stared in puzzlement at the deserted town.

Mort O'Brien, a redheaded Irishman, spoke with a rolling brogue. "Where be them folks?"

Grimes spotted smoke drifting up from the chimney of the Longhorn Saloon at the far end of town. "Someone's down yonder. Maybe they seen those hijackers."

Having slept late after the search for Slade, Tolliver had just downed his first whiskey of the day when a dozen irate miners led by a bandy-legged little man stormed in, guns drawn and blood in their eyes.

Grimes turned the muzzle of his six-gun on Tolliver. "Don't none of you boys move, you hear?"

Tolliver blinked at the sleep in his eyes and growled in a raspy voice, "Who in the hell are you, and what do you want?"

Ignoring the outlaw's question, Grimes asked, "Who else is here with you?"

For a moment, Tolliver started to argue, but the clicking of several hammers silenced him. "Three or four upstairs sleeping."

"Bring 'em down, boys."

Half a dozen miners scrambled up the stairs.

Holding his temper, the grizzled outlaw asked, "Now, do you mind telling me what's on your mind?"

At that moment, footsteps clattered on the stairs amid angry protests.

Grimes nodded. "We're looking for Frank Tolliver and a jasper named Hatch. We aim to hang them."

For a moment, Tolliver was speechless. Behind him, Hatch broke into a coughing spell. "Hang? For what? I ain't done nothing to you. I don't even know who you hombres are."

"Not you." Grimes shook his head emphatically.

"Frank Tolliver and Hatch Ahearn, that's who." He scanned the startled faces staring at him. Behind him, Mort spoke up. "I don't see 'em here, Al."

Al demanded, "This everyone?"

"Yeah, yeah. But what is all this?"

"I told you. We're looking for Frank Tolliver and Hatch Ahearn."

Tolliver snorted. "Well, you found them. I'm Tolliver and that one-eyed jasper over there is Hatch Ahearn."

The announcement struck the miners dumb. Finally, Grimes managed to stammer. "You—you're Frank Tolliver."

Mort spoke up. "He ain't the Frank Tolliver we met, Al. And that skinny one yonder ain't Hatch Ahearn."

Suddenly a tiny flame of suspicion flared in the back of Tolliver's head. He turned to Hatch. "The snowplow back?"

Grimes interrupted. "Hell no, it ain't. It's out yonder on the road where Tolli . . ." He hesitated, his face twisted in a frown. "Or whoever in the hell they are, where they left it when they stole the shipment. A hundred thousand dollars." His eyes grew narrow, measuring Tolliver and those behind him. "You know who them miscreants is? Just what do you know about all this? Talk up. We're in the mood to hang somebody."

The miners behind him muttered agreement.

For a moment, Tolliver stumbled for words, his brain reeling. A hundred thousand, and that lying Cooper told him it was only fifty thousand. He cursed the young gunfighter.

"Well?" Grimes prompted him.

Rolling his massive shoulders, Tolliver shook his head. "Not a thing, mister. Two jaspers by the name of Arch Simmons and Jess Cooper come to town recent."

Grimes narrowed his eyes. "What do they look like?"

Tolliver shrugged. "Cooper's young, blond hair. Simmons is getting long in the tooth."

"Sounds like them, Al," growled one of the miners.

"Yeah. It do."

Tolliver continued. "Me and my boys here, we was hired by a Mr. Wingate over to Santa Fe. We been waiting here for him to show up. Then the smallpox come in and all the townfolk went over to Las Vegas. I—"

Grimes took a step back. "Smallpox, you say?"

With a sly grin, Tolliver arched an eyebrow. "Well, they said it was. You couldn't prove it by me, but Wingate's paying us good money, so we told the folks we'd stay and keep an eye on things for them." He blew through his lips wearily. "You know how it is today, you can't trust nobody."

Grimes backed up another step and glanced around the saloon as if expecting a swarm of smallpox bugs to descend on him. "Yeah, yeah. When was the last time you saw those jaspers?"

"Cooper and Simmons? They rode out this morning with the snowplow, and we ain't seen them since."

"They didn't ride back this way?"

"Nope."

Grimes glanced at Mort. "If they didn't come this way, then that means—"

"Yeah," Mort broke in. "Santa Fe or the old trail."

Tolliver shot Mort a sharp look. "What old trail?"

"Outside the mine. Cuts through the mountain."

Tolliver's brain raced. "If you wait, we'll saddle up and ride with you."

Shaking his head emphatically, Grimes backed away. "No. That's fine. We'll find them. Besides, we don't want no truck with smallpox."

"Yeah, Al," Mort said. "That explains the two missing plow horses. Them two thieves loaded the gold on them." He paused and grinned. "Listen, Al. If they took the old mine, we can cut them off at the east end here."

Al arched an eyebrow. "I thought about that, but they'd already be through it by now. Tell you what. Mort, take half the boys and head for the east end of the mine. I'll take the other half back in case they headed for Santa Fe. If you don't see no sign of them, cut back through the mine and meet us on the Santa Fe Road. We'll do the same."

After the miners left, Tolliver growled, "Let's go, boys."

Hatch frowned. "We split up? Half one way and half the other?"

The hulking killer glared at the slender hardcase. "We stick together. Any argument? I been snookered once. It ain't going to happen again."

# Chapter Twenty-six

Sitting in his saddle just inside the forest of snow-covered pine and piñon behind the tonsorial parlor, Slade watched as half the miners wheeled about and raced north out of Juniper Pass. The other half headed south, the hooves of their galloping horses throwing up chunks of snow and ice.

Paleto glanced up at Slade. "What you think?"

Shaking his head, the young half-breed muttered, "I'm not sure. One thing—"

At that moment, Tolliver stormed out of the saloon and, with his four compadres tagging after him, headed for the livery. Within minutes, they were sitting deep in their saddles and raking the flanks of their ponies with one-elevens as they raced north.

Slade wheeled about and cut through the forest toward the mine road. With Right Hand and Paleto, he pulled up on a rise overlooking the road just as Tolliver and his gang sped past.

"You notice Cooper and Simmons wasn't with them, huh?" He glanced at his brother.

"Yes."

The two locked eyes.

Paleto simply said, "They take gold."

"Yeah, and that's what Jess meant when he said it would all be over by Friday."

With a wry grin, Paleto gestured to the south and east. "Him and the other have many hours. Like the bear, there are many dens in the mountains."

Slade waved them to the road. "Let's follow, but stay far enough back."

Right Hand stopped them. "You remember the white man I follow. He take the mine through the mountain." He nodded to the road ahead of them, torn by galloping horses. "We go back south to mine. We hurry, we get there before others. The snow is high, but I know trails that we can follow."

Jess and Arch reined up when they spotted Fort Union on the horizon. The older gunfighter glanced around. "Over there. That patch of aspen. I spotted it when we came through last week. There's a natural box canyon behind it with fresh water. We'll string up a fly against the weather. That'll be a good spot for tonight."

"Fine with me," Jess replied. "This Moriaty—can we trust him?"

Arch lifted an eyebrow. "As much as Phelps over in Santa Fe, about as far as you can throw your pony." The older gunfighter paused, then added, "In the morning, I'll ride in and set up a meeting with him."

Later, around their small campfire, Jess squatted on his haunches and sipped his coffee. "How much you reckon Moriaty'll give us?"

Arch pursed his lips. "I figure at least sixty or seventy percent. He has channels to dispose of it without much risk."

The younger man ran his slender fingers through

his blond hair. He eyed the older man slyly. "What do you figure on doing with your share, Arch?"

"Umm. That's a thought, you know." He stared at Jess for a moment, then gazed into space. "I figure on finding me a place down in Texas with good grass and a running stream. Just sit on the porch and let the world go by."

Jess laughed. "You? I'd have to see that."

The words jerked the older gunfighter back to the present. "Huh? Oh." He shook his head. "I'm getting too old for this kinda life, son. My hand's a tad slower, my eyes a shade dimmer. Nope, this is it for me. How about you? Want to go partners on a ranch? Settle down and stop running?"

"Me? No way. I'm catching a train to Chicago and blowing it all on women and gambling. Then I'll come back and start all over. After all, that's what money's for, ain't it?"

Arch smiled gently at the enthusiasm of the younger man, seeing himself twenty years earlier. "Yep, I reckon it is, Jess. I reckon it is."


The first two trails up which Right Hand led them were blocked by landslides. Finally, the third tortuous trail took them to the mouth of the mine, but too late for the first of the miners was emerging.

Slade muttered a curse.

From where they sat hidden in a thick copse of piñon, they watched as the second group of miners arrived from Juniper Pass. Al Grimes split them into three different groups, one for Fort Union, one for Las Vegas, and the other for Pecos and Santa Fe.

No sooner had the miners disappeared than Frank

Tolliver and his men rode out of the mine. After some discussion, the owl-hoots rode off together toward Las Vegas.

Slade studied the riders as they slowly vanished into the forest. He reined about. "We got a lot of riding. Let's get back to town and pick up some supplies."

Paleto grunted. "What about the ones in cave?"

"Pate and Henley?" Slade grimaced. "I'd forgotten about them. We'll drop them off in town." He chuckled. "Guess we best warn them about the rattlers."

Paleto and Right Hand smiled.

Two hours later, Slade climbed into the saddle and turned to Right Hand. He gestured to the northeast. "Can you take us through the forest to Fort Union without going back up to the mine?"

The diminutive Arapaho gave a short nod.

The wiry half-breed glanced at Paleto. "That's where Jess and Arch was heading when the Kiowa jumped them. I'm guessing that whoever they met at Fort Union sent them to Juniper Pass. As far as I know, he's their only contact."

The Mimbre Apache grunted and glanced at the overcast sky. "It be dark soon."

"Yeah." Slade eyed the sky. "But we can make a few miles." He nodded to Right Hand. "Lead out."

Al Grimes cursed as night came upon them. He glanced around at his two traveling companions. "We got ourselves in a fix here, boys. No grub, no blankets, and a cold night a-coming."

Mort O'Brien drew a deep breath and released it slowly, his breath frosty in the frigid air. "All we can do is build us a fire and hunker around it."

Several times during the long cold night, the miners found themselves wishing they were back in their bunks at the mine. Mort finally spoke up. "We ain't gone so far we can't turn back, Al. That way we can pick up some supplies, and then get after them hijackers."

"Not me," Al replied. "I'm going on. You two go back and get supplies, then catch up."

His eyes glued to the horse sign in the trail ahead, Frank Tolliver was a keg of black powder all primed to explode. His seething rage glittered in his icy blue eyes. That damned Cooper and Simmons had planned to double-cross him all along. Well, they sure as hell weren't going to get away with it, not if he had to track them all over the Southwest.

Behind him, Bull Gutierrez spoke up, his tone tentative, not wanting to aggravate the broad-shouldered outlaw. "We best find a spot to camp before it gets too dark, Frank."

Tolliver ignored him.

Red and Bull looked at each other. Red shrugged and kept riding.

An hour later, the dark night forced Tolliver to rein up.

Fumbling about in the dark, the outlaws laid a small fire and huddled about it. For the first time since early morning, Tolliver's rage subsided enough for him to realize they were not outfitted for their journey.

Across the fire, Red's stomach growled.

Hatch muttered, "Coffee would sure taste good right now."

Tolliver snorted. "Tighten your belt a notch. You ain't going to starve. We'll hit Las Vegas in the morning."

He shivered against the cold and rolled up in his blanket.

Slade's small party spent the night beneath a granite overthrust that reflected the heat of their small fire. Hot coffee and reheated venison filled their stomachs. As soon as they finished the coffee, they climbed into their soogans. Morning would come early.

Staring at the firelight reflecting off the granite slab above him, Slade muttered, "If the weather holds, we ought to make Fort Union by tomorrow night."

Next morning, Jess Cooper and Arch Simmons stood at the edge of the copse of aspen and studied Fort Union on the horizon. A frontier outpost since 1851, the fort had been laid out in a series of adobe buildings arranged to ward off any hostile attacks. One wing of the fort housed civilians, vendors who supplied the army with the various goods of commerce.

Arch cleared his throat. "You stay back here with the gold while I ride in and contact Moriaty. I'm not anxious to parade two horses loaded down with gold bars in front of all those Union boys." He chuckled. "Someone might get suspicious."

A faint smile played over Jess's lips. He drawled, "You sure you can trust me with all that gold?"

The older gunfighter grinned. "If I can't trust you, I can't trust anybody."

Inwardly, Jess winced at the compliment. "Don't worry, partner."

When Arch headed down the slope toward Fort Union, Jess returned to their hidden camp. As he stirred up the banked fire, a few flakes of fresh snow began falling. The young gunfighter grinned. New snow. Hope it's heavy enough to cover a heap of sins.

An hour later, the jangle of trace chains alerted Jess. Leaping to his feet, he shucked his Colt and peered through the aspens in front of the camp. He sighed with relief when he spotted Arch riding beside a four-in-hand wagon carrying several wooden crates. Next to Arch rode a stranger forking a red-speckled roan. He wore a gray Stetson and what appeared to be a spanking-new red mackinaw buttoned over an expansive belly.

Jess stepped out to meet them.

Arch grinned. "See you're still here," he called out jovially.

"Yep. Still here," he replied, his cold eyes fixed on the jasper at Arch's side.

The wagon rattled to a halt, and the bewhiskered hombre, bundled in a blue Yankee greatcoat, nodded from the seat.

Jess nodded.

Arch said, "Jess, this is R. G. Moriaty, buyer, seller, trader of just about any commodity a gent wishes."

Moriaty dipped his head. "Howdy."

The young gunfighter quickly appraised Moriaty. Clean shaven, new duds, good horse, and expensive saddle. No sidearm, so that meant he carried a hide-away. Average looking, but still, his angular face seemed to harbor a touch of evil. "Howdy. Climb down. Coffee's hot."

All four gathered around the small fire while the snow continued to drift down. Only George Barnes, the driver, reached for the coffee.

Moriaty cleared his throat. "Where is it?"

Arch gestured to the two large leather *bolsas* at the base of a boulder.

Shoving his Stetson to the back of his head, Moriaty knelt and opened one of the *bolsas*. A faint smile played over his lips. Without looking around, he said, "How much did you say was here, Arch?"

"Like I said, right at three hundred and fifty or sixty pounds. And we'll throw in the two horses to carry it."

Moriaty rose and turned to the two gunfighters. "I'll put it in the wagon with my other goods."

"Might as well take the horses anyway. They'd just slow us down."

With a shrug, Moriaty replied, "I can go sixty thousand."

Jess glanced at Arch, then muttered, "That's giving you quite a profit, ain't it, Moriaty?"

The fat man shrugged. "I'm taking a risk here. Besides, I got others to pay off."

Arch drawled. "If it's all right with my partner, it's fine with me." He looked around at Jess. "Up to you, son."

A sly grin erased the frown on the young gunfighter's face. "Well, partner. It's sixty more than we got right now. I reckon thirty ought to throw one hell of a party in Chicago."

With a rollicking laugh, Arch replied, "I reckon it will, son. I reckon it will."

"All right, George," Moriaty said to his driver. "Get this loaded while I pay the gents."

After the bars were loaded in the wagon, George stretched a sheet of canvas over the whole load and snugged it down.

Moriaty nodded, satisfied with the job. "You know where to take the load."

The older man nodded. "Yep."

"Then get started. I'll see you back at the fort."

Without another word, George popped the reins and sent the team plodding due east. The snow grew heavier, covering the deep ruts cut by the wagon wheels.

When Moriaty saw the puzzled expressions on the two gunfighters' face, he grinned. "I got me a little place over in the Vulture Mountains where I do some business with different tribes." He paused, then added with an ominous threat in his tone, "One that is well guarded."

# Chapter Twenty-seven

Jess and Arch watched from the grove of aspen until Moriaty, leading the two draft horses, disappeared over a small rise.

Arch grinned at Jess. "What do you say for a celebration drink? I picked up a bottle of whiskey at the fort."

"Sounds good to me, partner." Jess led the way back to the fire, glancing up at the falling snow. "Wish to hell this hadn't started. We can't afford to hang around here."

Arch squatted by the fire and reached for a tin cup. He splashed whiskey in it and handed it to Jess, then filled his own. "Don't plan to. There's a little hole in the wall about ten miles south of here on the Mora River."

Jess eyed him narrowly. "I never heard of one down there."

With a chuckle, Arch replied, "You're not as old as me, either. If I'd stayed holed up there, I'd never ended up in Yuma Prison." He downed the rest of his drink and pushed to his feet. "We start now, we can reach it by dark."

The young gunfighter looked around at the snow and frowned. "How are we going to find it in this?"

"Easy. If the weather was clear, from here, you'd see two peaks side by side. The hole is between them." He stuck his cup in his saddlebags and picked up the saddle. "Let's get moving."

"Whatever you say, partner."

Quickly, they saddled their ponies.

Jess went back to the fire and shucked his Colt and waited.

Arch tightened the cinch and spoke over his shoulder. "All right. I'm ready. How about you?" The old gunfighter looked around and froze. He was staring into the muzzle of Jess's six-gun. An uncertain smile flickered on his lips. "What are you up to? Point that thing some other way."

Pursing his lips, Jess shrugged. "Sorry, partner. It's pointed right."

"But—"

The roar of the six-gun cut off Arch's protest. The impact of the slug knocked him back a step. On instinct, the old gunfighter clawed for his revolver, but the next slug shattered his arm, and the third caught him in his chest.

He dropped to his knees in the snow, staring in disbelief at Jess. His lips parted. "Wh-why? Jess, why?" He fell forward, twisting onto his back as he fell. He stared into the gray clouds overhead, his blood staining the snow. As his brain began to shut down, he realized he had seen the signs that Jess had changed, but had chosen to pay them no attention.

Sneering, Jess stood over his fallen partner, ignoring the stunned disbelief on Arch's face. Without a word, the young gunfighter calmly fired again, blowing a hole between the older man's eyes.

Holstering his Colt, Jess knelt and pulled out Arch's

share of the payoff. "Sixty thousand will throw a hell of a lot bigger party than thirty, old friend."

He stared at the dead man a few moments longer, then mounting his pony and picking up the reins of Arch's horse, headed south to the Mora River.

Early morning, Slade and his compadres left the mountains and rode onto the Great Plains with nothing to break the north wind except miles and miles of rolling hills dotted with sage and beargrass.

Midmorning, Right Hand reined up at the base of a rise. He pointed to a single rider below them about a mile distant. At the same time, the rider spotted Slade. He waved and started toward them.

Paleto frowned. "He stranger."

As he drew closer, Slade remarked, "He was one of those three miners from yesterday heading for Fort Union." He peered beyond the oncoming rider, studying the countryside, but not spying the other two.

Grimes reined up a respectful distance from the three. He studied Paleto and Right Hand warily. "Howdy."

Slade nodded. "You lost?"

"No. Chasing some hijackers. They stole gold from the Boles Mine at Cimarron Gorge yesterday. We run off without any supplies. My partners are going back for some. They'll catch up."

With a grin, Slade fumbled in his saddlebags and tossed the miner a can of tomatoes. "We're after the same hombres."

Grimes frowned. "Who are you?"

Slade introduced them, then swiftly related the events of the last several days. "We knew something was up when they kept hanging around Juniper Pass. We was coming to warn you, but they moved too fast. That's why most of the town's over in Las Vegas. The two you're after is Jess Cooper and Arch Simmons. Gunfighters, and fast. They worked for Frank Tolliver, who planned to hijack the gold, but those two double-crossed him. Tilly told us what the gold meant to the mine and the town. She kept those waddies from hanging me, and so my brother here and me are trying to pay them back."

A smile wreathed the miner's face. "Then we're in this together."

Slade nodded. "Looks that way."

Just before dark, they spotted Fort Union. Slade reined up, looking around for a camp. "Me and Grimes will ride on in," he said to Paleto. "Those soldier boys down there might get uncomfortable seeing you and Right Hand down among them."

Right Hand shook his head. "No. Mexican Joe run stable. I with him when the Northern Cheyenne fight the bluecoats. We stay there."

It was dark when Slade and Grimes rode into the fort and pulled up at the hitching rail in front of the livery. Out back, Paleto and Right Hand reined up at the rear of the stable.

Tolliver and his gun hands rode into Las Vegas at dark and headed for the first saloon. After downing several drinks and asking around for Jess and Arch, they ambled down the boardwalk to the first café, where they put themselves around steaming bowls of beef stew and hot coffee.

The fat café owner studied Tolliver and his men as

they poked the chow down their gullets. He waddled over to their table and said, "You're the second bunch what's been in here starving to death and asking about two jaspers."

Instantly, Tolliver grew wary. "Yeah? Who was the others?"

"From some mine the other side of Juniper Pass." He gestured to the street. "They headed on up the street when they left here."

Tolliver considered the rotund man's comments. After he left, Tolliver muttered, "I say we find that bunch and join up with them. More of us looking, we'll find them two a heap faster."

Hatch looked up from his bowl. "Join them? But—"

"But nothing. They don't know us except from the saloon. It's Jess and Arch they're after." He paused. An evil gleam glittered in his black eyes. "Once we find them two, then we'll take care of the miners."

At the next saloon, they found the four miners, who gladly accepted Tolliver's offer to help in the search. By midnight, they had scoured the small village with no luck.

Outside the last saloon, Tolliver hung back as the miners headed down the boardwalk to a tonsorial parlor that rented bunks by the night.

Gutierrez leaned closed to Tolliver. "Now what, Frank? Them old boys is giving up and heading back to Juniper Pass."

Tolliver had been considering such a situation. He saw a chance to take the whole shipment for himself. His voice raspy, Tolliver replied, "We ain't. I reckon maybe two of us, me and Hatch, ought to ride over to Pecos and the other two up to Fort Union."

Gutierrez stiffened, and took a step back. "I say we

stick together, Frank. It ain't I don't trust none of you old boys, but a hundred thousand in gold is a mighty big temptation."

Beside him, Red nodded. Hatch just smiled at his boss. "I figure Bull is right, Frank. Let's all stay together." Besides, he told himself. I ain't anxious for a bullet in the back.

Suppressing the anger boiling through his veins that his little scheme had been foiled, Tolliver growled, "All right. We'll ride out at first light for Fort Union."

Red frowned. "Why there? There ain't nothing but bluebellies up there. Cooper and Simmons wouldn't go there."

"If they didn't come here, then that's where they'd go. Who'd expect them to run off with a hundred thousand in gold and head straight into the front yard of the Yankees?"

A slight figure bundled in a heavy coat came out to meet Slade and Al. He paused behind the closed corral gate. "You want horses in stable?" From the inflection in his voice, it was obvious to Slade the small man was an Indian.

"You called Mexican Joe?"

Joe stiffened, peering up into the darkness covering Slade's face. "I know you?"

"No, but you know an Arapaho by the name Right Hand."

For a moment, Joe remained silent. Finally he nodded. "I know him."

"He's out back of your livery with my Apache brother. We need a place to spend the night where no one will see us."

Without hesitation, he swung open the gate. "Come."

After closing the gate behind them, he disappeared into the darkness. Moments later, a door squeaked, and Right Hand and Paleto led their ponies inside.

Lighting a lantern, Mexican Joe led them past several horses to the end of the barn, where he indicated four stalls next to a small room. "That where I sleep. No one look in."

Quickly, the four unsaddled their horses and slipped into the room, in the middle of which was a potbellied stove putting out a welcome warmth against the cold of the night.

Later, as they sipped coffee and gnawed on dried venison, Slade said, "Tomorrow, Al will go over to the fort commander and tell him what happened. While's he's doing that, I'll prowl around the fort. See what I can stumble on. Paleto, you and Right Hand stay here, out of sight."

# Chapter Twenty-eight

The clouds had pushed out during the night, leaving a crisp, cold morning.

While Al Grimes visited the commandant of the fort, Slade questioned the civilian establishments, three saloons, two sutler's stores, the blacksmith, the freight line, and two cafés.

Al Grimes was waiting for Slade when he came out of the last café. One look on the miner's face told the rawhide-tough half-breed that Al had no more luck than he.

"Nothing?"

Grimes looked around in disgust at the headquarters building. "Sometimes I wonder what we pay them Yankee boys for. They don't seem to want to do nothing but sit on their butts in a warm office." He jammed his hand in his coat pocket and pulled out a rope of tobacco. Tearing off a chunk, he offered it to Slade, who declined. "He called in one of his officers and had me tell him the whole story all over again. They ain't seen nothing, but if they do, they'll take steps."

A wry grin twisted Slade's weathered face. "I didn't have any better luck." He looked around, focusing on the horizon far to the south. "Looks like we picked the

wrong place. Reckon we ought to pick up some supplies and head down to Las Vegas."

Grimes shrugged. "I'll leave word for my boys to
follow."

Back at the livery, Slade paused when he entered the
empty room, surprised Paleto and Right Hand were
not around. He glanced over his shoulder and spotted
the two at the far end of the livery, studying the stabled
horses with Mexican Joe, who was nodding emphatically.

He shrugged and reached for the coffeepot on the
stove. As he sipped the steaming black liquid, the Indians came in. Slade shook his head. "No luck. Reckon
we'll ride on down to Las Vegas."

The Mimbre Apache nodded. "First, see what we
find."

Slade frowned. "What do you mean?"

Right Hand motioned him to follow. "Here. Come
see." The slight Arapaho led the way to the end of the
livery where Mexican Joe stood behind several horses
standing hipshot in individual stalls, feeding quietly.

Slade instantly spotted the difference in two of the
animals. Big boned, they stood seventeen or eighteen
hands, and he guessed each weighed sixteen to eighteen hundred pounds.

Paleto dipped his head to the first horse. "Mexican
Joe say these two come in yesterday."

Puzzled, Slade stared at him; then he understood.
"You think—"

Paleto gave a slight shrug.

Mexican Joe spoke up. "White man called Moriaty
take out wagon early in morning. When he come back,
he have these horses."

"No wagon?"

The old Cheyenne frowned and gave a single shake of his head. "No wagon. These not same horses."

"Not the same?" Adrenaline coursed through the young half-breed's veins. "These weren't the horses that pulled the wagon? You sure?"

At his voice, the sorrel horse looked around. Slade stared at the animal, remembering the star and stripe, a patch of white on the forehead running down to the muzzle on the sorrel back in Burl Henry's barn.

Mexican Joe tapped a shriveling finger to his sunken chest. "I put horses in harness. I know."

"I know, too," said Slade, easing forward and rubbing the sorrel's neck while he studied the big animal's markings. "This one belongs to Burl Henry."

Paleto frowned. "How you know?"

"Here." He pointed to the star and stripe on the animal's forehead. "I saw it back in Juniper Pass."

Right Hand spoke to his Cheyenne friend. "You see where wagon go?"

Mexican Joe pointed to the southwest.

Trying to still the excitement in his voice, Slade asked, "How long before this Moriaty jasper came back?"

"Not long." The Cheyenne pointed to the eastern sky. "Sun one hand high."

An hour. Maybe more, maybe less, Slade told himself.

Paleto spoke up. "We see this one who is called Moriaty?"

"Not yet." He gestured to the southwest. "Let's ride that way a piece. See what's out there."

Thirty minutes out, they topped a rise and spotted a grove of aspen before a small ridge of granite harboring a small box canyon. Warily the four approached, guns drawn, but only animal sign disturbed the snow.

As they worked through the grove of aspen, two coyotes bolted, yelping in fear. In a rocky nook, Slade found the remains of Arch Simmons.

Al Grimes gagged when he saw the partially consumed body. The others simply stared impassively.

Slade stared at the hole between the old gunfighter's eyes. If Cooper had put any more slugs in him, Slade couldn't tell, for the coyotes had been feasting well.

Dismounting, Slade began stacking small boulders over the dead man. The others joined in, and minutes later, a mound of rocks covered Arch Simmons, a resting place far removed from that little place in Texas with good grass and a running stream of which he had dreamed.

Slade looked around at Paleto. "Now we see Moriaty." He paused. His eyes narrowed. His voice was cold. "The Apache way."

Paleto grinned. Al Grimes blanched.

Leaning back in his chair in his living quarters behind his general store, R. G. Moriaty puffed on his cigar in contentment. Business was good, even the legitimate part of it. His army contracts brought in considerable profit, but nothing like what he would make on the gold.

He patted his stomach. He'd put on some fat, but he still retained much of the muscle he had built in his thirty years of surviving in New Mexico Territory.

A tip of the cigar ash fell. He leaned forward, brushing at his vest and boiled shirt. Out front, his hired man, Walter, waited on customers, supplying them with whatever necessities they needed, whether it be rifles, tools, or rotgut whiskey made with raw alcohol, burnt sugar, and chewing tobacco.

Whiskey was one of Moriaty's biggest profit makers especially when he cut the 100 proof mixture with turpentine or ammonia or cayenne. More than one Indian or drifter had gone blind drinking Moriaty's whiskey.

Outside, the north wind rattled the windows and howled around the corners of the adobe building. The sun dropped behind the horizon, bringing a night filled with the promise of a hard freeze.

Moriaty shivered, grateful for the warmth put out by his stove. He figured a thick steak and a platter of potatoes for supper, topped off with a bottle of Old Overholt rye whiskey from his private store of alcohol. And who knows? he told himself. I might just hire me one of Dora's girls tonight.

Later, after a thick steak, he picked up Melissa, one of Madame Dora's choice girls, and the two of them headed back to his store.

As Moriaty had instructed, his clerk, Walter, had left a lantern burning after he locked up. Once inside, Moriaty took the young woman by her elbow and guided her through the clutter of items to his living quarters. He opened the door and had just ushered her inside when, without warning, the door slammed behind him, and the tip of a knife punched him under his chin.

Melissa spun. Her eyes grew wide when she saw a savage Indian holding a knife to R.G.'s chin. A stranger in buckskins whispered harshly, "Don't scream or else."

Melissa promptly fainted.

Moriaty sputtered, "What—"

"Shut up," Slade said. "One wrong move, and my

brother will drive that blade into your brain." He jerked open the rear door. "Outside."

Paleto backed out of the room with Moriaty following closely. Just outside, Moriaty made his move. Faster than a striking rattler, he knocked Paleto's hand aside and leaped for the rear door.

Slade jumped in front of him.

Moriaty swung, but the agile half-breed ducked, grabbed the larger man's arm, and spun him around. Among the Apache youth, swing-kicking was a avid pastime, the moves of which were ingrained in their brains as instinctive reactions.

Slade lashed out with his foot, kicking the back of Moriaty's left knee. The big man's leg folded, spinning him to the left and directly into Slade's well-timed kick to the chin.

Moriaty fell to the snow-covered ground silently.

A chilling cold awakened R. G. Moriaty. He was shivering uncontrollably. And then he realized he was naked. He tried to sit up, but his outstretched arms and legs were bound.

Lit by firelight, two white men and two Indians came into focus. Behind them was a mound of rocks, a grave. Suddenly he didn't feel the cold as a boiling flush of fear coursed through his veins. He fought against the ropes binding him. "What-what's going on? Who are you? What do you want?"

His double-edged blade in hand, Slade knelt by the trembling man. He touched the point of the blade to Moriaty's belly. He drawled, "I had a bet with my friends that you had at least three layers of fat over that belly of yours. My brother there says you only have two." He paused, then arched an eyebrow. "So I reckon we're going to have to find out." With a flick of his wrist, Slade sliced through the skin, bringing a tiny welt of blood two inches long.

Moriaty yelped like a stuck hog. "Stop! Stop! I'll pay you whatever you want. I've got money." He broke into sobs. "Just don't cut me." He fought the ropes futilely.

His eyes cold, Slade shrugged. "I don't know. Sometimes my brother is stubborn as a mule. And he likes the sight of blood."

The naked man stopped struggling against the ropes. His sobs grew louder. "Don't. Please. I'll do whatever you say."

Slade pursed his lips and moved the blade to the sobbing man's ear. "Where's the gold you got from Arch Simmons and Jess Cooper?"

# Chapter Twenty-nine

Moriaty swung his head from side to side. "I don't have no gold. I don't know what you mean. I just run the mercantile."

With a long sigh, Slade rose and nodded to Paleto. "You can have him."

Paleto and Right Hand knelt on either side of the sobbing man, an evil grin on their lips. The Arapaho ran his knife over Moriaty's genitals, and the crying man screamed at the top of his lungs and evacuated his bowels. "Vulture Mountain. Vulture Mountain. That's where the gold is. Please, please. Don't cut me."

"Where at Vulture Mountain?"

"On the south slope. A cave. You can see Wagon Mound from there."

Slade stared down at him. "What about Simmons and Cooper?"

"I don't know. I paid them sixty thousand. I never saw them again."

Paleto and Slade exchanged knowing glances. "You're right, my brother," the young half-breed muttered. "Jess has the money. Arch has a grave."

Moriaty whined. "What about me?"

"Cut him loose," the young half-breed said. He

stepped back from Moriaty. "Clean yourself up and get dressed. We've got a ride ahead of us."

While Moriaty dressed, Al Grimes whispered to Slade, "You wouldn't have cut him up, would you?"

Slade chuckled. "Only until he told me what I wanted to hear."

Grimes swallowed hard and nodded, mighty glad Slade was on his side.

Frank Tolliver and his three compadres had camped on the sandy bed of an arroyo south of Fort Union. After a spare breakfast of coffee and fried bacon on cold biscuits, they moved out, wanting to reach the fort before noon.

Midmorning, they rode into the grove of aspen.

Seeing the broken ground, Tolliver reined up. "What do you think, Frank?" Bull Gutierrez rode up beside him.

The broad-shouldered outlaw shook his head. "No idea. Hatch, you and Red look around."

Moments later, Red Sweet shouted, "Frank! Over here."

Tolliver reined up, staring down into what remained of Arch Simmons's face. He muttered, "I'll be damned. Looks like Cooper didn't hanker to share with nobody."

"Out here, Frank," Hatch called. "Someone left out of here not long ago. Four or five horses."

Wheeling his pony about, Tolliver raced to Hatch's side.

"There." The one-eyed outlaw pointed to the tracks.

Tolliver studied the sign. Cooper was leading three horses, all carrying gold from the deep imprints of the hooves. He grinned smugly. "Well, well, well. Looks like our Mr. Cooper has done had his string of luck run out." He squinted eastward following the trail until it disappeared in the distance. "Let's go, boys. We'll stay back here a couple hours. We can slip in tonight."

Just before noon, Slade spotted Vulture Mountain rising from the vast plains to the east. Another two or three hours, he guessed. He cut back north, planning on coming in behind the south slope. He paused to glance over their back trail, a puzzled frown on his face.

Paleto pulled up beside him. "What troubles you?"

Slade's gray eyes narrowed. "Someone's back there."

Al Grimes looked back. "I don't see no one."

The Mimbre Apache grinned at his brother. Slade replied, "They're too far back."

Grimes studied the wiry half-breed several moments. "Could be my boys coming after us or maybe just drifters."

"Could be," Slade replied, reining around and nudging his dun in the flanks. "We'll have cold camp tonight and move out early in the morning." He gave Moriaty a look of warning, then nodded to Paleto and Right Hand. "The gold had better be there, or I'll turn you over to those two, you understand me?"

Moriaty gulped. "It's there. I ain't lying. It's there."

Throughout the remainder of the day, Slade couldn't shake the nagging feeling that they were being tracked. And not by the miners.

That night over a supper of canned beef and water, Slade questioned Moriaty about the cave. "How many men you got there? And don't lie. You don't appear to be shy of brains, so you wouldn't leave that much gold untended. Now how many?"

Cutting his dark eyes at the Indians staring malevolently at him, Moriaty gulped. "Three. George Barnes. He's my driver. Vinegar Duncan and Boots Cabot is with him."

Slade studied the man a moment, then nodded.

After supper, he bound Moriaty's hands and feet. "You got a full belly now, storekeeper," he said, throwing a blanket over the supine man. "So don't move a muscle or one of us will run a knife through your brisket."

Gutierrez studied the dark silhouette of Vulture Mountain. "He's camped out on the mountain somewhere, but he ain't got no fire. We'll have to wait until morning, and then maybe we'll spot him."

Tolliver grunted. "Then we'll wait 'til morning."

An hour before sunrise when sleep is most sound, Slade awakened the others. He whispered to Grimes, "We're going to get the gold. You stay here with Moriaty." He glanced at the storekeeper, who was awake and looking on with calculating eyes. Slade turned to Grimes. "If he tries anything, kill him." He glanced around the desolate mountain slope. "By the time someone runs across his worthless carcass, the birds will have picked the bones clean."

The bandy-legged little foreman swallowed hard at the fierce coldness in the younger man's voice. He did not know if he would be able to follow Slade's instructions or not, but he still replied, "All right."

Slade paused to study the rolling plains to the west, searching for some hint of the source of his unrest. As an Apache youth, he had learned to trust his feelings, whether he saw concrete evidence of them or not.

Any other time, he and Paleto would ghost over their back trail and learn the truth, but there was a hundred thousand dollars in gold waiting less than a mile distant.

After mounting his claybank dun, Slade looked down at Al Grimes. "Keep your eyes open. Someone is out there. And it isn't your miners."

Lying on his belly just below the crest of a rise half a mile from Slade's camp, Frank Tolliver watched silently as three riders rode along the flank of the mountain. "Damn," he muttered, expecting only one rider, Jess Cooper. "That damned Slade again. What in the hell is he doing over here?" His cold eyes tracked along the half-breed's back trail until he spotted movement at the mouth of an arroyo on the north end of the mountain.

He glanced over his shoulder at his men sitting in their saddles below. He motioned to Red Sweet.

"Yeah, Frank," said Red when he squirmed up beside the grizzled outlaw.

"Over there. The north end of the mountain. See that arroyo? Watch and you'll see somebody move."

Several seconds passed; then Red exclaimed, "I see him."

"All right. Here's what we going to do. Bull, Hatch, and me are going to ride due north. When that jasper spots us, he'll keep an eye on us to see where we're heading. He won't be paying attention to his backside. You slip up and get the drop on him."

Red patted his six-gun. "Don't worry."

"No shooting. Slade's out there."

"Slade!"

"I don't know what he's up to, but him and two Injuns rode out south. Now, don't forget, no shooting. That hombre yonder can't tell us nothing if he's dead."

Unknown to Tolliver, a war party of Kiowa watched silently from a distant rise as Tolliver moved his men out.

Six-gun in hand, Al Grimes peered over the top of a limestone slab as three riders skirted the mountain, heading north. Without warning, everything went dark, and he dropped into the black well of unconsciousness.

Red grinned as Tolliver reined up and stared at the unconscious foreman. He recognized the man immediately.

Gutierrez said, "Hey, that's the old boy from the mine who came to the saloon."

"Yeah," Tolliver drawled, realizing the foreman's presence meant the small man either knew or had an idea as to the whereabouts of the gold.

"That ain't all, Frank," Red said, nodding at the bound and gagged man lying on the ground behind another boulder. Fear was evident in the man's eyes.

Tolliver nodded to Moriaty. "Take the gag off."

Moriaty thought quickly, searching for an explanation that would elicit the four men's help in recovering the gold. He looked up at Tolliver gratefully. "Much obliged, friend. I was beginning to figure no one was coming along to help."

The grizzled outlaw ignored the storekeeper's remark. "Who are you? Where did Slade go?"

"Moriaty. And—"

Gutierrez interrupted him. "Ask him about the gold, Frank."

If R. G. Moriaty was anything, he was a survivor. Immediately, he discarded any idea of gaining their assistance for only a token reward. In fact, from the hungry expression in their cold eyes, he had the sinking feeling that these four would not hesitate to kill him and take the gold. One of the reasons Moriaty had built the wealth he had was that he had learned long ago when things looked bad, cut your losses and move on.

Tolliver grunted. "All right, Moriaty. What about the gold? And don't tell me you don't know nothing about it." He cut his eyes to the unconscious foreman. "That hombre wouldn't be here if the gold wasn't. So, what about it?"

"Can you untie me?"

Tolliver nodded, and Red quickly freed Moriaty.

Rubbing his wrists, he pushed to his feet. "Thanks, friend."

"Now what about the gold?"

Brushing the dirt from his mackinaw, Moriaty heard the threat in the outlaw's gravelly voice. "Slade's going after it."

Though the response was that which Tolliver had hoped, it still surprised him.

Briefly, the storekeeper related the events of the last couple days, his eyes shrewdly cataloging the expressions on the faces of the four killers. Even as he spoke, he shivered with the realization they were going to kill him as soon as they got their hands on the gold.

# Chapter Thirty

Tolliver's hand rested on the butt of his six-gun. "Where is this cave?"

Playing for time, Moriaty replied, "The south end of the mountain. It's hard to find. I'll have to show you."

"Saddle up. We'll follow."

"What about that one?" Red pointed to Al Grimes, who lay unconscious.

"Forget about him. Mount up, and let's go."

As the storekeeper led them over the rugged slopes of Vulture Mountain, his brain worked feverishly for a plan of escape.

Slade crouched in an arroyo that led up the mountain slope, passing near the mouth of a cave at which sat an armed guard. Off to the south loomed Wagon Mound, a narrow, five-hundred-foot mesa shaped like one of the thousands of wagons traveling the nearby Santa Fe Trail.

Slade whispered to Paleto and Right Hand beside him, "Slip around and come in above the cave. I'll back out of here and come in from the front. If we're lucky, they won't pay no attention to their backsides." He glanced at the sun, not quite overhead. "I'll move out when I see you in place."

His dark hand clutching his necklace of bear claws, Paleto nodded,

Thirty minutes later, the Mimbre Apache and the Arapaho were in place, each above and on either side of the gaping mouth of the cave. Slade eased back down the arroyo to his dun, dumped the water from his canteen, and rode out on a portion of the plains keeping a serrated ridge of limestone between him and the armed guard.

As he came from behind the ridge and into view of the cave, the leather-tough young man saw the guard stiffen and peer at him. Slade rode lazily up the road to the cave, holding up his hand in greeting while still some distance away.

The guard spoke over his shoulder. Moments later, two more men armed with Winchesters appeared from the darkness of the cave. All three stepped forward.

Slade reined up within shouting distance. "Howdy."

The older one shouted, "Keep going, stranger. This is private property."

Nodding, Slade replied, "Just looking for some water." He tapped his canteen. "You know of any nearby?"

The older man pointed the muzzle of his rifle toward Wagon Mound. "Fresh water about ten miles thattaway."

One of the younger guards leaned forward and whispered to the old man, who listened a moment, then jerked away. "No. Nobody comes in this cave except us and Mr. Moriaty."

Slade held out his canteen. "Just fill it for me. I'll sit out here."

While the discussion took place, Paleto and Right Hand glided down the slope like ethereal wisps of smoke, each vanishing behind a shrub too small to hide anything except a rabbit.

The older guard shook his head and started to turn back. Slade, knowing the guard would spot Paleto and Right Hand, called out, "Obliged anyway, mister."

The guard hesitated, studied Slade another few moments, giving the two Indians enough time to come up behind them. He turned and froze, staring into the muzzles of a Henry and a Winchester.

"Take it easy, boys," Slade drawled, shucking his Colt and moving forward. "My Indian friends have mighty skittish fingers on those triggers. Now drop your rifles." All three Winchesters clattered to the ground. "And your sidearms."

Herding the guard into the large cave, Slade was surprised when he saw the time and effort that had been put into improving the utility of the cave.

A stable that could handle a dozen horses had been constructed in the rear. Racks of hand-hewn logs along one side of the cave held saddles and tack not only for riding horses but for draft horses. In a rough wooden crate, Slade discovered bandoliers of cartridges and half a case of dynamite.

On the opposite wall around a fire pit were half a dozen bunks. In the middle of the cave sat two green and red wagons, the top of one covered with white Onasburg canvas.

Slade ordered the three to sit in the middle of the floor. He nodded to Paleto and Right Hand to watch them.

Quickly, he loosened the canvas on the wagon and peered beneath it. A grin came to his face when he saw the gold bars. He nodded to Paleto, after which his eyes slid on down to the three sullen guards.

He turned and spoke to the three. "The man named Moriaty bought this gold from them that stole it from the Boles Mine a few days back. Now, I don't know if your boss knew it was stolen or not. I figure all you boys are doing is following orders. I've got no argument with you, but we're taking this gold back to the rightful owners. I got Moriaty out there, and he'll set things straight with you. Now, give me your word you'll sit there until Moriaty gets here, or I'll hog-tie you."

The older guard, George Barnes, shot a furtive glance at the other two, then replied, "You got our word."

Slade gave a terse nod. "Good. All right, Paleto. Let's get those horses in their traces."

While Slade pulled chains and collars from the rack, the two Indians went to the stable to retrieve the horses.

One of the younger guards, Vinegar Duncan, whispered, "Now's our time. Let's go."

George Barnes shouted, "Now!"

The three leaped to their feet and sprinted for the mouth of the cave.

Ten minutes earlier, R. G. Moriaty reined up and nodded to the cave. "There."

Tolliver studied the cave, then stared at the storekeeper suspiciously. "I don't see nobody."

Moriaty glanced at the cave again. His brows knit.

Red called out, "Hey, Frank. Down the arroyo. There's two horses."

"Slade." Tolliver's voice was a growl.

"That means he's got my men inside," said Moriaty. He looked at Tolliver. "This is the only way out. Put your men around the mouth of the cave, and we'll have them pinned down. They'll have to give up the gold."

Quickly, Tolliver barked orders, spacing his men. He glanced at Hatch, but the lanky gunfighter had slipped into a cluster of boulders out of the grizzled killer's sight. Tolliver cursed. He'd planned on killing Hatch during the upcoming gun battle, but the one-eyed killer had outsmarted him.

Moriaty's heart pounded against his chest as he swung to the ground and ducked behind a boulder. As soon as the shooting started, he'd light a shuck for Fort Union. To hell with the gold. To hell with his employees.

To his dismay, Red Sweet hunkered down beside him and gave him a leering grin. "We ain't letting you get away, boy."

At that moment, a shout came from inside the cave.

Slade jerked around when he heard George Barnes shout. He shucked his Colt, but held his fire. Let 'em go, he told himself. We'll be out of here in ten minutes.

Suddenly a barrage of explosions echoed through the cave as the three guards ran into the withering volley of lead plums Tolliver and his men were firing.

As soon as the firing began, Moriaty grabbed a heavy rock and slammed it into the back of Red's skull. He ripped the six-gun from the outlaw's limp fingers. His brain raced. Maybe he could salvage the gold.

Without warning, Red grabbed Moriaty's ankle. He snarled up at the storekeeper.

Panicking, Moriaty blew a hole in the growling man's forehead.

Across the hardpan, Tolliver shouted, "Red, Red! What's going on?" When he failed to get any response, Tolliver bellowed, "You're a dead man, Moriaty."

Without hesitation, R. G. Moriaty swung into the saddle and dug his heels into his pony's flanks, bound for Fort Union.

By the time the firing ceased, Slade, Paleto, and Right Hand had taken defensive positions covering the mouth of the cave. From where he looked on, Slade saw the three dead guards sprawled on the hard limestone outside the cave. He grimaced when he thought about Al Grimes, figuring the small man to be dead. Damned shame.

An excited voice called out, "We got 'em, Frank. We got 'em." In the next moment, Hatch was racing across the hardpan into the cave.

Behind him, Tolliver shouted, "Get back here, damn it. That wasn't them."

A two-hundred-grain slug powered by twenty-six grains of powder from Right Hand's Henry slammed into Hatch's chest, knocking the lanky killer off his feet. He hit and rolled to his knees, firing wildly as blood from a severed artery spurted through the hole in his chest. Right Hand fired again. This time, the slug took out Hatch's other eye and blew out the back of his skull.

With a satisfied grin on his face, Tolliver emptied his rifle into the cave, hitting nothing.

As quickly as it had begun, the firing ceased. A deathly silence settled over Vulture Mountain.

# Chapter Thirty-one

Leaning low over the neck of his galloping pony, R. G. Moriaty cast an anxious glance over his shoulder at the pop of gunfire. He sighed with relief when he saw he had no pursuit. Easing his horse from a gallop into a gentle lope, he squinted at the western horizon, beyond which lay Fort Union.

He had learned a chilling lesson, and thinking back over what consequences he could have faced, he figured sixty thousand was a cheap enough price to pay for his life.

As he topped the next rise, he spotted several Indians on war ponies. They stood on a distant rise to the south, merely watching.

The storekeeper's heart thudded against his chest and his mouth went dry when he spotted the braided hair on one side of the warriors' heads and the hair cut at ear level on the other side.

Kiowa!

He glanced over his shoulder. He couldn't go back.

Fighting panic, he kept his pony in a steady lope, slowly moving away from the Kiowas. All he could hear above the pounding of his heart was the steady thud of hoofbeats.

For a moment, a surge of hope rushed through his veins, quickly ended by a shrill war cry.

He dug his heels into his pony's flanks, but the Kiowa Wolf Clan quickly drew near.

Moriaty turned in the saddle. The Kiowas were close enough for him to see the cruel grins on their swarthy faces. He raised his six-gun and squeezed the trigger.

Nothing.

The hammer fell on an empty cartridge.

Sobbing in fear, he hurled the revolver at them and urged his pony to run faster.

A searing pain slammed into his shoulder, numbing his arm. He glanced at his shoulder and to his horror, saw an iron arrowhead protruding from his shoulder. He felt himself slipping from the saddle. He hit on his back, slamming his head against the ground and tumbling head over heels. He slid to a halt in the mud and snow.

Dazed, he felt rough hands grab him. Fingers yanked his hair and a pain like fire struck his skull.

A Kiowa warrior yelped and danced around, holding Moraity's bloody scalp over his head. Blood ran between his clenched fingers, dripping on his buckskin shirt.

A second Kiowa yanked the storekeeper's head back and slashed his throat. While Moriaty lay on the ground bleeding out, another Kiowa returned leading his pony.

Then the war party, jubilant and excited about their victory, turned to Vulture Mountain.

A guttural voice broke the silence. "Slade! Give me the gold, and I'll let you ride out. You ain't got a chance. I got a dozen men out here."

The young half-breed laughed. "Tolliver, you're not only a liar, you're stupid. You got three at the most. We got grub and water in here. We can wait you out."

Another barrage of slugs raked the interior of the cave, striking nothing but limestone.

Paleto looked across the cave at Slade and held up two fingers. Slade nodded. "That's what I counted." A wicked grin played over his face. He motioned to Paleto that he was going deeper into the cave.

A few moments later, the pungent odor of wood smoke drifted out the mouth of the cave. Soon, mingled with its tanginess was the delectable aroma of broiling venison.

Slade returned, grinning at Paleto and Right Hand. He called out, "Might as well relax, Tolliver. We're going to sit a spell and put ourselves around a heaping platter of venison and corn dodgers."

When Tolliver did not reply, the three inside the cave grinned at each other. Suddenly the crack of a rifle a short distance from the cave broke the silence. Tolliver shouted, "I just kilt one of them horses down in the arroyo, Slade. I'll kill the other one if you don't come out."

Slade held a steady rein on the anger threatening to explode into an impulsive and foolish response. That's what Tolliver wanted. "Do what you think best, Tolliver. The gold is going back to the mine."

Suddenly Bull Gutierrez shouted, "Frank. Out there! Kiowa!"

Tolliver peered around the side of a boulder and spotted six Kiowa warriors heading directly for them. "Damn," he muttered.

"What do we do, Frank?"

Slamming his Winchester back in the saddle boot,

Tolliver swung onto his horse and jerked the animal around. "I don't know about you, but I'm getting the hell out of here."

Slade and Paleto exchanged puzzled looks.

Moments later at the sound of retreating hoofbeats, the three hurried from the cave, wary of a trick. Back to the southeast, two riders were churning up snow and mud, bound for Wagon Mound.

"There," Right Hand announced, pointing the muzzle of his Henry at the oncoming Kiowas a mile out. "That why they run."

Slade barked, "Quick. Get the horse in here. We'll see what we can do to welcome our new guests."

As Slade swung a couple of bandoliers of cartridges over his shoulders, Paleto returned leading two horses.

The wiry half-breed chuckled. "At least the man likes horses."

Slade and Paleto found snug spots in the underbrush and rocks above the cave, providing them a wide field of fire. Right Hand remained inside, just in case any Kiowas made it past the two brothers. "You do the talking," he had said to the diminutive Arapaho. "No sense in telling them where we are until the right time."

The war party reined up a quarter of a mile distant. Two rode ahead, warily approaching the cave. They halted fifty feet out. "You. Inside."

Right Hand replied, "What does the Kiowa want?"

One patted his lean belly. "Food. Then we ride on."

"We have no food. Now ride on."

"We could ride in and take it from you."

"The Kiowa takes from women, not men. I say again, I have no food for you. Ride out."

From his vantage point above the cave, Slade recognized the suppressed anger on the two warriors' faces. He knew from experience, the Kiowa, mighty warriors that they were, preferred action to finesse. These two, however, were wise enough to recognize the hopelessness of their current situation.

One nodded. "We go."

After the small party disappeared to the west, Slade and Paleto descended. "They come back," Paleto said simply.

"I know." He studied his brother a few moments. "They figure on surprising us." He paused and added, "Unless we surprise them first."

Paleto grinned. He knew exactly what his brother meant. "Even though you live with the white man, you still think like a Human Being."

A voice arrested their attention. Down below, winding his way across the boulder-dotted slope, came Al Grimes.

"Never thought Tolliver would leave, and then, here comes them damned Kioway."

Slade grinned. "We'd given you up for dead."

The bandy-legged foreman touched the back of his head gently. "One of them coldcocked me. I woke up before they left, but I played dead for them. After they rode out, I followed." He paused, his eyes alight with anticipation. "What about the gold?"

Hooking his thumb over his shoulder, Slade replied, "In there, waiting to be hauled back to the mine."

Grimes laughed. "You mean Las Vegas. I'm taking it straight to Las Vegas."

Paleto grunted. "That good. Come morning."

"Morning." The stocky miner glanced at the sun. "We still got a couple hours."

The Mimbre Apache lifted an eyebrow. "And Kiowa."

Grimes frowned. Slade explained, "They'll be back tonight. When the Kiowa warrior wants something, he doesn't quit until he has it or he's dead."

The small man gulped nervously. "You mean, they know about the gold?"

"No. They just want in the cave. They reckon that since somebody is guarding it, there's something valuable inside."

"So, what do we do?"

Slade patted his belly. "I don't know about you, but I figured after covering all these bodies, I plan on a couple cups of coffee and some broiled venison. Then I figure on grabbing some sleep."

Paleto grunted. "That sound good."

Squatting around a small fire that evening, the Mimbre Apache looked up from his coffee. "A late moon tonight. We leave early."

"That's what I figure." Slade nodded to Right Hand. "I don't figure Tolliver will double back. Can't tell. So, you and Grimes here stay watchful."

Grimes cleared his throat. "What about you? What are you and your Apache brother planning to do?"

Slade grinned at Paleto. "We're going to give our Kiowa friends an Apache welcome."

During their flight from the Kiowa, Bull Gutierrez pulled up beside Frank Tolliver and shouted to be heard above the thudding of the hooves in the snow and mud, "Where we going now?"

Tolliver nodded to the tall mesa ahead. "We find us

a spot there to put up for the night." A grim smile split his heavily bearded face. "I got a couple ideas."

Gutierrez looked at him in surprise. "You ain't still thinking about that gold?"

Setting his jaw, the broad-shouldered hardcase growled, "Why the hell not? It's there for the taking if we can figure out how." He glanced at Gutierrez, and with a sly grin, added, "You wouldn't argue splitting a hundred thousand in gold, would you?"

Chuckling, the younger gunfighter shook his head. "Not a bit. As long as I don't get kilt getting it."

"Don't worry. You won't." Not until after we get it, Frank Tolliver added to himself.

# Chapter Thirty-two

Later that night, Slade dropped to one knee on the crest of the first rise beyond Vulture Mountain with Paleto at his side. In addition to a bandolier of cartridges over a shoulder, each carried three sticks of fused dynamite. They studied the rolling plains before them.

The stars cast a bluish silver light on the prairie. Dark blotches that were thick shrubs dotted the countryside. Large patches of snow glistened whitely in the starlight. Paleto muttered, "I see nothing."

Silently, the two brothers loped across the prairie to the next rise before pausing and studying the lay of the countryside around them. Moments later, they continued their search. After thirty minutes, Slade began to wonder if he'd guessed wrong, that the Kiowas had not planned on returning to the cave.

That's when Paleto grabbed his arm and nodded to a black line bisecting the prairie to the north. Slade studied it, seeing nothing until a flicker of light illumined the rim of the gully. "Yeah. I see it."

Paleto motioned that he would swing around and come in from the north. That way, they could come in from each side. "I call when I am ready."

\* \* \*

Five minutes later, Slade crouched behind a sagebrush and waited. Soon, the plaintive cry of a whip-poor-will echoed through the night. Slade answered with the coo of a dove, then struck a match and touched it to the fuse.

When he drew back to lob it into the gully, he spotted another burning fuse looping over and over as it arced through the night.

The first explosion shook the ground. The second followed almost immediately. Howls of pain and surprise drowned the dying echoes of the explosions as panicked horses stampeded, one or two dragging unfortunate masters who made the mistake of tethering their animals to their ankles.

The other warriors scattered in every direction as four more sticks of dynamite hurtled through the dark sky.

Back in the cave, Grimes and Right Hand gathered around. "We heard the explosions," said the small foreman. "You get 'em all?"

Slade laughed. "Scared the hell out them. You can sleep good tonight. Those old boys aren't coming back."

Before sunrise next morning with Al Grimes perched on the wagon seat handling the ribbons, they moved out for Las Vegas. Slade and Paleto rode swing while Right Hand took point. Frank Tolliver was still out there. After the gold was dropped in Las Vegas and credited to the mine, then they could stop worrying about the grizzled outlaw.

Slade was right. Frank Tolliver was out there. He watched through narrowed eyes as the wagon pulled out. Las Vegas, he told himself.

"What do we do now, Frank?"

Tolliver pursed his lips and studied Bull Gutierrez. "We swing south around them and wait for them hombres to come to us."

Because of the melting snow and the weight of the gold, the wagon made poor time, barely ten miles by noon. Late that afternoon, they spotted the Mora River, swollen high and swift by melting snow.

Right Hand rode in. He pointed in the direction of two peaks on the river. "Town, not much. There is ferry. Before mountains. We cross there."

When they rode into the small town, Slade shook his head briefly. Right Hand had not exaggerated when he said there was not much to the town. One saloon, one stable, one small general store.

Al Grimes aimed an arc of tobacco onto the mud squishing from beneath the wheels of his wagon. "Never knew this place was here. Wonder what they call it."

Without replying, Slade led the small party through the town and to the ferry. After pulling the wagon onto the ferry and tying it down, Slade and his compadres held their ponies so the undulating deck of the ferry wouldn't spook them. Just before the wizened old ferryman pulled away from the shore, two bearded hardcases, their ponies slinging up mud and snow, raced up from the direction of the mountains.

One shouted, "Hold on, there. We're going across." Without hesitating, they forced their animals to leap onto the ferry. When they dismounted, the older one spotted Paleto and Right Hand. His face grew hard, but his partner laid a hand on his harm. "Easy, Butch. We don't want no trouble."

Butch sneered and shouted at the ferryman, "What are you doing lettin' Injuns ride across?"

The old man shrugged. "They pay, they ride." He held out his skeletal hand. "That's a dollar for you and your friend."

The bearded hardcase snorted, "Get it from the Injun there." He paused, his eyes glittered. "No, never mind. I'll get it." He took two quick strides toward Paleto, who spun and directed a swinging kick on the side of the startled renegade's head.

With a scream, he tumbled overboard.

"Stop the ferry," his partner shouted. "Stop it."

Slade dropped his hand to the butt of his Colt. "We're stopping nothing, friend. Now, you owe the old man a dollar for you and the two horses. Pay up or join your friend back there."

The younger man eyed Slade several moments, his eyes reflecting his indecision. Finally, his shoulders slumped, and he nodded, tossing the old man a dollar and returning to the rear of the ferry, where he kept an eye on his partner climbing onto the far shore.

His eyes on the gunman, Slade muttered to the ferryman, "Reckon someone needs to teach those boys some manners."

The old man chuckled. "I'd wager that Injun friend of yours did just that."

Slade laughed mirthlessly, keeping his eyes on the younger hardcase.

"But," the old man continued, "I sees a heap of them kind around." He nodded to the two peaks a couple of miles to the northwest. "Them kind seem to flock to the

Hole." He shrugged and cackled. "Can't say I blame them. There ain't no law up there."

"The hole? What's that?" Slade glanced at the old man.

"A settlement of some sort. That's what they call it, the Hole. I ain't never been up there, but from what I hear, there's a heap of yahoos wanted by the law what fort up there."

Astride their ponies, Paleto and Slade watched as the ferry returned to the far side of the river. The Mimbre Apache spoke softly. "You hear what he say about the mountains?"

"I heard."

"What you think?"

Perched on the wagon seat, Al Grimes looked from one to the other, unable to follow the gist of their exchange.

"Could be. Best I figure, we found Simmons about twenty miles or so due north of here."

Frustrated, the bandy-legged little foreman interrupted. "What in the hell are you talking about?"

"Jess Cooper. Remember him? The one who stole your gold and killed Arch Simmons and took the sixty thousand Moriaty paid them?"

Grimes nodded. "I remember. What about him?"

Ignoring the question, Slade muttered, "Could be." He cut his eyes toward the twin peaks. "Could be he's up there."

The diminutive foreman snorted. "That don't make no difference. I got the gold. No skin off my nose."

"Maybe not, but come morning, you three are going on to Las Vegas. I plan to amble back to the little village and see what I can learn about the Hole."

"You're what? You can't leave me and the gold with—" He cut his suddenly frightened eyes to Paleto and Right Hand. "I mean—"

His gray eyes cold as ice, Slade cut him off. "You wouldn't have the gold if it hadn't been for those two, Grimes. I guarantee you, no jasper is going to touch that gold with them two riding shotgun."

Paleto nodded. "You may be right, my brother. But what of Cooper?" He cut his eyes to Grimes. "Like this one says, we have gold. I ask why you would do such a thing when it is not important."

For a moment, Slade studied the Mimbre Apache. He had no answer to the question, not even for himself. "I don't know. Part of me says no; the other, yes. Cooper gave me my life back. He could have killed me in the barn that night. Maybe I should be grateful and forget about him. But I can't. He's like the badger that robbed our traps when we were boys. Remember? He continued to rob them until we killed him. Cooper is like the badger. He won't stop robbing traps. Maybe us once again."

A couple of miles farther on, they pulled into a cul-de-sac on the west side of a small mesa. Paleto glanced over their back trail and nodded to Slade. "They come."

Grimes looked around in alarm before he climbed down from the wagon. "Who?"

Slade replied, "The two jaspers back at the river." He grinned at Paleto. "I don't reckon he appreciated the lesson my brother taught him."

"But—but," Grimes sputtered.

With a grin, Slade waved him to listen. "Paleto and me will be out there tonight. You and the gold will be safe here with Right Hand. Now, let's put coffee on to boil and fry up some bacon and biscuits."

As they squatted around the small fire sipping coffee and sopping biscuits in the bacon grease, Slade nodded to the sagebrush-dotted prairie before them. "Where do you reckon they'll come?"

The Mimbre Apache gestured to a small rise to the southwest, then to a line of dead vegetation marking the course of a shallow arroyo some hundred yards distant. "One will slip down the wash to the rise. He will look straight into the camp."

"That's what I figure," Slade replied, wiping his greasy fingers on his buckskins. "The other one will hide behind the small ridge of limestone to the north," he said, indicating a shallow ridge some thirty yards distant.

"And we will be waiting for them," Paleto said.

Slade nodded.

Al Grimes listened to the matter-of-fact discussion with increasing confusion. "How do you know that's where they'll be? They might come in from another direction."

Grimes's obvious frustration amused Slade. Patiently, he explained, "The Apache studies the animals and birds about him. He knows their habits; what they like; what they don't; how they move. You can point out the antelope a mile away to my brother here, and he can tell you the direction of the animal's next move. You see, the Apache is one with those about him."

Slade waved his arm at all before them. "We chose this place to camp because it offered only those approaches. As soon as darkness begins to settle in, we'll slip out there and be waiting for them." He nodded to the Arapaho. "You remain here, with Right Hand. Stay behind the wagon. Don't move around, but talk."

"What if they don't come?"

Paleto chuckled. Slade replied, "They will. They're too dumb not to."

Grimes gulped. "Will—will you kill them?"

Somberly, Slade replied, "Only if they make us."

Paleto rubbed one of the bear claws strung on his necklace.

## Chapter Thirty-three

# Chapter Thirty-three

Just as the darkness settled over dusk, Slade and Paleto shucked their heavy coats and slipped out, their
silhouettes fading into the hazy shadows of the coming night.

Colt in hand, Slade ducked behind a sagebrush
growing at the end of the slight limestone ridge. More
than once as a youth, the young half-breed had hidden
within arm's reach of others. Tonight would be no different, only simpler for the white man never saw what
lay before, just what he wished to see. These two would
be no different.

Behind him, he heard the muted voices of the Arapaho and the mine foreman. Time passed slowly. His
eyes grew accustomed to the darkness, and from time
to time, he spotted feeding rabbits. One paused just beyond the sage to nibble at some grass. The tiny crea-
ture looked into Slade's eyes for several seconds, then
resumed feeding.

At that moment, the clink of a spur came from the
darkness. The rabbit froze, stared over its shoulder, then
bolted.

Seconds later, a shadow appeared from the night
and eased in behind the ridge. Slade smelled the sweet

stench of whiskey and the foul odor of the hombre's unwashed body.

The shadow slid a rifle over the top of the ridge. The bushwhacker eased the hammer back. The click of the cocking hammer sounded like a gunshot in the brittle silence.

"Touch that trigger, and you're dead." Slade's words froze the man.

Without warning, the owl-hoot screamed and whipped his rifle around. Slade fired twice into the darkness below the jasper's hat.

With a grunt, the would-be bushwhacker jerked backward, his rifle discharging a streaking jet of orange fire into the darkness.

Quickly, Slade rolled to his right, away from the ridge, and spun on his belly, peering into the darkness where the second killer lay.

Moments later, a whip-poor-will called. Slade responded with the coo of a dove.

Paleto emerged from behind the rise like a wraith, wiping the bloody blade on his thigh. He nodded as Slade approached. "Best we throw them in arroyo and cover with dirt."

"The animals will find them tomorrow."

The Mimbre Apache shrugged. "But we sleep tonight."

Slade laughed.

After removing the dead men's gun belts, they rolled the bodies into the arroyo and kicked the steep bank over them. Paleto nodded to the dark prairie. "I get horses."

Back in camp, they tethered the horses with the others, tossed the saddles and tack along with the extra weapons in the bed of the wagon, and rummaged through the saddlebags.

The wiry half-breed grinned when he pulled out a pair of denims and a linsey-woolsey shirt, worn but clean. Quickly, he shucked his buckskins and slipped into the fresh duds. He turned to Grimes. "Let's you and me swap horses. No one back there will recognize yours."

Mounted on Al Grimes's sorrel next morning, Slade watched as the wagon pulled out for Las Vegas. Paleto turned in his saddle. Slade waved, then headed back to the Mora River as a cover of clouds pushed in from the north.

Instead of taking the ferry, Slade swung east, fording the river some two miles downstream and riding into the small village just before noon.

Two well-used horses stood hipshot at the hitching rail in front of the saloon. Slade pulled in across the street at the general store.

It was cold and empty except for a single clerk wearing a dirty white apron and sleeping in front of the potbellied stove. Slade scanned the store. It appeared typical of the ubiquitous mercantiles of the West, filled with a vast assortment of items and goods for those passing through.

He ambled over to the shelves of canned goods and pulled down a can of peaches. Using his knife, he opened it and drank the juice.

Back at the stove, he tapped the clerk on the sole of his boot.

The rail-thin man jerked awake, staring up in surprise at Slade, who held up the can of peaches and said, "I'll take a couple more of these if you don't mind."

"Yeah, yeah. Sorry I was asleep. There ain't much to do around here except sleep."

Slade laughed and speared a peach. He ordered a few more items, bacon, coffee, and flour. While the clerk filled the order, Slade casually questioned him, "I'm supposed to meet a friend here. About an inch or so taller than me. Blond hair. About twenty-six or so. Goes by the name of Cooper." He watched warily for any reaction from the clerk. There was none.

"Nope." He slipped the items into Slade's saddle-bags. "Ain't seen no one like that. Maybe across the street at Lester's saloon. He serves up a good steak, too, if them peaches ain't enough for you."

A few more disreputable-looking hardcases had drifted into Lester's by the time Slade pushed through the doors. Several sets of wary eyes studied the slender newcomer at the door, then dismissed him.

Quickly Slade scanned the dim interior, spotting no familiar faces. A slight man with a long nose, mutton-chop sideburns, and bald head nodded from the bar. "Howdy, stranger. What'll you have?"

The man reminded Slade of a bald-headed sheep. He ordered a steak and whiskey, carrying the latter to a table in the corner of the room.

Outside, the clouds grew thicker.

The saloon owner lit a couple of lanterns over the bar to chase away some of the gloom, the light of which served to amplify the murkiness in the rest of the room.

A few minutes later, Lester plopped a thick steak and another whiskey on the table before Slade. "More where that come from, stranger."

The young half-breed nodded and dug in.

To his surprise, the steak was as good as the store-keeper across the street had claimed.

Halfway through his steak, a blast of cold air swept in as the doors swung open. Slade glanced up and his eyes went cold as Frank Tolliver and Bull Gutierrez stomped in.

Shucking his Colt, Slade eased deeper into the shadows of the corner as the two gunnies bellied up to the bar and ordered a bottle of whiskey. Tolliver growled at the bar owner, "You seen a red and green wagon go through here sometime yesterday?"

Lester shook his head.

A cowpoke at the end of the bar eyed Tolliver narrowly. "Maybe."

The heavily muscled outlaw glared at the grinning cowboy. His voice belied the twist of anger contorting his grizzled face. Tolliver slid his bottle of whiskey down the bar. "Help yourself, friend." He paused, then asked, "What time did it come through?"

For a moment, the cowpoke studied Tolliver and Gutierrez, then grinned and filled his glass. "Couple hours before dark. Heading south." He slid the bottle back. "Obliged."

Tolliver turned to Gutierrez and cursed. "If them damned Kiowa hadn't popped up again yesterday afternoon, we'd'a been here in time."

Gutierrez downed his whiskey. "Reckon you're right, Frank. But we was lucky we spotted them first. Our scalps would be dangling from their belts right now."

The cowpoke at the end of the bar called out, "Hey, Lester. Coop been around today?"

Slade stiffened when he heard the name Coop.

At the bar, Tolliver froze at the question.

Gutierrez whispered, "You hear that?"

Tolliver cleared his throat. "Listen."

Lester nodded. "This morning."

"Damn. I's hoping he'd buy me a drink. I'm broke. How about some credit?"

Lester grunted. "Hell's bells, Slim. You owe me over twenty dollars now."

Frank Tolliver slid the bottle to Slim and ambled down the bar. "Have one on me, friend. Hate to see any jasper go thirsty."

"Thanks."

At his table, Slade strained to hear the conversation, but their words were garbled.

Tolliver nodded. "I couldn't help hearing you ask about a cowpoke called Coop. I used to work with an old boy over in Juniper Pass named Cooper, Jess Cooper."

The slender cowpoke frowned. "I don't know his Christian name. We just called him Coop." He paused and grinned. "But he's got money to burn, I can tell you that."

Tolliver laughed. "Sounds like old Jess." He tossed down a drink and poured another, and one for Slim. "Maybe one of these days I'll run into him again, and we can have a drink to the good old times."

"Hell," exclaimed Slim, his slender face flushed with whiskey. "No sense in waiting. Old Coop, he's up at the Hole. Been there the last few days."

A frown knit Tolliver's forehead. "The Hole?"

"Yeah. I guess you'd call it a fort up in the mountains. Law never sticks its nose in there. A rough place." He shouted to the saloon owner, "Ain't that right, Lester? The Hole is a rough place?"

Lester nodded indifferently and wiped at the bar.

"The Hole," Slade muttered, remembering the old ferryman's tale of the outlaw hideout.

Shaking his head, Tolliver asked, "Whereabouts in the mountains? Reckon I could find it?"

Slim poured another drink and downed it. "Hell, I'll do better than that. Buy me a bottle of whiskey, and I'll show you where it's at."

After the trio left, Slade moved quickly to the bar and paid his bill. Pouring another glass of whiskey, he sauntered over to the front window and peered outside, ostensibly studying the weather while he nursed his drink.

He spotted the trio riding northwest out of the small village toward the mountains a couple of miles across the rolling prairie. He grimaced and shook his head in admiration at whoever had selected the Hole as an outlaws' retreat.

Anyone on the mountain could see riders approaching from five miles away. Instinctively, Slade knew he would have to go in at night.

And then, one or two flakes of snow drifted down.

Lester came to stand beside him. "Looks like we got us a storm coming. You need a bed for the night, stranger? I got some out back for fifty cents. Stove to keep things warm."

Slade shook his head. "No, thanks. Reckon I'll ride on out."

The slight saloon owner shrugged. "Bad weather to be out in."

"Maybe so, but I got a couple compadres waiting for me."

The snow grew heavier.

* * *

Lester scratched at one of his muttonchop sideburns and watched as Slade swung into the saddle and headed east out of the small town, away from the mountains. He grimaced, thinking to himself that there was nothing out there but sagebrush and wild Kiowa. He shook his head. "Good luck, cowboy," he muttered, turning away from the window and heading back to the warmth of the potbellied stove.

Outside, the snow grew heavier.

# Chapter Thirty-four

Slade swung wide around the village, coming into the mountains from the north, riding more by Apache instinct than sight, for the snow had cut visibility to less than a hundred yards. He leaned forward and patted the sorrel on the neck. "That's good and bad for us, fella," he muttered. "They can't see us, but come dark, we best have us someplace to fort up for the night."

Then, like a ghost, a tower of weathered limestone rose before him, its top lost in the falling snow. Beside the tower appeared another, and another, a wall of the mountain made up by a series of gigantic limestone towers, each separated from the other by a narrow chimney opening onto the rim of the limestone wall.

The ground began to ascend. Minutes later, Slade reined up, staring into a gaping opening between two towers. He grinned with satisfaction when he realized he had stumbled onto the trail leading deeper into the mountains. He studied the upward trail. It was well traveled. He rode inside and glanced over his shoulder. Beyond the mouth of the trail was a veil of white, as if a giant curtain had been pulled.

Though he did not expect any guards along the trail during such inclement weather, he rode warily, the rawhide loop off the hammer of his Colt.

Two hundred yards up the trail, the outside wall of limestone fell away, revealing a steep slope of pine and piñon, the needles and branches of which were crowned with pristine snow.

The snow grew heavier.

Another few hundred yards up the trail, Slade cut off onto the slope, searching for a snug hole out of the weather. With the snow and swirling wind, a small fire would bring no threat of discovery.

Soon he found an ideal spot, and within minutes, a small fire blazed beneath a limestone overhang, warming the small area comfortably. Slade strung a fly over the opening on the remote possibility of a curious eye spotting the fire.

A night blacker than a flock of crows had settled over the Hole when Slim, with Tolliver and Gutierrez at his side, pulled up at the hitching rail in front of one of the six rock-walled houses perched beside a small lake in the middle of a valley.

"In here," Slim announced, ducking his head into the falling snow and hurrying into one of the houses. "He stays here."

Unseen by the slender cowboy, Tolliver and Gutierrez checked their six-guns, ready for their confrontation with Jess Cooper.

To the two hardcases' anger and disgust, once inside, they learned Jess Cooper had ridden out earlier that day for Las Vegas. One of the four outlaws seated at the poker table nodded. "Yep. Rode out this morning."

Tolliver glared at Slim. He wanted to smash the smaller man's nose into his face.

The slender cowpoke shrugged. "Sorry, boys. I didn't know he had pulled leather."

"Yep," said another of the poker players. "He just up and took off. Hadn't even talked about it. Just up and gone."

Clenching his fists, Tolliver cut his cold eyes to the four hardcases sitting at the poker table. He tightened the reins on his temper. No sense in taking his frustration out on Slim. Besides, there was five of them against him and Gutierrez.

The snow ceased during the night, and next morning before the sun rose, Slade lay at the base of a twisted piñon on the rim of a limestone bluff overlooking the small community below.

As soon as false dawn lit the sky, Tolliver and Gutierrez emerged from a stable on their ponies and headed for the trail leading out of the Hole.

Slade hurried back down to the trail, eager to cut them off before they reached the prairie below.

Below a curve in the trail, he slipped behind a large boulder. The icy wind swirled through the pine and piñon. From up the trail, a horse whinnied. Slade tightened his finger on the trigger of his Colt.

With Tolliver in the lead, the two rounded the bend. Slade jumped out. "Hold it right there, Tolliver."

"Slade!" Tolliver jerked on the reins. His horse reared, pawing the air. The sudden movement startled Gutierrez's horse, causing the animal to stand on his hind legs and paw frantically at the air.

The pony staggered back, then fell, crushing Bull Gutierrez, breaking his ribs and driving the broken bones through his lungs. A fit of coughing seized him, spraying blood everywhere.

Slade dodged the flying hooves.

As soon as Tolliver's pony had his feet on the ground,

the broad-shouldered outlaw spurred him. The horse leaped forward, stumbled, and fell head over heels. Frank Tolliver leaped from the saddle and hit the ground hard. He jumped to his feet, snarling, and grabbed for his six-gun. His holster was empty. The fall had sent his revolver flying.

He turned on his heel and scrambled up the wall of the trail. Slade leaped after him.

At the rim of the limestone wall some hundred feet up, Tolliver turned and hurled a heavy rock at Slade. The wiry half-breed pressed up against the limestone just as the boulder brushed his shoulder.

He looked up. Tolliver had vanished. Quickly, he scaled the remainder of the distance to the rim, spotting the grizzled outlaw running into the forest. He cocked and raised his Colt. "Hold it there, Tolliver, or I'll put a slug in your spine."

The big man jerked to a halt beside an ancient pine.

Slade approached warily. "Now turn around."

His face contorted with fury, Tolliver turned. "You best kill me. I get the chance, I'll kill you."

Ignoring the threat, Slade said, "Where's Cooper?"

"Go to hell."

Without warning, overhead, a loud pop like the crack of a rifle broke the silence. Slade glanced up as a dead limb, weighted down by snow, came hurtling down. He jumped back just as the limb slammed into the ground.

In that instant, Tolliver leaped on him, knocking the Colt from the smaller man's hand and wrapping fingers the size of sausages around Slade's throat. Through clenched teeth, Tolliver growled, "You caused me enough trouble already, you bastard. I'm going to tear your damned head off."

Slade seized Tolliver's wrists, then threw himself backward, pulling the large man after him. When he hit the ground, the wiry half-breed threw his feet up, catching Tolliver in the belly and flipping the big man over onto his back.

Slade leaped to his feet and, as the outlaw climbed up, slammed a bony fist into Tolliver's grizzled jaw. The big man's head whipped around, but in the next second, he swung a massive fist that caught Slade in the ribs. Slade staggered back.

Like a hulk of rock, he stood glaring at Slade. "You're a dead man."

With a laugh, Slade shot back, "It'll take a better man than you, you worthless piece of trash."

With a scream of rage, Tolliver charged. Apache bloodlust coursed through Slade's veins. Agilely, he darted aside and slammed a fist into the big man's left cheek, splitting the skin. Before Tolliver could turn, Slade drove another sizzling punch into the grizzled outlaw's kidney.

Shaking his head and gasping for breath, Tolliver glared at Slade. This time, instead of charging wildly, he stalked forward like a mountain puma, his fists the size of hams.

With a growl, Tolliver swung a roundhouse right. Slade ducked under it, only to run into a left uppercut that knocked him back on his heels. Sensing blood, Tolliver waded in, throwing one crunching punch after another.

Calling on his training as an Apache youth when one was forced to defend himself against three, Slade parried the punches with his arms and shoulders, but each one jarred him, drove him back step by step.

Suddenly he backed into a pine.

A shout of triumph tore from Tolliver's throat, and he threw a straight right at Slade's head. Slade ducked. The punch brushed the top of his head and slammed into the tree.

Tolliver screamed and jerked his hand back.

Slade kicked him in the knee, then when the big man ducked, slammed half a dozen slicing punches into the man's face. Tolliver backed away. Slade took a running jump and smashed both his feet into the big man's chest, sending him tumbling head over heels.

Rolling onto his hands and knees, Tolliver remained motionless a few moments, his head hanging. Then a savage growl sounded from deep in his throat, and he raised his head, his red-rimmed eyes glaring at Slade like a sow grizzly.

He lunged to his feet, glanced around, and spotted a dead tree limb ten feet long and as big around as his massive biceps. He picked it up, broke it in half over his knee, grabbed one piece with both hands, and wielded it over his head like a club. His face was a mask of rage and blood. "I'm going to kill you, you son of a bitch."

Slade backed away, futilely searching the ground for his Colt. His feet touched limestone, and he knew he was only a few feet from the rim of the wall. He eyed Tolliver warily. The big man flexed his massive shoulders, and a cruel sneer twisted his lips.

Suddenly a bloodcurdling scream ripped from Tolliver's throat, and he charged Slade, swinging the massive club back and forth.

The wiry half-breed ducked the first swing, grabbed a handful of snow and mud, tossed it in Tolliver's face, and threw himself aside as the second arc of the massive club swung back, catching Slade a glancing blow in the back and hurtling him into a pine tree.

His head felt like it exploded, and for a moment, he couldn't move.

Then he heard a terrified scream and looked around in time to see Frank Tolliver balancing precariously on the rim of the wall. His eyes wide with fear, the grizzled outlaw thrust out his hand to Slade, but before the young half-breed could react, Tolliver toppled down one of the gaping chimneys.

With a sigh of relief, Slade leaned back against the tree and closed his eyes, wincing as his muscles began to throb from the beating his body had taken.

He dropped his hands to his side, and one of them fell on his Colt. He picked it up and grinned ruefully. "Now you show up," he muttered, wiping the mud and snow from the revolver.

Slade peered down the chimney, but the shadows within the gaping hole were too dark to spot Tolliver. Slade shook his head. No one could have survived the fall. Both Tolliver and Gutierrez were dead.

He clambered down the wall.

Moments later, the cowpoke who had led the two hardcases to the Hole the night before rounded the bend. He jerked his pony to a halt when he spotted Slade in the middle of the road. "What the—" His startled gaze slid over to the sprawled body of Bull Gutierrez.

Slade drew down on him. "Sit easy, friend."

Slim eyed the Colt in Slade's hand and grinned wryly. "Don't worry, mister. I'll sit as easy as I can."

Then Slade recognized him. "You were with this jasper in the saloon yesterday."

"Yep. That was me."

"You brought two of them up here to see Jess Cooper."

Slim nodded. "Right again, mister."

"Did they?"

Slim glanced at the body of Bull Gutierrez. "Nope. Cooper rode out yesterday. Las Vegas. That's where this hombre and his partner . . ." He paused and glanced around for Tolliver.

Slade indicated the chimney down which the outlaw had fallen. "He's in there."

The young cowpoke gulped and nodded. "That— that's where these two jaspers was going until . . ." He paused again and shrugged. "Well, until you decided they wasn't."

Slade studied him another moment. "Drop your hogleg and saddle rifle, then turn around and ride back. I got no trouble with you unless you want to make some."

Slim grinned boyishly. "Hell, mister. I ain't trouble for no one. Especially if he's holding a gun on me."

Slade chuckled. "Maybe you best consider another line of work, friend. Otherwise, you might end up like these old boys here, deader than a beaver hat."

Slim studied Gutierrez a few moments, then nodded. "You got a point, mister."

# Chapter Thirty-five

As soon as the young cowpoke disappeared around the bend in the trail, Slade raced down the slope to his camp. Five minutes later, he was boiling down the mountainside to the plains below, cursing as he envisioned Jess Cooper running across Grimes and the gold.

The chance of an encounter between the two was remote, but not impossible. After all, both Cooper and the gold were headed to Las Vegas, and a red and green wagon stuck out like a fox in a henhouse.

Wedged in the chimney, Tolliver groaned. From somewhere beyond his narrow confines came voices. He shouted.

Moments later, a rope was dropped to him.

Slade kept Grimes's sorrel in a gentle lope, putting seven or eight miles an hour behind him. Just before noon, he spotted smoke drifting into clear sky, one that seemed even a deeper blue because of the crisp edge of the north wind.

Its bed empty, the wagon sat in front of the New Mexico Territorial Bank. Slade saw his claybank dun at the hitching rail beside the ponies that belonged to Right Hand and Paleto.

Before he could dismount, the bank door opened and Paleto came out, followed by Right Hand and Al Grimes.

The bandy-legged little foreman grinned up at Slade. "All done. Thanks to you and your friends, the Boles Mine will stay open."

"And with it, Juniper Pass," said Tilly O'Connor as she and Rose Perry emerged from the bank.

Grimes laughed. "They spotted us soon as we rode in." He nodded to them. "Sort of like a family reunion."

Paleto's somber voice broke and silenced the gaiety. "He is here."

A cold hand squeezed Slade's heart. "Cooper?"

The Mimbre Apache nodded to the Red Bull Saloon across the street. "He knows we are here."

Right Hand stepped forward. "He stand on porch and watch us take gold inside."

Tilly came forward and leaned against the hitching rail. "Paleto told us what you had in mind. Give it up. Let the law take care of him."

The skeptical young half-breed lifted an eyebrow. "The law can't prove nothing on him. The only one who saw it all was Arch Simmons, and he's dead. We can't even prove Cooper killed him. So, what is the law going to do?" He paused. "I don't know of any other way."

The small woman looked up at Slade, her eyes pleading. "We ain't lost no money. With the gold in the bank, the mine can keep operating and the town will stay alive. Forget about Cooper."

Slade arched an eyebrow. "So he can rob again, kill again?"

Before Tilly could reply, a voice from across the street froze the small group. "Slade! Jake Slade!"

The leather-tough cowpoke remained motionless. He glanced at Paleto. "Move aside. All of you."

For a moment, they hesitated, then quickly moved out of the line of fire.

Hands held out to his side, Slade slowly turned. His heart pounded against his chest.

Standing on the porch of the Red Bull Saloon, Jess Cooper grinned at him. "Figured you'd be here when I seen them unloading the gold. What are you plans?"

Every muscle taut with expectation, Slade kept his eyes fixed on the smiling, but dangerous gunman. The speed of Cooper's draw that day in the Perdenals Mountains flashed into his head. "You."

Cooper's smile froze. "I reckoned on that. You ain't got a chance, you know. Not by yourself." His cold eyes cut to Paleto and back.

Keeping his eyes on Cooper, Slade replied, "He isn't part of it. Not this time."

The gunfighter's eyes narrowed in suspicion.

Slade continued. "You take me, he'll come after you. Not today because I say so. But later. That's the way of our people."

A cruel laugh rolled off Cooper's thin lips. "Maybe I ought to take both of you now."

Every nerve in the young half-breed's body tingled with a mixture of anticipation and fear. He forced a laugh. "You're good, Jess, but not that good."

Several moments of silence passed, each pregnant with growing tension. Finally, a crack appeared in Cooper's confidence. "What if I ride out now? Leave the territory."

Slade took a step toward him. "I'd come after you. Or you can give yourself up."

Cooper snorted. "Ain't no way I'd do that."

"Then I don't see no other way out."

The lean gunfighter studied Slade another moment. "You don't leave a jasper much of a choice, huh?"

Slade swallowed hard. "That's about the size of it, Jess."

Cooper drew a long breath and stepped off the porch. "Well then, I reckon we ought to get the ball rolling."

On the boardwalk in front of the bank, Paleto's fingers rubbed his bear-claw necklace.

Easing to the middle of the street, Slade used his thumb to remove the leather thong from the hammer of his Colt. "Reckon so."

A crooked smile played over Cooper's lips as he seemed to glide to the middle of the muddy street. He halted, flexed his fingers, then eased down into a gunman's crouch, his right hand above the butt of his six-gun.

Slade planted his feet, flexed his knees, and waited, his eyes fixed on Cooper's.

Without warning, Jess Cooper's hand blurred. In that moment, Slade knew he was a second too late. Even as he was pulling leather, he anticipated the impact of a slug.

To his surprise, a rifle cracked from behind him.

Cooper jerked back, his eyes filled with surprise. The rifle cracked again and Cooper spun to the ground.

Slade wheeled around just as the rifle cracked a third time. The slug slammed into his shoulder, sending him staggering backward, but not before he glimpsed the leering sneer on the grizzled face of Frank Tolliver.

Tolliver stepped from behind the corner of the general store and clacked another cartridge into his rifle. Before he could throw it to his shoulder, a barrage of gunfire from in front of the bank slammed into the outlaw, killing him instantly as Paleto and Al Grimes emptied their rifles.

# Chapter Thirty-six

A week later, his arm in a sling, Jake Slade reined up on the rim of the canyon overlooking the valley in which his brother, Nana, had died.

Instinctively, his steel gray eyes focused on the charred tree on which Nana had been impaled. Snow covered the limbs, and to his dismay, he saw no evidence of his brother. The *sentir perdido*, the bad feeling he had felt so strongly, washed over him. "There," was all he said, nodding to the tree several hundred yards below.

Paleto, followed by Right Hand, urged his pony down the slope. "Let us put our brother to rest."

Nature had followed her inexorable course, but searching the snow below the charred limb, they found most of their brother's bones and a few shreds of his clothing.

In Apache tradition, they transported his remains to the crags of a nearby mountain, burying him in a crevice with his worldly goods. Before stacking rocks over his remains, Slade removed his double-edged knife and scabbard and laid them beside his brother. Paleto removed the necklace of bear claws about his neck and draped them over the bones.

Then they stacked rocks high over their brother so the animals could not get to him.

At the base of the mountain, they paused to look back. Slade's memories of his youth flashed through his head. Without looking at Paleto, he said, "What do you think our brother is doing now?"

Paleto chuckled. "If I know Nana, he's sitting around a fire with a young maiden laughing at us."

Slade looked around and grinned. "I reckon he would be." He drew a deep breath. "Well, let's get ourselves back to Arizona Territory. You got a wife to tend to. I got a stage line to run. And," he added, "maybe I'll see that little Coyotero maiden you told me about."

# ☐ **YES!**

Sign me up for the Leisure Western Book Club and send my FREE BOOKS! If I choose to stay in the club, I will pay only $14.00* each month, a savings of $9.96!

NAME: _____

ADDRESS: _____

TELEPHONE: _____

EMAIL: _____

☐ I want to pay by credit card.

☐ **VISA**   ☐ **MasterCard**   ☐ **DISCOVER**

ACCOUNT #: _____

EXPIRATION DATE: _____

SIGNATURE: _____

Mail this page along with $2.00 shipping and handling to:
**Leisure Western Book Club**
**PO Box 6640**
**Wayne, PA 19087**
Or fax (must include credit card information) to:
**610-995-9274**
You can also sign up online at **www.dorchesterpub.com**.
*Plus $2.00 for shipping. Offer open to residents of the U.S. and Canada only.
Canadian residents please call 1-800-481-9191 for pricing information.
If under 18, a parent or guardian must sign. Terms, prices and conditions subject to change. Subscription subject to acceptance. Dorchester Publishing reserves the right to reject any order or cancel any subscription.